COMING
AND GOING

COMING AND GOING

PETER STEPHEN BENTON

Novels by Peter Stephen Benton:

Brownstone & Ivory

Beyond the Blue Serenade

ISBN: 0692477101
ISBN 13: 9780692477106
Library of Congress Control Number: 2015910277
Night Sky Productions, Longmeadow, MA

Dedication

This one is for the boys
Ben, Derek, and Andy

Cover concept: F. Gaylor and P. S. Benton

Cover photography, with permission, and design: F. Gaylor

Acknowledgments

It is no secret that William Shakespeare was particularly clever at defining the human condition in very entertaining terms through the use of metaphors, allegory and ebullient characters who, at some level, become everyman. Still, life remains mostly a riddle and no man (or woman) can exist in a vacuum without others. Ergo, there are those in my world who I wish to recognize because they had something to do with this book or the stories herein.

First and foremost, of course, is my wife Betsy. She is tolerant, accepting, unselfish, and encourages my literary pursuits. I'm not certain that the catchphrase "opposites attract," is appropriate, or necessarily true, but we still seem to possess sufficient commonality to have withstood one another for over three decades.

I must mention some people who have played a part in my endeavors. The multi-talented and erudite Deb Hall has, from time to time, skillfully led me to places that I needed to go in my writing, and again provided an invaluable female perspective; Kathy Freme, one of my oldest and best friends, has encouraged me in ways that she is probably unaware; Stu and Cheryl Benton, who provided me with access to venues as well as support with and for my efforts; Lucy Atkinson for taking an interest and being so dear, sweet, and generous - we love you; William David Barry, for favorable, though unofficial, reviews; Fred Gaylor, long-time friend and fellow parent, professional photographer and artist nonpareil, for obvious reasons; Lisa Bullock and Jay Seyler for their inimitable photogenic contributions; Gina Golash Kos, for overwhelmingly enthusiastic endorsements of my previous two novels, likewise Alice Sazama; A.B.C. Whipple, posthumously, again, for validation and initiation into the fraternity of authors; old New England inns; and the Bard of Avon - thanks, Bill.

Prologue

BRYANT PARK, EARLY MAY

The sun was out, mostly.
Midafternoon; the park was busy but not crowded.
My back to the library, he was on my left,
Facing the new grass upon which none could yet tread.

His white hair was long and flowing,
Swept back gracefully: wavy.
He sat alone on a green metal chair,
As did I—observing, remembering the coming and going.

The green hooded sweatshirt,
For him, matched the maroon socks.
Late seventies, I guessed—isolated: no one near him.
His soft expression seemed distant, confused perhaps.

His lips moved silently as he glanced from side to side,
Nodding his head in mild affirmation.
Carefully he folded his arms across his chest,
A solitary snowy lock wisped in the cool spring breeze.

Under the shadows of new leaves he stared pensively
While his right hand rose to cover his mouth.
It was as if he had recalled a feeling
Long time gone, lingering still; somewhere.

Was it the tender touch of the hand that was once softly held?
Or the gentle voice that now only whispers in his soul?
What do I see in this vague reflection?
In Bryant Park, early May.

P.S.B.
New York City
May, 2004

THE VILLAGE

But, soft: behold! lo where it comes again!
I'll cross it, though it blast me. Stay, illusion!
If thou hast any sound, or use a voice.
Speak to me.

—WILLIAM SHAKESPEARE, *HAMLET*

I watch the distorted flames reflected from the fireplace to my right dance seductively on my sparkling martini glass. A waitress supporting a full tray of steaming slabs of prime rib on her shoulder with controlled inertia bustles past our table and momentarily disrupts my tranquil reverie. The clear Beefeater gin, embellished by the vaguest suggestion of dry Martini and Rossi vermouth, ripples against two partially submerged olives skewered on a red plastic sword. An enticing olfactory scent of cooked beef wafts my way, exciting the carnivore in me. The slim, tapered stem of the crystal vessel just beyond the tips of my fingers glows in the soft candlelight that flickers between my wife and me, and one of the many smaller dining rooms of the Publick House in Sturbridge, Massachusetts, reverberates with pleasurable sounds as diners enjoy a cozy midwinter feast at the rustic New England Inn.

"End of January…they still have their Christmas decorations up. We shouldn't feel so bad," I announce quietly, eagerly—the first words spoken since we were seated and became immersed in our very individual menus. Without moving her head, Taylor rolls her eyes upward and over the top of her reading glasses, quickly glancing around the room. She utters a throaty, barely audible "uh-huh," and then her attention quickly returns to her Saturday evening dinner selection. The leather portfolio is perched on her lap and leans against the edge of the table.

My comment was intended to solicit a kind of reassuring appeasement, knowing that on this night the interior of our home forty miles away looks exactly as it did on Christmas morning. I do the outside decorating and the tree; she does the rest. In her defense, time is a rare and cherished commodity in our lives. I did get the validation that I had sought, however, even if it was a somewhat less than enthusiastic grumble.

Fortunately our conversation is minimal—we have been together for twenty-four hours on this rare weekend hiatus together. It's not that I don't want to talk to her; rather, I suspect I am still in a state of shock. My world and reality were appreciably jostled a few hours before. Actually any small talk instigated by me is more of an attempt to snap me out of my preoccupation. Perhaps enough liquor will assuage the incredulity of the latter part of my day. Now musing over my martini, loosened memories and feelings swirl in a convoluted eddy, agitated by something that was completely unexpected and quite unabashedly bizarre: I waited decades hoping it would happen, and now that it really has, I find that my initial euphoria has become shrouded with wispy disappointment. No…that's not it. More like interested indifference. I never thought I would feel this way. Not ordinarily reticent, I seem to be tonight. I am sure my wife appreciates the rare peace and quiet from her normally loquacious husband. But after all of these years, there seem to be more questions than answers still. That has left me introspective—thinking; once again.

⊶⊷

The day began innocuously enough. It was a gray day: expected for late January but not this January, at least not in New England. Winter had been unseasonably mild thus far this year. During the night the cold and the frail, silent snow had crept upon us with the utmost stealth while we'd slept. In our hotel room this morning, I watched Taylor, sweet and still laughing at my constant attempts at humor, struggle with her long underwear that had been long lost in a dresser drawer until rediscovered and packed in a getaway rush yesterday after work. It was good that they are stretchy, having been acquired many years before in a pre-Weight Watchers era, probably for skiing. Clothes that are not worn for a while do have this odd characteristic of shrinking when in drawers or hanging in closets. There must be a scientific explanation. We both chuckled at the rips in my wool socks—scars from a Vermont hunting trip, probably an encounter with a wild end table.

The Weather Channel had predicted the arctic conditions. We do show our age these days by our new obsessions: Who would have imagined twenty years ago that weather could be so entertaining? It's true—we are becoming our parents. As for weather broadcasts, now the all too familiar scene of someone screaming into a microphone while slogging through the latest natural disaster has become routine.

On the way we had stopped at a local convenience store on Route 20 where I was forced to pay a king's ransom for my daily fix of Advil. We found the entrance to the Old Sturbridge Village quite easily—it was as if my Ford Explorer knew the way. The delicate snow swirled and billowed in front of our windshield as we turned into the deserted parking lot. Just as we had expected—the fifteen-degree temperature (with a single-digit wind chill factor) had discouraged all but the heartiest souls. There were no more than ten cars. We are native New Englanders—so we fancy that the elements are something to be ignored, simply an ordinary inconvenience. Ho, hum. That is until our feet or fingers freeze.

Despite the spaciousness of the parking lot, I had trouble deciding where to park—that was until an exasperated Taylor cajoled me. There are some things about me after more than two decades of marriage, or perhaps because of, that still annoy her.

Soon we were standing beside the car in our L. L. Bean parkas, gloves and thermals; my warm shoes, her lined boots and heavy cotton socks, prepared to challenge the elements, stubbornly refusing to permit the harshness of the bitter New England winter, now here late and somewhat begrudgingly, to spoil our plans. After all this was my idea—what better way for a colonial-era history buff to experience what people endured every winter day in the early 1800s? It was peculiar how the inspiration had popped into my head last week when Taylor had announced that both of our kids would be away on trips and that we had the time to go somewhere—alone. I had responded without hesitation as, truth be known, I am always salaciously hoping for an opportune tryst but also possess the wisdom to know that we need a worthy and relevant destination in addition to a room with a Jacuzzi or hot tub. Surprisingly my first suggestion was acceptable to her. I was a bit chagrined when I found room availability tight. The trade-off was that the only accoutrement, if it can be called that, was a king-sized bed. Oh, well. *Where are all of the people?* I now wondered.

As we strolled hand in hand across the sandy, black-asphalt parking lot streaked unevenly with whirling white clouds of snow, our car beeped twice behind us. My keyless remote locked the doors. One beep was sufficient: The second was intended to inspire a reaction. Taylor rolled her brown eyes dismissively—apparently she had expected it. Once again I realized that as I have grown older, I have become extremely predictable. That sounds boring, although Taylor claims I am anything but—I hope that equates to something like *endearingly reliable spontaneity*. I dropped the keys into one of the many pockets of my parka and zipped it shut.

As we walked by the shops just in front of the entrance, I solicited a kiss—not unusual at any time of day for me. Taylor acquiesced obligingly, and with a heavily insulated glove I patted her bottom softly—also something I do quite frequently, although usually behind closed doors and definitely without gloved hands. It's reassuring—exclusive; there is a deeper meaning—I know she gets that. She quickly scolded me for my public display of affection or indiscretion: maybe both. I abruptly stopped and faced her. I turned my head from side to side, looking around—emoting, of course. There was not another soul to be seen. It was my best Marcel Marceau impersonation. Then she smiled warmly and nudged me toward the entrance. She likes structure and predictability, mostly.

Lively traditional music of fiddle, mandolin, and guitar emanated from small outside speakers mounted on the walls of the newer buildings that house the gift shops and bookstore.

"Clogging music," I said as we playfully scrummed for position along the sidewalk, the light covering of snow sliding mildly underfoot—two boomers on a lark. I suppose we looked silly...I didn't give a damn. Taylor became serious again as we proceeded under the archway and approached the ticket window. She gathered maps and such as I extricated two twenties from the eclectic pile of bills, credit cards, licenses, and papers and all the other crap scrunched in the front pocket of my jeans. They are a little snug—the jeans, that is. I try to stay fit. We both struggle with our weight. Guys do seem to have an easier time of it as they head for the far reaches of middle age. There seems to be fewer ominous physical transformations—gravity being especially insidious. I try to reassure Taylor every day, in some way, that she is still attractive to me. I suspect she is equal parts appreciative and skeptical. I don't know how to convey my sincerity—I just know she doesn't believe me completely. Still, I find her just as appealing as ever because she is who she is. Today I am thrilled to be with her. She isn't particularly interested in history—she was being a good sport this day, for me. I had made a very strong pitch. I felt drawn to this place and its history.

Past the admissions gate, we hiked up the dirt road—tan gravel, really, sprinkled with a white, confectionery-sugar dusting of snow. We stopped, and I helped pull the hood of Taylor's parka over her head, navigating her white fluffy earmuffs. Her hair is almost completely gray now. Stepping back I saw that her turned-up nose and round cheeks were already pinkish in the frosty air. Fragile snowflakes continued to puff around us as we passed the first structure, an aged wooden building under reconstruction and as yet unidentified on the map. Taylor had had our itinerary and timelines for the entire day already set by the time we left the entrance, which was predictable. Another blue building was to our right—also under reconstruction. All of the buildings within the village are authentic and have been moved there from all over New England.

Our first destination, the white church—otherwise known as the community meetinghouse—was just ahead. We quickly climbed the stone steps; we didn't want to miss the eleven o'clock pipe-organ concert. Both being from old Yankee heritage, we felt as though we were in the midst of the spirits of our Puritan ancestors. The ambience, the sights and sounds and smells, immediately transported us to another time and place.

Before unlatching one side of the double doors, we looked back at the deserted town green, or common, as the open area in the center of the village was known back then, so called because the general public could use the area for grazing livestock, hence common area. Billows of light, windblown snow clouds scudded swiftly across the brown and white surface that was surrounded by houses and other period structures. White smoke streamed from most of the chimneys, filling the air with one of my favorite smells—wood fires burning in well-stoked fireplaces.

"That must be what the green back home looked like a hundred and seventy years ago," I observed. Taylor nodded her concurrence and continued on.

Inside the meetinghouse I dawdled in the foyer and read the historical snippets displayed on waist-high wooden stands while Taylor slid behind the door leading to the sanctuary. Eventually I followed her. There were eight people inside. I saw that Taylor had occupied a pew, an enclosed box-seat affair with a door, about halfway down the center. In a bygone era, the proximity of one's purchased pew to the towering pulpit was an indication of social and economic status: closer, hence more prominent. I suppose extreme prominence might unwittingly entitle the occupants to a shower of spittle if the preacher was of the emotionally charged fire-and-brimstone variety. That would certainly encourage an attitude of prayer for the privileged throughout the sermon.

Not unexpectedly, my lady's choice in the empty church was typically moderate—middle of the church. She is by nature strong and forthright yet modest and humble, unassuming and unpretentious. I admire that about her. She is a good person; I do adore her, especially her laugh. We were both silent now, however.

The organ was in the front, next to the pulpit. From behind, the organist seated there presented an ominous impression stirred by recollections of old horror films. His frizzy black hair flared to his shoulders and rested on the black-felt collar of a blue waistcoat with tails draped to the floor. In my very fertile imagination, I envisioned that *it* would suddenly spin around on the stool and reveal itself to be a Lon Chaneyish ghoul or some *Night of the Living Dead* hideous half-rotted corpse that would leer with macabre lechery and clack its loosely hinged jaw at the sparse audience.

To our delight the unseen organist played familiar hymns. The sound of the ancient instrument evoked fanciful visions of those who once had worshiped in and governed from this building when it was nearby in the center of the town of Sturbridge. But the musty smell of oldness inspired imagery of the dark, dank interiors of long-buried coffins of the now-dead congregation that once had occupied the very cushioned seats upon which our living, heavily insulated derrières now rested. I thought the whole scene was thrilling.

There was a pause, and the organist's arms dropped to his sides. I stiffened as he began to rise, wondering if we would be horrified or repulsed. He stood and turned slowly—I assumed for effect. To my surprise I was looking at Frank Zappa dressed in nineteenth-century period clothes. Of course it wasn't really him—Frank himself had been dead for several years—but I turned to my wife and grinned mischievously. Trying to whisper, I somewhat immoderately articulated my humorous observation and was instantly met with a flinty rebuke from Taylor. Nonetheless, our host was congenial and offered a brief explanation about the music selection as well as a history of the various functions of meetinghouses nearly two centuries before. It seemed the building had been aptly labeled then.

We would soon discover that few of the buildings in the village were electrified. Two that definitely had to be were the general store and the cafeteria located in the back of the tavern on the common. We were told, eventually, that many had alternate heat sources. I then encouraged Taylor to remove her coat, as I had done, so she wouldn't be cold when we went back outside. Then I asked "Frank" about the relatively comfortable temperature in the room. He informed us that back in the early 1800s, there probably would have been no or perhaps only meager heat in the meetinghouse. Then Zappa twirled with a flourish, flipping his waistcoat tails in the air over the bench, and re-seated himself. He resumed playing. After his final hymn, a somewhat dirge-like rendition of the familiar Protestant "Doxology," he stood and quickly exited through a doorway to his right. Taylor and I traded smiles and quickly prepared to continue our journey. This day together promised to be a grand adventure.

Next we descended from the gradual rise upon which the meetinghouse was perched and approached the first house on the common, to our left. It was snowing harder. Typical of most homesteads in that era, it was a small work-ing farm that produced enough sustenance for a family as well as something extra to barter for other necessities.

"How many years ago were we here?" I wondered aloud as I surveyed the property inside the wooden split-rail fences that were pervasive throughout the village, all hewn on the premises in the largely self-reliant recreated com-munity. It was a living museum.

"I don't remember ever being here with you," Taylor disclosed. "I think I came here when I was young, maybe on a school field trip or something, but that's the only time," she added with an air of deferential certainty.

I quickly wracked my brain, trying to recall who it had been. I knew it wasn't my ex-wife. I narrowed down the suspects—most likely it was Maryellen, a girl I had been with for three years before Taylor. That was nearly three decades ago. Inexplicably, a chill ran down my back, causing me to shudder.

"Are you OK?" Taylor asked.

"I just got a chill. Chilly, that's all," I replied. It was odd; I wasn't particu-larly cold. For a moment I felt a weird sensation—a touch of vertigo, perhaps. Taylor headed for the door of the house. I wandered away toward the pigsty.

"I'll see you inside," she announced as she opened the back door. "Don't fall in," she added with wry grin.

Recovered, I looked under a covered pen and saw three large, spotted sows huddled together on a bed of straw. I heard the back door of the house close. There was an old, white mare grazing by a single tree inside a small, hilly corral in the back: pale-yellow straw was strewn everywhere. I turned and started for the house just as an older man, maybe twenty years my senior, was coming up the walk holding the hand of what I presumed to be a granddaughter. We politely exchanged greetings as they passed me, headed for the pigs. I went into the Feno house—the name of the original owner displayed on a plaque posted by the door that contained a pithy history of the place.

"These ceilings must be this low for heat," Taylor mentioned as I came inside. She had been waiting for me and warming a bit. With an affirmative nod, I acknowledged my tacit agreement, and, as I removed my gloves and knit cap, I noticed there was no fire in the fireplace, yet the room was tepid.

"I think people were shorter then as well," I added.

We walked around the corner to find a woman in the other room, about my age I surmised, spinning wool into yarn on a wheel. She was, of course, dressed in period clothing and wore a bonnet; she was delightfully friendly, as one would expect of a docent portraying the living history of the museum. She had a long pointy and was probably somewhat bored on this day of rather sparse attendance. The three of us had a lively discussion. Taylor and I learned about the process of spinning wool, which the woman, no doubt, had told countless times before. She was very nice, although she spoke in clipped phrases, often stuttering as if her mouth couldn't keep up with her brain. We also learned that Martin Van Buren had been president in 1838, the year represented in the village, and that "Frank Zappa" was really an affable and multitalented local character named Roger Worthington.

Then we were off to the farm outside of the village proper (beyond the common) to "meet the oxen" at noon. As expected Taylor had allowed time in our schedule for diversions (she knows me well), and we explored the one-room schoolhouse then perused the shoemaker's shop. We bumped into a younger man, tall and wearing a black outback hat, escorted by, we assumed, his two little daughters. We had seen them at breakfast at our hotel earlier.

The farm was nestled among several acres of partially snow-covered working fields with an occasional haycock scattered here and there. We learned that oxen are not a separate breed of animal but neutered bulls over four years old that have been trained for heavy, laborious work. Much to my surprise,

I discovered that they have their own set of commands, and a command of "gee" means go right. Unfortunately, soon afterward, I couldn't remember the word for left. I suppose my oxen would trudge around in circles.

From there it was on to the cooper's shop and the farmhouse kitchen, where some irresistible smelling pies were being made from scratch, using authentic ingredients and then baked in a wood-fired brick oven in the kitchen. Then on to the blacksmith shop. It was all very fascinating, and I was especially pleased to see that Taylor appeared to be enjoying herself. The thought crossed my mind that people ate better back then—all natural ingredients.

Characteristically, Taylor wanted to stick to our schedule, and with a mention that her feet were getting cold it was imperative that we get to the parsonage on the common for tea at one o'clock. We traipsed up the road and around the corner to the white saltbox. The smell of the wood smoke that promised a cozy hearth was motivation for us to hasten our lockstep pace along the road. Suddenly, mysteriously, I felt queasy, and my legs became rubbery. Weakening, I stopped. Taylor pushed the latch open with a mittened thumb then quickly glimpsed back when I hesitated just before the bottom step.

"What's wrong?" she implored with a puzzled gaze. I must have looked piqued because she immediately closed the door and came toward me. I moved forward, but the momentary unsteadiness and disorientation were discomforting.

"It's really nothing," I answered unconvincingly. I swept past her and pushed the door open. We were met by a welcome blast of heat from the crackling fireplace to our right. There was Frank Zappa again, who was now Roger. He remorsefully explained that the reverend was away for the day, and he was filing in and serving the tea. Taylor and I glanced at each other and exchanged smirks. I was aware that there were two other people sitting across from us by the fire, but initially I was more concerned with adjusting Taylor's chair so her feet would be warmed by the crepitating blaze. Then I helped her with her jacket. As I was wrestling with my parka, I happened to glance over at the woman sitting on the other side of the fireplace. I froze.

My heart pounded in my chest, and I swallowed hard. I could feel my hands shaking. I was stunned and didn't hear Taylor tell me to take the cup and saucer that Roger was offering. I mumbled something gratuitous and sat back, staring straight ahead. I squirmed in my chair. *Could it be?* I thought. *No. No. Impossible. She's heavier now—the last time I saw a picture of her she definitely looked her age. Most people in their fifties do except Taylor. No…wait… Good God, it could have been her fifteen or so years ago, though,* I concluded.

She looked like the same Maryellen who, just over twenty-five years prior, had been in her midtwenties. We had been madly in love and lived together for nearly two years: we had planned to get married. Then things happened, and our relationship unraveled. Maryellen broke it off with abrupt finality and left me in the lurch. She moved to Portland, Maine, and was married within a year. At the time I thought it was the worst thing that could ever happen to me. I was shattered.

I tried to sneak another discreet, furtive glance at her, but the woman caught me this time and smiled courteously then averted her eyes.

Damn, if this isn't Maryellen, this woman could be her double. Wow—she is absolutely resplendent, radiant in the yellow-orange firelight. My God, the likeness is startling, with her strawberry red hair just a little more than shoulder length. But that face, that beautiful face with those full cheeks, lovely full lips, and silky smooth alabaster skin, those soft eyebrows, and most of all those big, blue eyes. But her expressions and mannerisms—the resemblance is eerie. Goddamn it, if it's not Maryellen, she could be her twin sister, I thought. Having searched the Internet out of curiosity about a year before, and with the help of Google, I knew that Maryellen now lived just north of Boston in Lexington, so it could have been possible that it was her except that this woman seemed so much younger and thinner than logic would abide. And she was too old to be Maryellen's daughter.

With a blast of cold air, the father with the two girls came bustling in from outside—I used the commotion as a diversion to scrutinize the man who was with "Maryellen." I almost dropped my cup and saucer and realized I was trembling. Beneath a wide-brimmed felt hat, he appeared to be at least five or ten years older than she was. His hair, at least what I could see, was grayish.

Strangely, he seemed to be about my age, which chronologically wouldn't make any sense at all. Maryellen was the same age as I was.

If it is her, what is wrong with this picture? I know that this would probably be Maryellen's second husband, who is older than me, so he does fit this younger Maryellen. What the hell am I thinking? I must be flipping out. This is stupid, I reasoned. *I'm seeing what I want to see.* I quickly decided this was a case of mistaken identity, coincidence—an illusion I had created. *I had better snap out of this fast,* I resolved. It was very dangerous. I sensed that Taylor was now aware of my misplaced attentiveness.

I timorously espied the woman once more before I ceased my voyeuristic urge, but not before noticing she was dressed in brightly colored clothes, looking more like summer style—odd for the dead of winter. Draped across her lap was a black cashmere overcoat.

Maryellen had always looked fabulous in black—and the color and style of her coat were perfect for her. They were my favorites on her, and I used to tell her that. It just can't be, I decided and then diverted my attention back to Taylor and Roger. I noticed that the group had grown to nine or ten.

I stared at the fire, and thousands of images bombarded my mind. We had been young and probably not as smart as we'd thought we were. Although I had been summarily jilted and suffered through a painful severance, my feelings for Maryellen had drifted into an emotional limbo. She had lingered with me at times, and I had felt terribly uncomfortable with that despite the passage of so many years. Still, I had forgiven her a long time ago. I had truly hoped that she would find happiness. For some strange reason, the song "Love Street" by the Doors was playing in my head.

Taylor had known about Maryellen since day one, although she never expressed any jealousy or suspicion—only fleeting curiosity occasionally. But that was all, really. That's Taylor—confident and trusting. But then, I have never given her reason to doubt my commitment or loyalty to her, either. She's secure and has every right to be. It was just this secret fixation, this obsession—I'd never had a chance to talk with Maryellen at the end—to make it right. The lack of closure was distressing. Somewhere inside I had never been able to let go completely. I had things to tell her that had gone unsaid or were disbelieved long ago. Time was now my proof—the affirmation. Not that anything would change, but if I could just get a few things off of my chest it would set things right, at least, I figured. Who knows what the "real" Maryellen thought, or felt, now.

I began sweating as I went through the motions of conversation. The room was hot, and I was beginning to wonder if I was coming down with a cold or something. Out of the corner of my eye I saw Maryellen's escort remove his hat. As soon as Taylor finished her tea, I anxiously began prodding her gently to leave, which was met with a certain resolute resistance—she likes to move at her own speed and not be rushed when she is at her leisure. It's a game we play after all of these years being married. I used to be a mule (maybe an ass?); now I'm more like the oxen. I guess that's what maturity is all about—realizing that cooperation is not necessarily plodding obedience, at least in theory.

The woman, "Maryellen," remained taciturn, and with a hurried final glimpse I made eye contact and realized she was on to me. Had I gone too far? Was I acting like a fool, a stalker, or a lecher? *She seems much younger up close. I have to pull myself together. I'm on the verge of embarrassing myself and Taylor,* I postulated. I was very uncomfortable.

As soon as I hit the brisk winter air outside, I came around. *What was I thinking? She was such a convincing lookalike. And was it just a coincidence that she is with a guy who fits the circumstances, or rather the situation? The juxtaposition of years is too farfetched, anyway. Wake up,* I silently demanded of myself. Taylor threaded her arm in mine, and we set off for the small tin knocker's shop next door. My angst dissipated as we walked. The cold air and the walk were refreshing.

"Not any warmer out here, sweetie," I announced. "Did your feet warm up?"

"For the most part," Taylor replied. I looked down at her boots and then at my own waterproof leather shoes that I had found on sale earlier in the month. With a pair of heavy cotton socks, my feet were snug and toasty.

"I love these new shoes. My feet are perfect," I added.

"I know. That's the third or fourth time you've told me," Taylor answered laconically as she led the way into the tin shop. That's another thing I do these days—repeat myself. It comes with the territory, I'm told.

"I'm not sure what they'll do if the snow gets heavier," she added.

"Are you suggesting the Weather Channel could be wrong?" I quickly retorted.

"Perhaps," Taylor announced boldly.

"Blasphemy," I growled playfully as we reached our destination. She purposely bumped me lightly with her hip.

The visitors' gallery was tiny, separated from the workshop by a counter with a door to the outside at either end. There was an acrid burning smell that partially masked a pungent metallic odor. Two men in dark-blue aprons toiled at workbenches. One was about forty and garrulous, outgoing; the other was all of seventy-five and appeared to be curmudgeonly. Nevertheless, they jousted amicably with one another. Both were busily plying, or portraying, their special trade. The shop was covered with a variety of handmade, shiny tin creations—mostly lanterns and no two exactly the same.

The door behind us opened and closed. Taylor and I turned simultaneously—it was "Maryellen" and her partner. I was much more at ease this time; the initial shock of her striking resemblance had finally subsided. She stood next to me. I noted she was the same height as the real Maryellen. Now I could also see, with the brightness of a window behind her, that this woman's profile was exactly that of Maryellen.

Interestingly, this Maryellen's man and I engaged the younger, more voluble tin knocker in conversation, and at one point Maryellen's man and I actually addressed one another. He was friendly and was every bit as inquisitive as I was. I used the opportunity to study "Maryellen" up close as much as I dared, frantically hoping that she would say something. I tried to manipulate the conversation to draw her in. I wanted desperately to hear her voice.

The voice. That would be proof positive—prima facie evidence. It would foil the ruse of this most effective though unwitting imposter. Although I last heard it so very many years ago, there is a danger that if her voice, its cadence, tone, or timbre, is within a suggestion of Maryellen's, I will freak out. Then all of those thousands of "I love yous" and "good nights" whispered so intimately will be resurrected and haunt me once again.

Wait a minute. Maryellen was never reserved. That's it! She wouldn't have been so quiet—she would have waded into the conversation long ago. This is all just a fantasy, I fought to convince myself. As I tried to rationalize this cruel hoax I had perpetrated upon myself, I envisioned myself as a silly puppet dangling precariously somewhere in limbo between reality, the past, and wishful thinking. Curiously, an aroma of lavender wafted through the shop.

Lavender? Is someone wearing strong perfume? I wondered. Taylor tugged at my arm and motioned noiselessly toward the opposite door. It was time to move on to the cafeteria for a quick bite to eat before songs and storytelling at two o'clock in the main room of Bullard's Tavern.

After a quick lunch, we made our way up a back staircase that led to the smaller of two large rooms at the front of the tavern. The wide planking of the unfinished wooden floors was secured with hand-forged spikes, no doubt smote at the nearby blacksmith shop. Earlier in our travels, we had learned that in 1838 there would have undoubtedly been a finish or some form of covering on the floors, but they were purposely left this way to withstand the high volume of visitor traffic and the wear and tear that that engenders. We rounded a corner and were in the main room, where the fireplace glowed and crackled welcomingly. Taylor and I looked at each other and grinned. There was Roger again.

"He's a busy guy." Taylor chuckled softly as we went forward and exchanged pleasantries with our now not-so-new acquaintance. So far there were only five other people seated in a semicircle around the fireplace. That included the dad and his two daughters. I piled our coats on a table next to the antique settee that we about to occupy.

With fife and guitar, the gifted and peripatetic Roger entertained us with several songs of the era and then concluded this particular performance with a long-winded and especially peculiar yarn about a lazy cheapskate from "the village" who ended up hanging upside down inside of his fireplace, one foot tied to a rope that was lashed to his cow, which had fallen from the roof. I was aware that others had arrived late—Roger had subtly acknowledged the unseen stragglers behind us with a nod while he sang. At the conclusion I stood and turned to retrieve our parkas.

She was sitting directly behind me. Her escort was seated next to her with his arms folded across his green sweater as he gazed casually out the front window. This time her eyes were waiting for me. She smiled softly and maintained eye contact for longer than I expected. I wasn't sure if I was embarrassed, frightened, or surprised. Now I knew she had Maryellen's eyes. I fumbled with our things and then stumbled against the old couch when I stepped on a sleeve of Taylor's coat.

"What are you doing? Pay attention to what you're doing," Taylor snarled with mild annoyance, her voice controlled so her comment stayed within my earshot but below the lively murmur that now filled the emptying room. I felt like an oaf. The fire popped mockingly as beads of sweat welled upon my upper lip. I was completely unnerved.

"I...I bumped the chair. Here, sorry," I muttered as I straightened clumsily. In my peripheral vision I saw "Maryellen" putting on her overcoat by the front door. Taylor was wrestling with her puffy down parka, and I reached over to help it over her shoulder. While Taylor had her back to me, I stole another surreptitious glance. I knew I was obsessed.

Damn, she is stunning in that coat. Just like Maryellen. This girl is Maryellen's twin. I wish I could hear her voice, but she won't talk. Why?

Taylor and I went down the stairway in the back and stopped to check our map. Our next stop was to be the "Towne House" at the end of the green. Towne was the name of the New Hampshire family who had built and lived in the colonial manor two hundred years ago.

The sky remained steely gray, and the temperature had dropped; there was an unrelenting, biting, blustery breeze. Naked tree branches swayed and clicked together like hundreds of elongated skeletal fingers, ethereally waving and pointing as if urging us on in the direction of the large, darkened mansion. The wind chill must have dipped below zero. An occasional nomadic snowflake now meandered on the air and then flittered away on a gust to some random final resting place. I could smell snow in the air as the damp wind buffeted my face.

I pulled my oatmeal-colored, knit woolen cap farther down over my ears as we stumped up to the front door at a somewhat less than casual pace. Daylight would soon be waning, and we both seemed to sense that time was of the essence. There was a fenced-in enclosure to the left of the white clap-board house. I could see a light-brown calf eating hay. Beyond the animal was a rolling, windswept pasture that flowed to the edge of white-purple wood-land. The snow had accumulated on the ground—there appeared to be an inch or so.

The house looked deserted. The front door was securely bolted.

"Look," Taylor exclaimed, pointing a mitten-covered left hand toward the ground. "Footprints going around to the side."

For someone who had been theretofore only marginally interested in his-tory, she was now eager to find a way into the old house. Maybe that was the operative term—*house*. Women always seem to be interested in houses and, more specifically, homes. Or perhaps it was her inherent curiosity that was aroused. We scurried along, following the path of someone who had recently gone before us. The snow started coming down heavier as we rounded the corner.

The back door was open. A ghostly quiet met us as we crept inside—we seemed to be alone. The air inside was still…and dead cold. There was some-thing about this musty old place. I was spooked but didn't know why. I looked around nervously.

Once upon a time, this had been the residence of a wealthy family, depict-ed in this village as the most affluent. Surprisingly, most of the floors other than the kitchen were carpeted. This place was old, and the crinkled paint and faded wallpaper needed restoration. After exploring the first floor, we climbed the staircase in the front foyer, each baluster ornately carved. The an-cient stairs creaked and groaned under the weight of our footfalls. My leather gloves swished along the railing.

When we reached the second floor landing, we turned left, and I guided Taylor through a bedroom doorway. The wooden trim was painted pink, and the walls were covered with faded gold, pink, and green patterned wallpaper. There were period bedclothes laid out, just as if the home's occupants would be soon returning to slumber after nearly two centuries. Once again my pecu-liar propensity for morbidity resurfaced, and I envisioned them, or what was left of them, reposing in their respective graves, still and silent. They would not be returning. I heaved slightly with a macabre cackle. *Will others think the same of us two hundred years from now?* I wondered.

We returned to the landing and headed into a much larger room with what I guessed to be a higher ceiling. This room had moveable walls and could be easily partitioned. It ran the width of the house, front to back.

There was an easel with a brief history of the room near the middle of the railing that separated the furniture and other objects from the general public. Not only had it been used for individual bedrooms, but it had also served as the village meetinghouse until one was constructed in the parish from where the house had been moved. For many years the room had been used for meetings of local Freemasons. In front of some antiquated memorabilia and artifacts, there was another placard that discussed the secret rites and mysteries surrounding the Masons. Being a member of the Craft, I was fascinated by the display.

"I have to pee. I had hoped there would be a bathroom in here," Taylor said in a needy but not quite desperate tone. I quickly observed that her need for comfort was more urgent than not—more like imminent as evidenced by the frenetic pace of her jiggling legs. Ever since giving birth to our kids, she has had little time from first impulse to really "gotta go" mode.

"They had outhouses in 1838. Most houses didn't have indoor plumbing, dear," I teased.

"Well, I am not going in any damn outhouse, especially today," she snapped back.

I chuckled. "Yeah, your fanny would probably freeze and get stuck. You'd have to sit there until I showed up with some hot water!"

"Very funny. Listen, I have to go, dear," she countered.

"They don't have any that I've seen, anyway," I said. "I guess you'll have to go back to the tavern," I offered. "Sorry I can't help you this time," I added a bit more sympathetically, yet with just a hint of my ever-present mischievousness.

"I was afraid of that," she whined. "I really have to hurry—now," she declared in a low squeal and then scurried back toward the door, retracing our steps. "Wait for me here," she shouted over her shoulder as she bounded down the stairway.

"Do you want me to come with you?" I called out after her, knowing that we were alone in the place.

"No, no. Just wait here," she answered, her voice fading in the distance as she clambered down the final stairs.

I listened to her rapid shuffling footsteps, the old, scarred wooden floors complaining as she raced through the house. Then I heard the back door open and then slam shut. The noise echoed loudly throughout the old building; a deafening silence followed.

It was a solemn stillness. Then I felt the emptiness. *I know this feeling*, I realized. *It's the silence of loneliness and sadness I once knew all too well. I remember the isolation—being left alone after years of companionship. Without her. A cold winter day, alone, listening to Pink Floyd's "Wish You Were Here" on the stereo over and over and staring out the windows as I paced. When it was over, my heart ached. It still does, sometimes*, I finally confessed to my most inner self.

This was all about Maryellen. I knew that. Her memory had been unexpectedly awakened in the last hour. I knew it had been ignited from seeing that woman and letting my imaginings get the best of me. Her startling likeness kindled old memories and emotions decades dead—or so I thought. Suddenly a bone-chilling draft swept through the room. I shivered and realized that the cold, oddly, had somehow penetrated my insulated parka. I became aware of the subtle scent of lavender again. I looked around quickly, expecting to see someone—one of the women I had seen before and suspected of wearing that particular fragrance. It was sickly sweet.

Then I heard a sound. A soft swoosh, barely noticeable at first, as if a door downstairs had been quietly opened and then carefully closed. Then, after a pause, gentle footfalls on the tired, creaky stairs. *Someone else is in the house. Strange, I didn't hear anyone walking across the floor as I had when Taylor left. But then again, Taylor was a tad hurried*, I noted.

Each step was slow, rhythmic, purposeful. Whoever it was approached the top of the front stairs, the delicate sound coming closer. I was curious. *Is it a caretaker, just another visitor, or something else?* My fertile imagination had always gotten the better of me in situations like this, since I was a kid and old enough to be aware of my surroundings. Then the footsteps stopped.

I realized I was holding my breath. There was no talking—no sound at all. My heart raced, and I felt it beating in my throat. I listened circumspectly.

Slowly "Maryellen" came around the corner, entering the large room.

"It's her," I gasped under my breath as a persnickety ray of late afternoon sunlight, the only one to pierce the overcast sky all day, chose that particular moment to come streaming through the front windows and paint a brilliant orange swath across the floor between us. She had her hands in her coat pockets as she moved forward steadily, deliberately. She traversed the blazing sunbeam and it seemed as though she disappeared momentarily. Our eyes were locked this time. She was alone. I knew those eyes—there was no mistaking who they belonged to. I had gazed into those eyes ten thousand times.

It HAS to be my mind playing tricks on me—I'm probably creating a delusion from something that was long forgotten because I want to, I need to. I'm about to make a fool of myself, I thought as I tried to retain a final vestige of reason and logic. *There's no way—I know what she looks like now. This woman is too young. It's impossible. It's not her, you goddamn fool. You idiot.*

"Hello."

I started when she spoke. Then my body tensed, and I set my jaw firmly.

"I thought you recognized me before but wasn't sure," she said softly.

Holy Mother of God. It IS Maryellen's voice. I was stunned. There was absolutely no doubt now.

"Don't be nervous. We're alone. I saw Taylor heading—rather scooting toward the tavern, and my husband is outside talking to the animals out back. So…I took this opportunity to talk to you alone. I wanted to—I had to. It's been a long time coming. I hope you don't mind. Do you?" she asked graciously.

I had no idea how she knew Taylor's name. In fact I had no idea how she could have known me unless she had used the old Google trick like I had done with her.

"Oh…my…G-God," I stammered, now paralytic. "I…I had no idea, Maryellen. I mean you have no idea how…well, I'm…glad…happy…I'm happy to see you," I blathered.

"I thought you would still be upset with me—not want to see me again. I took a chance…"

"No, not at all. I mean I'm not mad or anything. You did what you thought you had to do. I get that now," I answered, getting over the initial shock.

"You look good," she said with that coquettish smile of hers that always sent a jolt of electricity tingling through every cell in my body. It still did.

"You're as pretty as ever," I declared, the words escaping before I was capable of exercising any discretion whatsoever. My filter had failed. It was a more mature pretty, at least that much I kept to myself. It could be taken the wrong way, for sure.

"Do you remember the day we came here? We were in this room. There was no one else, like now. We embraced, kissed, and vowed that we would love one another forever. That was a long, long time ago," she said contemplatively. A sudden melancholic countenance washed over her like a wave as she softly glanced at me. I thought I heard regret, remorse in her voice.

"I thought we did," I answered with vague certainty, hopefully concealing my faulty recollection. That was an anomaly: I remembered most of the things that Maryellen and I did together with fastidious detail. But this was a blur.

"That was a wonderful day. One of our best," Maryellen continued plaintively, as if ruminating on a fond reminiscence of a far-distant past. "We had fun. We were so in love…" She sighed.

"We were…" I replied cautiously, deliberately letting my voice wither on the last syllable.

"I wanted to tell you how sorry I am," Maryellen offered humbly. "I didn't mean to hurt you the way I did. I was doing what I thought was best for me, and you, at the time. I did love you and knew you loved me. I want you to know that. It was very hard for me to do what I did. It was very painful," she added with a sincerity and sensitivity that was clearly evident in her expression—her eyes especially. This was much more than I had ever expected from her. She was never one let herself reflect emotionally on her past. She would never go there, wherever that was.

"Oh, baby…oops…that slipped…sorry," I retracted.

She smiled understandingly and nodded nostalgically. "I thought I detected a glimmer of fondness, a recollection of a tender memory."

"Maryellen," I said, pausing thoughtfully. "It wasn't just you. I made some terrible mistakes. I did and said some stupid things—some bad things. You must know now that wasn't me. I don't want to make excuses, but I was scared and very desperate. I was deathly afraid of losing you. Then, when I felt you slipping away, I became resentful, and I fell apart. It's absolutely true that desperate people do desperate things. I did desperate things. I was young, and wrong. Emotions were bombarding me from every direction. I was inconsolable. But I *never* fell out of love with you. Never. It may have seemed otherwise, but it's true. Back then in that mess I was unable to express my feelings verbally, maturely, so I acted out my emotions in destructive ways. I became insecure, I lost my confidence. I didn't think I could hold on to you—"

"Don't apologize. It's OK. I forgive you. That was a lifetime ago. And I could tell from the letter you sent me a few years ago that you forgave me. A bit of a shock, but I was touched and flattered after all of those years," she said.

"I apologize. That was a weak moment. After I did that I was afraid you would think I was stalking you or something. It was meant to be an olive branch—to set things right. By the way, I shared the letter with Taylor. That's the only way it had any legitimacy. I had to be open and honest. She is a very understanding person and knew my feelings ran deep. Anyway, I've always wanted to see you again, to talk to you. God, here it is closing in on three decades later. Can you believe that? By the way, do you mind if I ask why you look so different from the photographs I've seen lately on the Internet? Did you have something done?" I asked, trying to be as tactful as possible.

"No, no. Let's not waste time talking about how I look. That's not important—"

"But you look so young. And you have always been so pretty—"

"Now stop. You flatter me, but that's quite enough. Beauty is fleeting. Trust me on that one. Listen, I understand a lot more about what happened with you and us as well. Hindsight is always twenty-twenty. We were both young. Since I've been through a divorce and had children, I can empathize with what you had to endure. Many years later I came to understand that you were trying to deal with a lot of stuff I didn't understand at the time. I didn't help much. I was dealing with issues of my own. I do feel very bad about what happened. Yes, I was able to put it behind me, but I did think of you—us—at times. There were some very wonderful, happy, funny times. That was such a sweet love. But I fear I wasn't right for you then, and I'm afraid I would have made you unhappy. I needed to grow. We were both very different people back then. It could have been a lot worse than it turned out. Like most things in life, timing is everything."

"Maryellen, I truly wanted to marry you—to spend my life with you."

"I know. But I'm afraid I had to vilify you to get through it. And, I couldn't let myself look back. No way: I shut you out. There was no other way for me."

"We had such passion. And I don't mean only lust."

"There was passion, that's for sure," she confessed with an impish grin, her blue eyes flashing. "But you have Taylor. I've watched the two of you together today—you are obviously very happy and love each other. And look, married for over twenty-five years. She's been good for you—better than I could have been. She's very strong and well grounded. You needed someone like her. You were fortunate. Consider yourself very lucky."

"You know a lot about me too, I see. Yes, I'm very happy and I believe Taylor is too. I know things worked out for the best—that always seems to happen. And yes, I was very lucky. But, your memory, and I guess that's the key, your memory has lingered—I wanted to have better closure than we had. It's just something I've needed even after all these years. It can't be helped. I still have dreams about you—always chasing you but never catching up."

"Well now you've caught me. Still, sweetheart, you can't live in the past. You can never go back. And you shouldn't have tortured yourself with this obsession about something that might never have been," she entreated compassionately, thoughtfully. Her eyes seemed to caress my very soul. "Don't dwell—remember?"

How well I recalled that expression having heard her say it many times.

Then, for a split-second I wondered if this whole scenario was something I had concocted in my head. But I blinked hard, and she remained in front of me. The room had grown darker, the only illumination being the fading light from the windows. The gray, bilious clouds had congested again, inhibiting any sunlight from penetrating their veneer. Maryellen seemed cloaked in an aura; the glow as well as the incongruity of her youthfulness remained surreal and disconcerting.

"That's just the way things turned out. You can't change history. And yes, you have Taylor…" She sighed, her tone somewhat despondent as her voice faded. It was almost as if she had purposefully stopped, leaving a thought unsaid. I grasped the finality in her words, yet I could also perceive that there were special feelings implied. There was no malice or uncaring in her voice, only empathy—I might have perceived a tinge of wonder, fantasy. I now understood that Maryellen knew that I had truly loved her, unconditionally. And I realized how much she had loved me.

"I do love Taylor very much and would never do anything to hurt her. You're right again, Maryellen. My relationship with Taylor is solid—we are the best of friends. We've been through a lot together and have survived. I can't imagine my life without her. But I still get sad when I think that I should have been more mature in our relationship and more of a friend to you. I didn't get it back then. Understand that it wasn't because I didn't love you or care about you. I did want you to be happy."

"I know. I cared about you too. At one point I wanted badly for it to work, but it just wasn't to be. Neither one of us was ready," she declared resolutely.

"I guess that's the bottom line, isn't it? Timing. I know that only too well. It's just too bad the stakes had to be so high. I paid dearly for losing you."

"Don't look at it that way. Everything worked out. You have a nice family. That's nothing to regret now. Maybe we couldn't have been what you think we could have for each other—not like you and Taylor and your kids. We'll never know. Some things just *don't* work. We've both had bad marriages to prove that."

"Taylor has taken good care of me. She means the world to me. I'd be lost without her. We've been lucky—our lives have grown around each other."

"That's sweet of you to say. And she's lucky, too. You're not such a bad guy." Maryellen grinned. "You're very special."

"No question about that," I stated humorously. We both laughed out loud. *I can't believe that this day has finally come. I have waited almost thirty years for this*, I contemplated.

Suddenly the back door opened and closed downstairs, and Taylor's unmistakable footsteps moved through the rooms below and neared the stairway.

"I must be going. I'm glad we had this talk. Take care of yourself. And I did mean it when I said I'll always love you and what we once had. I will," Maryellen whispered as she came closer. "God bless." The fragrance of lavender was stronger.

Must be her perfume, I surmised. I also noticed a faint odor of a fire—not wood but rubber and other materials. *Probably from the blacksmith shop or something*, I assumed.

"I'm thankful that we got to share part of our lives together," she added. I reached for her hand, but she recoiled from my touch and turned away, retreating quickly. Then she moved toward the narrow back stairway. She glanced over her shoulder as she began to descend the steps. Maryellen smiled warmly. It was then I realized that although we may never see each other again, we parted as friends this time.

"Maryellen, thanks for everything. Health and happiness always," I called out softly. She looked over, dolefully, and then I watched the top of her head, that beautiful red hair, disappear down the dark stairwell. I was choked up and fought back tears. I cleared my throat loudly and attempted to regain my composure as best I could.

Seconds later Taylor strolled back into the room, slightly winded.

"All set?" I asked with a new feeling of confidence in my voice. I felt relieved. In the last few minutes, I had done something I had been wanting to do for half my lifetime—something that had kept me from completely surrendering for more than a quarter of a century.

"Was someone here?" Taylor asked. "I heard you talking."

"Yup. That was someone who was in the tin shop with us," I answered indifferently, belying my true emotions. "I was explaining about Freemasonry," I tacked on that comment for effect, mostly to keep Maryellen's identity concealed. I don't tell fibs as a rule, but I felt this was a necessity in case the last ten minutes had been a figment of my imagination.

"Let's keep going. I'm getting cold, again," Taylor urged, taking hold of my gloved hand. We reached the same back stairs that Maryellen had used. I glimpsed out of the small window to my left and saw Maryellen reunited with her husband by the pasture fence. She was petting the young calf through the fence posts. To my surprise she turned and looked up at me. She smiled and waved carefully. I turned and followed Taylor carefully down the narrow, dark stairway.

When we emerged from the back of the house. The snow had stopped. I looked over to where I had seen Maryellen and her husband just moments before. They were gone. As Taylor and I began to walk, I hesitated—curiously there were no footprints in the new snow. I glanced over at the fence next to the pasture and the path that led to the road where they had been. They should have been in sight. I saw no one. In fact I never saw them again in the waning hour or so that remained of our day at the village.

⧏⧐

The turkey dinner was exceptional, and Taylor raved about her duck. In the tiny lobby area of the Publick House, I help her with her coat. We are preparing to venture into the frigid darkness and back to our hotel. I anticipate the rest of our evening with revitalized excitement and peace of mind. The wine will work its magic with Taylor, hopefully before the tryptophan kicks in completely on me.

As Taylor continues to ready herself, I glance at a small table near the maître d's rostrum. A newspaper is lying face up. I read the headlines of the Saturday morning, January 27 edition of the *Boston Globe*: "Democrats Balk at Iraq Plan." I feel compelled to flip the paper over and look at the rest of the front page. When I do, a black-and-white photograph jumps out at me. It is the charred, twisted wreckage of what was once an automobile. My eyes are inexplicably drawn to the smaller headline beneath the gruesome picture:

"Fiery Route 9 Crash Claims Lives of Lexington Couple."

ROOM 24

Hereafter, in a better world than this,
I shall desire more love and knowledge of you.

—WILLIAM SHAKESPEARE; AS YOU LIKE IT

The black Cadillac Escalade was heavy enough to resist the occasional nudging from the winds coming out of the east—the SUV was cruising north via Route 128 on the Boston beltway. Still, vigilance was needed to make steering corrections when the vehicle was buffeted.

"—I haven't heard, have you?" Brian Winslow glanced down at the speedometer and then looked back up at the road ahead as he spoke over the car's hands-free telephone. Traffic was light—it was late on a Sunday morning in mid-April, and he was traveling between sixty and seventy miles per hour except when the force of intermittent gusts, like invisible ramparts, pushed him back. Cruise control was of no use under these conditions.

"Only that they're saying it looks like a nor'easter." The voice resounded throughout the passenger compartment of the sizable vehicle.

"Hey, Bill, whadaya mean 'like' a nor'easter? I was always under the assumption—and by all means, correct me if I'm wrong—that you either have a nor'easter or you don't," Brian responded mordantly. He pictured Bill holding his cell phone to his ear, wavy russet and silver-streaked hair combed straight back, his beaked nose jutting prominently from his perpetually tanned face. Brian knew that William Bryant Howe would be impeccably dressed—a crisp cotton oxford shirt, probably blue, and British tan gabardine slacks, most likely.

"I'm not a goddamn weatherman, for Christ's sake. I'm only telling you what they said. That's the latest I've heard," barked Bill at the other end of the conversation.

"Well, anything about the parades tomorrow?"

"Only rumors and hearsay around this place."

"This place" was Concord, Massachusetts—Brian Winslow's destination. Tomorrow was Patriot's Day, and the parades were the annual Concord and Lexington parades commemorating the commencement of hostilities that began the American Revolutionary War. Although the actual anniversary was the nineteenth of April, the following Thursday, for this year, April sixteenth, a Monday, was the date designated on the calendar to celebrate the holiday. Now, a few years into only the third century since the republic's initial bloody battle for liberty and independence, Patriot's Day had become a lackluster and somewhat forgotten celebration in most of the United States other than Eastern Massachusetts, Wisconsin, and Maine. Still, in the towns of Lexington and Concord and the surrounding communities where the lives of native sons, the original patriots and Minutemen, served as collateral for an idea that was supported by roughly one third of the population, the memory was relived once a year. Winslow and Howe belonged to a select group of individuals who, by virtue of their heritage—they had ancestors who had fought in the war—sought to keep the history and memory of their forefathers, the original patriots, alive. Both were members of the Color Guard of Massachusetts Sons of the American Revolution, a state section of a national organization chartered late in the nineteenth century and ratified by an act of Congress.

"Rumors and hearsay? You sound like a lawyer," Brian said, chuckling.

"Of course I do—I am." They both guffawed. "But I am not a goddamn weatherman, although I like the odds they get way better than any odds I ever had. Sorta like major league hitters—success thirty percent of the time means you'll probably be in the hall of fame. If I had that kind of record, I would be starving and waiting for the phone to ring."

"Who else is there? Is the color guard banquet still on?"

"Listen, where are you?"

"Um…just past Waltham on one twenty-eight."

"Just get here. You're less than twenty minutes away, for Christ's sake. There may not be enough for a quorum, but the inn is staying open. And both bars are definitely good to go tonight. Ron is here from Connecticut and was asking about you, so you know those guys are somewhere around here. They're diehards. And I suspect the Lincoln men and women will show up later, as usual, since they live just up the street, and their town is dry," Howe declared.

"Yeah. I went to a wedding in Lincoln a while back. The Pierce House, I believe. Tough to get a drink in that town unless it's a function. Gotta go to Concord or Lexington. OK. See you soon."

"Hey…keep your powder dry."

"Don't say that—may be bad luck."

"Good-bye."

There was a loud click, and a gust of wind battered the Escalade just as the radio came back on—the Doobie Brother's "Listen to the Music" blared from an XM classic-rock station. The palm of Brian's left hand slid down the arc of the black-leather-wrapped steering wheel, his thumb finding the button that lowered the volume—it had crept up slowly before the call, the digit nibbling to higher increments as each decibel level became assimilated or a song just needed to be louder. The call had automatically muted the radio. He smiled, realizing it was the same phenomenon that occurred when starting a car—the radio blasting, as the setting of the volume was where it had been when the vehicle was last running. Or a clock radio in the morning that had been barely audible when set the night before.

Ahead and to the east, the clouds looked like layered granite with the lower, lighter clouds scudding quickly northward, the upper layers murky, unforgiving, unmoving. Other than a few sprinkles here and there, the rain had held off. Brian Winslow was optimistic. There would be familiar revelers at the Concord Inn in the center of Concord tonight regardless: the hardcore. And he knew that the Concord and Lexington parades had been cancelled only once in the past one hundred or so years—that for a freak April snowstorm.

A red Ford pick-up truck passed him on his left, its driver hunched over, with both hands clutching the steering wheel.

"That jerk is just asking for trouble going that speed," Winslow instantly opined to no one but himself. Talking to and about other drivers while he drove was normal.

Today, Massachusetts Route 128—also Interstate 95—was as barren as he had ever seen it, which was a relative concept as it would still be considered busy by the uninitiated. It had a reputation as one of the most congested thoroughfares in the United States, particularly during the heaviest commuting times to and from the Boston area on weekdays. Also one of the most treacherous.

Minutes later, as he approached the right-hand exit 30B to Route 2A east, large raindrops began to splatter across the windshield, blown sideways from a battering squall. He traveled along the Jersey barriers to his left and then right onto the actual exit. Along route 2A he made a scheduled stop at the "Minute Man Historical Park" visitor center in Lincoln where he purchased a book on the battles of Lexington and Concord for for his youngest daughter. Then he got back on 2A. Immediately to his right he passed the spot where Paul Revere had been captured by a British scouting party, now commemorated with a circular stone monument. Brian turned left onto Bedford Road and followed it until taking a right onto Route 2. Soon he came to a set of traffic lights that were red. On green, Brian, the second car in line, proceded straight through the intersection and pulled into the Mobil station there where he used his Mobil Speedpass to fill up for the ride home. Brian took a left out of the station and headed to the center of Concord.

Monument Square, the Concord green, lived up to its name—there were statues, markers, and obelisks that had been placed there over the 230 plus years since destiny had fated Lexington and Concord as hallowed ground in the American struggle for independence. Brian Winslow's Cadillac skirted along the long, narrow island like a sleek black cat. The Concord Inn was at the end, facing Monument Square.

As was the case in recent years his wife, Meredith, hadn't accompanied him—being the chairwoman in perpetuity of the annual plant sale for their home town garden club always seemed to interfere, as it was also on Patriot's Day weekend. And she had seen the parades many times before, with her husband and all of the others decked out in replicated period colonial militia clothing of all sorts—an assorted collection of waistcoats, great coats, breeches, linen and cotton shirts, neck stocks, hunting frocks, and varied footwear, stockings, and hats. There was also an array of colorful officers' uniforms that were particular to specific colonial units, some remnants of the French and Indian War, as well as a smattering of Colonial Continental Army uniforms, most of which had the basic buff and blue coat but also variants of breeches, vests, stockings and cockades. There were also the decorative feathers and round patches of ribbon or brass on tricorne hats that identified them as belonging to a unit from a particular town or colony.

Parking behind the inn was usually tenuous—tight corners and limited spaces—but today, and at this time of day, not so much. Once settled he struggled to haul his Battenkill duffel and garment bag through the basement door and up the stairs to the lobby then over to the front desk. Entering the lobby, a smell became more noticeable but not overpowering. It was an old smell: this part of the inn, the original building, dated back to 1716. The ancient wooden floors creaked loudly with each step.

"Hello. May I help you today?" asked the slim, black-suited, pale young man of about twenty-five. He had unruly dark hair and blue eyes.

This kid definitely has Celtic ancestors, Brian observed, having seen many such souls with Celtic blood on his trip to Ireland the prior October.

"Yes. Reservation for Winslow," Brian said firmly, almost defensively— the tone could be interpreted as insinuative—expecting there would be some unexplained oversight, that his reservation from a year ago would be lost and the inn now filled to capacity. He stood next to his bags, his knees stiff as he readied himself for battle, poised for a skirmish. He always did this. Once a hotel somewhere in Texas hadn't had his reservation, which led to nightmarish experience and, despite a precautionary telephone confirmation two days prior this time around, the memory of that Lone Star state incident was indelibly imprinted on his psyche. It had made him forever unjustifiably apprehensive when checking in anywhere.

The clerk rummaged through the computer, pressing buttons like he was playing a piano—so many that it seemed impossible that they could all be relevant and necessary.

Why not one button just for "reservations?" Brian thought.

"Ah…Mr. Winslow. Yes. One night?"

"That's right—tonight, I hope," he said, serious.

A woman in her mid to late forties, he guessed, wearing a white blouse and with streaked, dark-rooted blond hair tied back in a bun, popped up from a small desk behind the clerk. She furtively glanced over the desk clerk's shoulder. Mostly devoid of makeup, her face was without blemishes, though distinct crow's feet dashed away maturely from both of her dark eyes. "Helen" was neatly embossed on a nametag worn just above her left breast.

"Yes, sir. The fourteenth," the young man answered calmly, missing or intentionally deflecting the intended humor.

"That's right," Brian answered curtly.

"And in the old part of the inn, preferably overlooking the square?"

"So far, so good."

"And the note here says a room with a ghost? Is that correct?"

An elderly husband and wife standing at the house computer on the far end of the front desk abruptly looked in the direction of the clerk and Brian, as did two fiftyish women with gray hair—one tall and boney, the other squat—who had been perusing the books for sale on the shelves behind Winslow. From behind the counter and to the side, Helen now stepped forward, smiling. She had a three-by-five index card in her hand. The young man, who Brian could now see was John, as announced on a name tag affixed to his shirt at about the same location as Helen's, snapped up a paper from the printer of the computer.

"Hello, Mr. Winslow. Don't think for a moment that we don't take our guest's requests seriously around here," she intoned easily, grinning. "In fact that very request is written on this card from last year! You have the best room in the house as far as ghosts are concerned. Room twenty-four."

Brian allowed himself a wry grin.

Suddenly, beyond the desk and to the left, the front door was nearly ripped from its hinges by a burst of wind, and a bearded man in a navy blazer, who somewhat resembled Captain Edward Smith of the Titanic, lurched after it. Then, inexplicably, his hand was cast away as the door changed direction and slammed shut. The man stood straight up and steadied himself, staring at the door. From beyond the foyer, Brian heard muffled voices whose intonation described the situation in disbelief. The only words that he could discern were those that sounded as if they were uttered by a terrified elderly woman who repeated the phrase "good Lord" several times.

"Great. Should be perfect tonight with the storm." Brian smirked as attention focused back on him.

"Oh, yes. Indeed. Too bad we can't take credit for that too," Helen said, laughing and placing the room key on the counter after sliding the printed sheet that the clerk had handed her across to Brian. "Vehicle information and such," she added perfunctorily.

Brian completed and signed the form, picked up the key, and then turned to pick up his luggage.

"Thank you, Mr. Winslow. I hope you have a *wonderful* evening," the woman proffered cordially with a hint of affable irony. "Good luck."

He stood up with his garment bag over his shoulder and duffel in hand, smiling.

"Thanks. We'll see how it goes." He chuckled. "Should be a ghastly evening." He glanced quickly at the others in the room and grinned as he turned toward the lobby door that led to the stairway, and rooms. Their expressions were mixed—a few were curious, the others skeptical.

⊰⊱

"They cancelled both of them," Stu Warren bemoaned as he hung up the lobby telephone. "First time in who knows how many years."

An unfamiliar voice from nearby chimed in, "According to the Weather Channel, we're going to get slammed tonight. It's a full-fledged nor'easter, all right. Tomorrow looks like a washout. There are already flash-flood and high-wind warnings."

"So, how many of us are here?" asked Ray Glover, commander of the color guard, he of red bulbous nose and head that was mostly flesh encircled with what looked like a snowy wreath, but was actually the remnants of thin, white hair. "They had no problem with us cancelling the banquet—I think they told the waitstaff to stay home."

"Some waitstaff," fired back Stu Warren. "It's always Jack and one other kid every year anyway. How many do we have here, did you say?"

"Enough to still get dinner," Brian Winslow responded. "Let me throw my stuff in my room, and I'll be right down. Stu, you know my flavor, right?"

Through the small-paned windows, Brian saw that dusk was approaching. There were five of them as they retreated, the floors uneven and creaking underfoot, in the direction of the small bar just around the corner from the front desk. On the other side of the small bar was the dining room, with only one couple in a corner, and they were about to leave. The lighting was dim, mostly from electrified oil lamps on the tables and replica coach lanterns on the walls.

"They said the kitchen's open and both bars until ten." Ray added optimistically.

"That'll work," someone in the group piped up, to everyone's delight as evidenced by an ardent, collective chuckle.

"Guinness tonight, I presume?" Stu inquired, the question unnecessary, the answer expected.

"You presume correctly, my friend," Brian answered.

"It will be settled and ready for consumption, at least the first, by the time you get back downstairs," Stu said with a wink and a nod.

"Where's Bill?" Brian asked, glancing around the lobby.

"Had to make some calls on his cell and needed better reception..." Stu stated as he silently studied some of the memorabilia on a wall, most of which depicted the singular most celebrated event in history that put Concord on the map, eclipsing the people and places in the area of significance to early American literature.

"I get great coverage here—who's his provider?"

"T-Mobile or something, I think."

"Lawyers are the cheapest—"

"Cheap, eh?" It was Bill's booming voice from behind Brian as he made his grand re-entrance into the lobby with his typical élan. Brian turned, and, under the yellow-with-age framed lithograph of Paul Revere's engraving of the battle at Lexington, they shook hands heartily.

"Tighter than a duck's behind," Brian avowed. Both men laughed as Bill slapped Brian on the back. The others chuckled as well.

"Hey, listen, I have to get upstairs and get rid of my stuff, and the boys here are headed—"

"For the bar. What a surprise," Bill interrupted. "I'll see you later."

As he was wont to do, Bill Howe began to quickly muster the men in the lobby in his customary, boisterous manner while hijacking the thought of heading to the bar for a cocktail and making it seem as if it was his original idea. Brian picked up his bags once again and headed for the narrow stairway. The steps were steep and creaked with cries of the secrets of antiquity, and the wallpaper looked as if it should have been in an inn from the colonial period in the United States. The fact was the inn hadn't been opened in the building until the late 1800s but had been a destination for sojourners and history buffs ever since. The restaurant in the front had been added later—information that Brian knew, yet he still marveled at how relatively new the building seemed in the context of a young America. The fragile history was but a blink of the eye compared to the saga of mankind and the rest of the world.

He reached the second landing, and, stumping toward room twenty-four in the corner at the end of the hallway, he noticed that the door of the small room straight ahead was open. A silhouetted figure was seated at a desk.

Drawing nearer he could see that it was a large man with his back to him. As soon as Brian was beneath the brass chandelier in the hallway, with bulbs resembling candles that emitted a dim yellow-whitish glow that crawled weakly down the patterned wallpaper, the man quickly spun around—alerted, no doubt, by the sound of Brian's footsteps on the wood floor. Brian recognized him immediately as the inn manager, Joel Meyer.

Pushing his Windsor armchair back with an ear-shattering shriek on the wooden floor, Joel stood and looked at Brian. Over the years the two had made an acquaintance, and a faint smile of familiar recognition spread across each man's face. Joel was a large man with round features and sunken eyes. He was big boned and carried far more weight than was healthy. His hair was wavy and jet black, with specks of gray; he appeared to be in his late forties or early fifties. He had been managing the inn for ten years.

"Welcome back," Joel announced and offered his right hand to Brian, who quickly put down his two bags outside the door of room twenty-four.

"Hi, Joel. Great to see you again. Is this your office?"

"One of them. Our official offices are in the basement, but since space is at a premium around here, I use this old storage closet that's too small for much else to get away from it all. Here again for the festivities, I see."

Brian nodded and poked his head inside the former closet. There were bookshelves attached to the wall, filled with notebooks and papers, while newspapers and computer reports covered the surface of the battleship-gray metal desk. There was a small, octagonal window high on the wall straight ahead, with delicate white-lace curtains that filtered the light from outside, which was becoming increasingly meager despite the afternoon hour.

"Yup. Patriot's Day again. I'm back to march, but there will be nowhere to go this year except to the bar," Brian said with a smirk. "Too bad we had to cancel the banquet. Sorry about that."

"Yeah, that's a real bummer for you guys and us but understandable nevertheless. By the way, you're staying here?" Joel asked as he pointed to the number twenty-four affixed to the closed door that they faced to their right.

"Yes, sir. I asked for the room with a ghost, and I got what I wished for."

"So it was you, eh? I wondered about that reservation—we all did. What do you know about the history of this room?" Meyer asked, smiling easily.

"Well, that there's a ghost," Brian answered pensively.

"Hmmm. OK. Sometimes we should be careful what we wish for." Joel then turned and retrieved a DVD from the back of his desk. "Are you aware that *60 Minutes*—you know, the CBS show—did a story on this room, on the entire hotel?"

Brian stopped and stood erect. "No."

"And one of the reporters on the show slept in this room with paranormal equipment and cameras. They also had a medium here, and paranormal researchers set up equipment all over the hotel."

"So what happened?" Brian asked as matter-of-factly as he could, trying to appear blasé; he hadn't known any of that.

Joel raised a guarded eyebrow, although his countenance remained generally relaxed. He displayed no malevolence but rather retained the manner of a good-natured host informing his visitor of a mysterious yet infamous room in his own house.

"You'll have to watch the video to find out," he declared. "Diane Sawyer was the one who actually spent the night. Do you want to see the video? Obviously you know they picked room twenty-four because it's considered one of the most active paranormal rooms in America. There has been quite a bit of history."

Joel stopped. His eyes darted from Brian to the door of room twenty-four and then back twice, almost anxiously.

Brian paused. Their eyes met again. "I'll tell you what. I'll watch it tomorrow. Is that OK? I don't want to be influenced by others," Brian answered calmly.

"Suit yourself." Joel came out into the hallway and closed the door to the small office. "Gonna be a wild one tonight. They're saying this storm is going to be a ripsnorter. And with this wind, a lot of things will go bump in the night. We could lose power. Sweet dreams…" He locked the door to the office and then turned and smiled sympathetically at Brian. Then the big man hulked toward the narrow stairway.

"Thanks. Hey, what's your cell number? That way you can be the first to know if Marley wakes me up in the middle of the night dragging his chains and cash boxes," Brian called after Meyer. His tone was jokingly sarcastic.

Joel smiled and waved as he disappeared around the corner down the stairs, his footfalls heavy and labored.

"They have it at the front desk—I'll tell them to give it to you if you need it," he answered obligingly as his voice faded, echoing as he descended the stairs accompanied by the squeaks and exclamations of tired old wood responding to the thudding cadence of his heavy steps.

Brian swiveled and fished in his pocket for the room key. Finding it, he slid the key into the deadbolt lock. He remembered the Guinness that was waiting for him downstairs. *Must be flat by now*, he concluded.

⢀⡀

"Where did the night go?" Bill Howe asked, standing with one foot on the brass rail at the bar in the hotel lounge known as The Blacksmith's Shop. He cast an imposing figure standing at six foot five, and his demeanor certainly let everyone within earshot know he was in the room. He, like everyone else, was settling his bar bill. Ten o'clock had arrived swiftly. Earlier, after dinner in the smaller pub at the front of the inn, the men from the Massachusetts, Connecticut, New Hampshire, and Vermont chapters of the Sons of the American Revolution had weathered the storm indoors while the Lincoln men and women, dressed in their Lincoln-green colonial garb, had stood outside across the street in the pouring rain and howling wind. They and a few brave others others had hovered over the grave of an English soldier killed on April 19, 1775, and performed a memorial service. The soldier, retreating from the skirmish at the North Bridge, was buried where he had dropped dead, which was now next to the sidewalk across from the inn. Their ceremony this year was abbreviated, and even a few of the SAR members had decided to participate in their authentic colonial uniforms or clothing, holding umbrellas that were mostly useless. As soon as they finished, all filed back into the pub.

Brian looked down at his bill in disbelief. It was $13.13. A chill ran down his spine. All of what Joel Meyer had told him began swirling in his head.

"Is this right?" he asked, handing it to the bartender with the square face and dark, heavy beard.

"Ha—it looks like you're hexed tonight," Ulysses S. Grant shot back unceremoniously. Brian thought the response was unnecessarily mordant. He was simply questioning the amount.

"No, I mean it seems low. I bought more than that, I thought."

"Well, I stand corrected—it's your lucky night. Either you didn't get charged, which I highly doubt, or somebody was picking up the tab, which I suspect is the case. I think that gentleman over there…" He pointed to Bill Howe, now milling around and still carrying on a conversation with Stu and another man from New Hampshire dressed in traditional colonial clothing, as were many in Concord. "He picked up a lot of drinks on his own tab tonight."

"OK. Thanks," Brian muttered. He'd had a few Guinnesses but not enough to make him tipsy. He glanced at the others remaining in the room.

"See you in the morning. Breakfast at nine." he announced to the group.

"Sleeping in, eh? Hey, watch out for the goblins," Howe bellowed, followed by a collective chortle.

Brian left a twenty-dollar bill on the counter and started out toward the stairway. With each step Joel Meyer's voice echoed through his head.

That's all bullshit, Brian thought. *With all the places I've stayed that were supposedly haunted, I've never had an experience. And I would welcome it. Maybe Marilyn Monroe could visit me in the middle of the night,* he mused.

As he approached the door to his room, he heard the wind howling outside. The deadbolt clicked, and after a concerted twist of the doorknob he pushed the door open. Knowing it would be dark when he returned, he had left a few lights on when he left—when the gray glow from the darkening sky had still seeped through the curtained windows and provided some illumination. He looked around cautiously. As soon as he closed the door, a gust of wind battered the side of the outside wall, and he heard a thump.

"Time to explore this dump," he mumbled.

In the bathroom he plopped his shaving kit and contact lens paraphnalia on the counter. Without thinking he glanced out of the door of the bathroom and peered carefully around the room.

Brian removed his contact lenses and put them in a small vial filled with fresh disinfecting solution. Then he put on his glasses—bifocals. He looked up in the mirror at himself and then over his shoulders to the shower behind.

"Damn," he said. "That son-of-a-gun Joel spooked me."

He walked back into the room and looked at the bed. Brian recalled a story he had read about someone seeing an imprint, as if someone were lying on the bed. Had it been about this place or somewhere else he had stayed? *Maybe Kinnity Castle in Ireland. That whole place is haunted as well, but nothing happened when I stayed there, again in the most notorious room.* He wasn't sure. Another gust of wind sent bulky raindrops tapping against the windows like hundreds of tormenting fingertips. In the distance he could hear a shrill squealing and banging, as if the storm were tearing at something, greedily ripping it from its hinges.

Good God…what if we lose power? he thought. *I have a small flashlight, but that's it. Matches, a few, but no candles.*

The television was on wheels—it was an older model and nothing like the new flat-screen high-definition televisions that had recently become so pervasive in the TV market. There was already a scheduled phaseout from analog to digital reception scheduled nationally. He found the remote, turned it on, and began flipping through the stations, looking around the room from time to time when the wind exploded against the building and the lights flickered.

Ali MacGraw and Steve McQueen suddenly appeared on the screen. Brian moved over to the side of the bed and took off his shoes, his eyes focused on the television. He had two bottles of ginger ale with him that he had brought up from downstairs, now cool but no longer cold. He loosened his shirt and pulled up a chair. A commercial came on; it was then that he realized, excitedly, he had stumbled upon the classic 1972 movie *The Getaway.*

This is the perfect diversion, he decided and made himself comfortable. The late '60s and early '70s cars looked ancient—as antiquated as the Buicks and Fords in movies made in the thirties and forties.

⊰▤▧▱⊱

His head snapped up abruptly, and Brian realized that he had nodded off. Now he had a bladder that needed attention. As he stood he looked at his wristwatch and saw that twenty minutes had passed. The storm was raging like a feral animal just beyond the walls of the room. *I should be more worried about getting killed by the weather than being spooked by dead things.*

Walking back through the room from the bathroom and past the end of the bed—which was covered with a blue bedspread that was not especially taut, only wrinkled a bit—Brian sat back down in the chair and quickly glanced around. Satisfied that he was still alone, he turned his attention to the movie again. His eyelids became heavy, and he was fighting the urge to doze off, a battle that in his last conscious thought, he knew he was losing.

Suddenly, frantic pounding at the door behind him startled him awake. His chin had been resting on his chest—he realized that he had, in fact, drifted off again. The room was pitch black, and the only light he could see was flickering faintly behind drawn curtains. It was an eerie orange-yellow glow that ebbed and flowed—like fire.

"Isaac. Isaac."

Still groggy, he heard a large bell begin to peal nearby and then what sounded like the booming of a distant cannon and reports of black-powder rifles, maybe muskets, being fired. *Or is it the storm and thunder influencing a dream?* he wondered. Though it had stopped for a few moments, the pounding on the door began again in earnest.

"Isaac. Isaac. The regulars are out. The regulars are heading this way."

What the hell is going on? Have the re-enacters gone haywire? he pondered, now realizing what was happening.

"Who...who is it?" he growled. In the middle of his question, he cleared phlegm from his throat, which had been idle a while, and groped around his surroundings in the darkness. Nothing was where he had known it to be before he had nodded off.

"It's Timothy. Dr. Timothy Minot. You have to arise, sir. The men are coming—this is a real muster."

Brian didn't move. He could hear a great deal of commotion outside. Gone was the wind and rain.

"Timothy, tell the guys to go ahead without me. I'm just in the color guard."

"The only color soon to be seen will be red—our blood. I'm telling you, the lobsterbacks are on their way here. Sir, this threat is very real, and I know that you are aware of the munitions that are in the back of this building and elsewhere. We must take what we can and try to get as much of the remaining to Colonel Barrett's farm. Several divisions of regulars are in full march. This time we suspect they are truly headed here to destroy our cache and quite possibly us and our homes. There is no time to waste."

Brian's eyes were beginning to adjust to the darkness as he stumbled, moving to where he thought the bed had been. Instead what he could make out vaguely in the indigo shadows was the outline of a table; reaching out to touch it, he realized it was covered with a leather top.

What in God's name? This is an examining table, he realized. *What the hell?*

"OK. OK. Give me a minute, damn it." He reached for the door and fumbled, looking for the key on the bedside table. There was no bedside table where one had been before he'd fallen asleep, he thought only briefly. He felt the door—a skeleton key was in the lock—a lock that had not been there before. The deadbolt was gone as well. He turned the key and heard a click. Then he pulled the door open.

He gasped. Standing before him with an oil lamp was a slim gentleman, a man he had never seen before. He was bald and bespectacled and his clothes were of the colonial era: stockings, breeches, waistcoat, and a linen shirt with a black neck stock. But there was something perculiar about the clothes—they had an unfinished look to them, the material rough and buttons inconsistent in size and shape, as if produced individually. Looking past Dr. Minot, Brian saw that the hallway outside the room was not at all as he remembered it not an hour before—no chandelier, only sconces on the plain walls holding candles flickering scant yellow-orange radiance. He could see where the wax had dripped onto the bases of the sconces.

"Isaac. You are needed downstairs, and I fear I will need my operating room for medical purposes later. Young Prescott arrived and announced that the regulars on their way here to capture our arms. They are in Lexington now, after Adams and Hancock and mean to hang them. We do not know, but they may have enough rope with them to decorate all of our trees should we not escape. We fear that this time it is no false alarm. Hurry, man," the person who had identified himself as Dr. Timothy Minot explained hurriedly.

"Doctor, hold on a second. I'm sort of confused here. First of all, is this a joke? What happened to the storm? And why are you calling me Isaac?"

"Would you rather that I refer to you as Mr. Monroe, sir? Isaac, if you wish to have a storm, I can assure you that one is absolutely approaching—a storm of destruction, confiscation, pillage, ravaging our women, and holy death. This is no fool's errand. Perhaps the fog of your slumber is the explanation for your present muddled nature. Indeed," Minot blustered impatiently.

"Well, why am I in this room, then? I've heard of elaborate hoaxes, but this tops them all. Bill Howe is behind this, isn't he?"

"Howe? My dear young Mr. Monroe, I do not have time to stand here and discuss such folly. We are being attacked, man. I have told you they might hang those of us they cannot slaughter with ball or grapeshot, of that I am certain. The loyalists will sabotage our every plan. We stand to lose our means of defending ourselves, save for shovels and pitchforks, which are certainly no match for the regulars of the British Empire. You must start out at once. This is my house, and you have stayed in the only room available since I examined you last night. You were tired, and we thought due to the late hour you should stay and not travel, considering your circumstance."

"Examined me? For what? What circumstance?"

"Pain and itching in your lower bowel; bleeding—"

"You mean hemorrhoids?"

"I was going to operate today. That is the least of your worries now. All of our lives and property are at risk. Get dressed and come along. Now light your lamp so that I may continue on."

With that Minot removed a crude match from his waistcoat and dipped it into his lamp—it flared, and he handed it to Brian and then scurried toward the stairs. There was only one staircase. Brian did notice discomfort where there had been none before, yet that problem had been taken care of years before.

This is nonsensical—must be a dream, he reasoned.

With the harsh glare of what appeared to be an oversized match Brian located an oil lamp, removed the chimney, and lit the wick. He replaced the chimney and adjusted the flame with the small, round pickwick. Outside, a large bell, like that heard only in churches, continued to clang, and gunshots resounded throughout the center of Concord. He could also hear voices and movement below the stairway—brisk shuffling and shouting. In the street beyond his windows, there was what sounded like great confusion, chaos.

Glancing around the room, he noted that everything was different. His suitcase was gone. There was no bathroom where one had been only an hour before. His glasses had become small spectacles and not bifocals. Feeling them, he knew immediately they were primitive—he removed them and found that they were crude but functional, just as they would have been in the eighteenth century. His cell phone was gone.

"Goddamn it. What is going on here?" he said, his voice raised. Dr. Minot had moved away from his door. "I need a bathroom and in a hurry," Brian entreated. Moving the lamp, he spotted a chamber pot under a chair where clothes, presumably his, were draped.

After relieving himself into the pot, he began to dress. The clothes were his own replica colonial clothing, or at least that was what he thought. Strangely the Jas. Townsend labels were missing, and the material of the navy-blue waistcoat, white vest, and tan breeches had a coarser texture. The white-linen shirt and black neck stock also seemed to be of heavier consistencies. Upon closer inspection the pewter buttons on all of the garments appeared to be the same, or closely consistent, suggesting that each size was made from the same mold, though they were not necessarily as he remembered them.

"Isaac. Hurry. There is no time to tarry."

Brian had no idea who had shouted that message up the stairs, but be buttoned his breeches swiftly and threw on his vest and waistcoat. His leather garters might have been a bit tight, but that was a small price to pay to have his stockings secure. The only shoes in the room were his heavy buckle replica shoes. They, too, had a strange feel from that to which he was accustomed. Rising from the chair, he turned and stalked through the mysterious portal and into the hallway. Without the lamp he never could have navigated the stairs, and without warning he felt a tight pain exactly where the doctor had said it would be.

Such an elaborate production. Isaac who...? he ruminated.

When he reached the last step, he was awestruck. The entire scene was surreal. Dirty, scruffy men rushing back and forth—the odor told him immediately that many of these people had not bathed lately or definitely without any regularity. It was the most eclectic group of men imaginable. There were no women or children in sight, and the light of day had barely seeped from the eastern horizon. The layout of the building was different, and there were great caches of mostly muskets, fowling guns, and an occasional blunderbuss strewn throughout the rooms. There was a range of quality among the weapons, from relatively new forged steel to rust-covered pig iron to homemade and imported French muskets. There was an occasional coveted English Brown Bess among the muskets. They were being carried in bunches out of the front door by the throng of men, young and old.

"Isaac. Good that you were so close."

Brian turned and was greeted by a whiskered red face wearing a seedy, floppy hat, a hunting frock, and a mouth half full of bad teeth. He had a large scar just above his right eye.

"Now, grab some of these and stick with me—we'll have plenty of powder and ball later. Get a good one for yourself, as you'll not be traveling home anytime soon. Here."

Brian walked a few steps to his left and retrieved a Brown Bess musket leaning against the wall. He looked at it and gasped—it was an original first model, and if serviceable it could fetch upward of twenty to thirty thousand dollars.

"If it weren't for Revere and his warnings over the last few weeks, we never would have been able to move most of the stuff out of here to Barrett's farm, Acton and Stowe, like we have and still are. That is except for a few buried cannons. We knew the redcoats were a comin', but we didn't know just when. Damn them if they find them. The king's buggers," floppy hatted bad teeth spluttered.

Suddenly, from somewhere in the building, a booming voice rang out above the din. Brian was unable to see who the orator was.

"Gentleman, gentleman."

A hush fell over the crowd in deference to the speaker's appeal.

"We have met with the reverend Emerson. The alarm has gone out to muster the militia, not just here but in Stow, Bedford, Acton, and Sudbury. As the Committee of Safety has planned, alarm riders have been sent out to our neighboring colonies as well. Reuben Brown has been sent down the road to see what the regulars are up to, particularly in Menotomy and Lexington. All are to gather in the meetinghouse as soon as this work is finished here. Make haste, men." The speaker, a man possessing a sturdy, confident baritone timbre, as yet unseen and unrecognized, stopped. The frenetic, desperate activity resumed.

Stepping into the middle of the turmoil and the shouting, Brian glanced at the door and saw torches outside and the heads and shoulders of men above the curtains in the wavy glass windows. He put his lamp on a table nearby and placed his black tricorne hat upon his head. Looking back into the hallways and room that just a few hours ago had contained the counter where he had checked into the inn, he saw by candlelight, mostly, a diverse collection of men bustling about, men of all ages and backgrounds, many obviously farmers, carrying and dragging all forms and shapes of armaments and ordinance out of the door.

Suddenly he froze in his tracks. Looking straight ahead he saw his image, or at least the reflection of someone in a large, almost full-length mirror in a gilded frame. Brian shifted his weight and moved his head slightly to one side—the figure followed as if in pantomime. He did it twice again with the same result. He removed his hat. It didn't look at all like him—at least twenty-five years younger and a full head of bushy, sleep-tousled blond hair.

Those eyes; the nose and chin...Who is this stranger I'm staring at? he pondered.

"Here, Isaac, take these, and let's get over to the tavern. There'll be time for primping another day but not today, I'm afraid. Doesn't matter what you look like if you're dangling from the end of a rope or have your brains and arse splattered about the countryside from ball and grapeshot."

The stranger was tall and lanky and wearing what appeared to be a home-spun woolen vest. His shirtsleeves were rolled up to his elbows and revealed strong, sinewy forearms; he was one of the few not wearing a hat of some kind and sported a tussled head of thick, wavy light-brown hair. He handed Brian three muskets. Brian stumbled slightly with the weight of the now four muskets and started toward the door. Suddenly he was jostled, and the bar-rel of one of the muskets hit the doorway jamb as he careened clumsily. The cobwebs of sleep in his head had cleared, yet his still-waking body lagged from the brusque awakening minutes before.

"Oh, sorry, Mr. Monroe."

Brian turned his head and was face to face with a strapping lad wear-ing a brown woolen vest and a soiled ticking shirt. He was not a day older than sixteen, with blond hair and grease, or something resembling grease in the dim gray shadowy light, smudged across his forehead and left cheek. He was clutching a new French Charleville musket in his large left hand; both hands were blackened with the same substance that was on his face.

"I have to get to the tavern immediately. The Minute Company is muster-ing now. I think we're going out to meet Tommy on the road and give him his comeuppance."

Brian stopped abruptly and let the boy through. He was obviously a min-uteman. Then, rebalancing the guns, Brian nodded to no one particularly, turned sideways, and lurched through the foyer and front door. Several other men and one woman were queued outside, waiting for the doorway to be passable. Brian looked up at the square. His mouth fell open in disbelief.

"Oh my God," he muttered just above a whisper. The sight had taken his breath away.

There were no monuments and no grass—in fact no discernible parameters of the square. No cars, no wires, no streetlights, no sidewalks, and few trees. The hill on the other side of the road was not covered with graves, as it had been only hours before. There were none of those old tilting, weatherworn, and aged stones, many that once had legible names and dates and words that had long since been lost to the ravages of time.

Am I seeing the living faces and hearing the voices of the patriots who will fill that hallowed ground? he considered incredulously.

Though the area was topographically recognizable, not much else was familiar. Across the murky air, he espied the Liberty Pole and flag waving in the early morning breeze in the square, just where history had said it was. His knees buckled at the sudden realization of what he was witnessing—whether created in his mind as he slept or, by some quirk of paranormal activity, having passed through a dimension or some portal of time travel, it was the early hours of the morning of April 19, 1775.

The center of the square was a large dirt area teeming with wagons of all sizes and shapes, drawn by oxen and horses. It was a chaotic scene of disorderly order: small groups of people who seemed to be acting in concert. By flickering orange torchlight and the fading indigo-pastel yellow of the creeping early spring dawn, overloaded carts filed with armament were sent plodding down what was not much more than a rutted pathway in the direction of the North Bridge. A sickly, pungent odor of burning tar and corn husks mixed with fresh manure permeated the air.

Brian was sweating—it was cool but not cold. The bell continued to peal, and he could still hear the indiscriminant musket fire, which reminded him vaguely of muffled firecrackers heard in the distance on the Fourth of July. Instinctively he knew that muskets and other black powder gunshots have a distinctive sound.

Beyond the square, veiled in a haze of smoke and dust, he recognized the church, or the meetinghouse, however it was not where it had been earlier in the day when he had arrived—and it was facing a different direction. That was the source of the bell, unquestionably loud enough to alert the countryside. Wright Tavern was still where it should have been, and he noticed a crowd gathering there as well as in front of the meetinghouse. Somehow the night had cleared, and despite the brightening sky, some stars were still visible. Looking over his shoulder, he saw the moon prominent in the sky. It looked no different, yet he knew men, Americans, had walked on it in his lifetime.

"Isaac, put those in the nearest cart, and let's get to the tavern," urged a new voice coming at him from behind and to his right. Turning, Brian saw that the speaker was a stout man accompanied by a slender woman dressed like a camp follower. A bonnet shaded her face. Her dress, made of good-quality cotton, billowed slightly as she quickened her pace toward him. A pair of burly arms that came at Brian from his left relieved him of all but the Brown Bess just as the woman threw her arms around his shoulders and pressed her face against his chest.

"Oh, Isaac. I am fearful. This will be bad business. I fear for your safety, my dearest," she declared affectionately, desperation clear in her tone.

"Mercy. Please. Remember your probity. You are in the public square," admonished the stout man, who was nattily attired. Judging by the quality of his apparel, which could have been imported from England, as well as his manner and bearing, he must have been someone of affluence and importance. Unlike any of the other men Brian had seen since being rousted from his room, this man had clean fingernails.

Brian hadn't seen the woman's face, but her voice had an eerie familiarity: the cadence, the rhythm. He held her loosely, and then she pulled away. Their eyes met. He started—he knew this woman. And it wasn't just their eyes that met. Their souls touched. They were kindred. Brian Winslow realized that he was in the presence of someone to whom he was very close despite the fact that, as far as he could know, they had just met. Her touch; her clean, soapy-fresh smell—she had an aura that enveloped him like a cocoon.

"I wish your duty was with me. Only goodness would come of it, Isaac, my love." she said softly, pulling away, dropping her hands down, and grasping both of his hands. Hers was a velvety, warm touch. Glancing down, he observed that her hands and fingernails were also unsoiled.

He watched her carefully as she reached into a pocket of her high-collar, full-length cotton dress—other than her hands and upper neck, not an inch of flesh was showing. The skin on her face was porcelain white and smooth

No hair was showing, but her dark eyebrows led him to believe she was a brunette. Her nose and chin were graceful, sculptured, her lips pouting with fleshy tenderness. Winsome cheeks ran along the ridges of high, delicate cheekbones. Brian Winslow knew this face.

The stately man stepped forward. Brian could now see a resemblance to the woman.

"Now, Mercy, despite the fact that Isaac is your betrothed, a public display of such affection is reserved for those of a much lower…" He glanced around quickly as his voice fell off and the back of his right hand rose to cover his mouth. "Shall we say…ahem…position than is ours. Dear sister, please try to control yourself, and have a bit more discretion."

"In these times, my brother Jacob, in spite of our STATION AND STANDING, I have no intention of abiding by your principles in the face of such danger to the man I adore with all of my heart."

Brian watched her intently as she delivered her declaration. *The way she moves, those eyes, her mannerisms, the very feeling that has possessed me being near her—everything about her I know. My God, who is this woman? How could I feel such affection…no…maybe even love?* He wracked his memory, trying to figure out this bizarre situation and his inexplicable feelings while trying to assimilate the juxtaposition of events swirling around him.

"Mercy, why do I know you so well? And we are to marry?" Brian asked carefully.

"Oh, you are playful to the end. I love that about you. But I cannot laugh this morning. Please, I beg of you. Be careful," she implored. "I want you to keep this with you at all times."

He held out his hand, palm up, into which she carefully dropped a metal object. He looked down—it was a small silver cross.

"May it protect you, and may you think of me when you touch it or look upon it. Through God's grace, my sweetest of men, please return to me."

"Isaac, we must get over to the meetinghouse. Mercy, get on now. You must go to safety—to the Buttrick Farm on Punkataskett Hill," demanded her brother, Jacob.

"Oh, Isaac. My heart will be with you. No matter what happens, I will love you forever and ever."

Brian hugged her and then, releasing her, turned away and began walking.

"Isaac," she said. "Do you not wish to at least bid me farewell?"

He stopped and looked back at her. There were her eyes, waiting. Eyes that had been watching him intently and hoping for another glimpse as he moved toward the meetinghouse—toward destiny.

"Mercy, may God do his will," he said. Brian had no idea where the words had come from, but he felt them. Then he joined the throng headed for the tavern. He stopped and spun around; she ran into his arms once again and raised her lips to his ear.

"Oh, my dearest Isaac," she whispered, loud enough to be heard over the shouting and mayhem, but only by him. "God bless you, dearest, and may he return you to me so that you may father more of our children—more than your child who now lives and grows within me. Oh, Isaac, come back safely, and help me satisfy this unquenchable desire to bear as many of your children as I may, all that you wish to give me."

❧❧

"Men…" The voice was deep and resonated throughout the hall; it was measured and calm. Brian recognized it as the same voice from the inn. "The regulars are definitely coming this way."

A murmur rumbled through the crowd as the realization that this was the very moment every member of the Concord militia and minutemen had anticipated—and for which, over the previous months, they had been training.

"Now is not the time for undisciplined action or thoughtless provocation. Therefore we must decide as a group what we are to do so that we may act as one body. Time is very much of the essence."

"Major Buttrick, why don't we all meet them on the road? We have the training and numbers," shouted a younger voice. There was a supportive cry from several clusters gathered in the back of the crowded tavern.

"Major, what are the numbers of the regulars?" asked an older man, salt-and-pepper hair sticking out from under a wide-brimmed brown hat. He was sitting closer to the front and wore a well-seasoned hunting frock.

"We don't have a count, but when Reuben Brown returns we should have a better idea. Young Prescott said there were several regiments of foot, marines, and grenadiers. Could be as many as a thousand."

"Then we are outnumbered, and to face them would be folly, and surely there is no quicker way to meet our maker," shouted a hardy gray-bearded man standing on the side and holding an older firing piece.

Buttrick quickly glanced at the men assembled in front of him and shouted, "Those favoring a stand right here, so say aye." There was a loud response but far from unanimous.

"Then those suggesting a more defensive position down the road and leaving scouts here in town, so say aye." It was obvious that the first set of ayes were in the majority. It was clear that the older men in the militia had made their decision from experience and wisdom, the younger men from emotion. The former desired to wait to see how events unfolded before committing to a particular course of action, and the vote reflected that fact.

"Then let us form our lines outside immediately. I will be discussing our battle plans more closely with the other officers. However, no man should feel that he cannot speak up and voice his opinion. We are not tyrants like bloody King George."

"Huzzah, huzzah, huzzah," shouted the men, and then they streamed out of the building into the common.

"Wait, wait, wait," Buttrick shouted above the commotion. But now it was too late—the throng had piled out into the street, some into Wright's Tavern. As Brian bumped and moved, he responded to greetings and nods of heads indicating familiarity without hesitation, knowing only that he was among the most revered of American heroes, the original patriots. These were the men whose graves he had walked upon; he had read their names on weathered headstones. Some he had honored posthumously with wreaths, accolades, and prayers as a member of the Sons of the American Revolution.

Looking into their faces, he saw not only their commitment but also the gauge of their generations: the youth, reckless and eager; the young fathers and husbands, careful yet determined to protect home and family; and the older men, wise and calculating, centered in reality, many veterans of the Seven Years' War, otherwise known as the French and Indian War, which had been waged some two decades prior.

Somewhere close by a skunk had let go—the odor now permeated the air.

⇥⇤

A red-orange hue had risen in the east as the blue-black sky retreated westward. Without trees the horizon was observable—most of the colonies had been defoliated, as the tall, strong trees were a valuable and needed resource. Brian knew that before the cutting had begun in the seventeenth century, the canopy in the New England wilderness had been, in many places, as much as one hundred feet high, with timber standing as tall and thick as western sequoias. The common in Concord was now clear except for a single wagon and the several companies of militia and minutemen.

Word had arrived in the form of saddler Reuben Brown, upon his return astride a frothing, sweaty steed, that there had been shots fired in Lexington. The minutemen had formed up and headed down the road toward Lexington, their plan to engage the regulars before they reached the town.

"But were the regulars firing ball?" Brian overheard Buttrick ask Brown, just as history had recorded the conversation.

"I do not know but think it probable," answered Brown, panting and trying to catch his breath. To the east the sky, clear and cloudless, lightened to a more golden, presunrise glow. "I did not tarry for fear that harm or capture should befall me, and I would not be able to complete my mission."

"Good, good," Buttrick growled, though unsure if long-anticipated mortal hostilities had commenced in the cool April dawn, therefore giving reasonable cause for deadly defense. "Men, we will hold our position for now," he shouted.

Brown had righted himself in the saddle, having caught his breath after a feverish gallop.

"How many regulars, Mr. Brown?"

"Many. Several regiments from my estimation."

"Thank you, sir." Buttrick turned to the militia. "Do not load ball quite yet, men. Advance up the hill."

Brian, unsure of what he was doing, followed the man in front of him and snuck an occasional sideways glance to see what the others in his company were doing as well. They all seemed to be well trained and moved together. So far his behavior had not belied his ineptness and lack of training. Whatever disorder there had been initially had been channeled into ordered military precision. They stopped at the top of the hill, and all of the Concord companies were now positioned in reformed lines.

The Reverend Emerson suddenly emerged from the meetinghouse as the men climbed the steep hill that Brian knew only as a cemetery but without a grave in sight on this morning. As soon as they had reassembled on the hill, a clamor quickly spread through the ranks with the news that the Acton, Bedford, and Sudbury militia were assembling on Punkataskett Hill just beyond the North Bridge. There were smiles and sounds of growing confidence as most realized their strength, though somewhat fractured at the present time, had probably doubled from approximately 250. The top of the sun peaked above the horizon.

All heads turned as the first sounds of fifes and drums wafted over the cool morning breeze.

Brian glanced over his left shoulder and saw a group of men at the top of the hill embroiled in a heated discussion. They were out of earshot. He noticed Major Buttrick reacting with deference to an older gentleman dressed unexceptionally and wearing a wide-brimmed, floppy hat. From his knowledge of the skirmish at Concord, Brian sensed it must be Colonel James Barrett, commander of the Middlesex regiment. Another younger man, well dressed in comparison to the other members of the militia companies, seemed to be arguing rather demonstratively with the older members of the cabal. To Brian's right the minister William Emerson was working his way along the lines toward him, encouraging the men and patting them on their arms and backs. The fifes and drums were growing louder and more distinct.

Across the barren fields, the Minute Company was marching in formation in the direction of the common via the Boston Road. Not far behind the minutemen, the distance hard to estimate, was an endless column of red, white, and glistening steel. It was the regulars, now clearly visible.

"What in God's creation are they doing?" an anonymous voice boomed nearby. "Escorting the redcoats into town?"

"Who are those guys up there?" Brian whispered to the lean, wide-eyed, whiskered farmer to his right, one of only a few wearing suspenders. A lifetime of toil in the rugged New England climate was etched into his leathery, unshaven face. His sloping bumpy nose was speckled with dark hairs. He turned his head owlishly toward the top of the hill, squinting, and then glanced back disgustedly at Brian.

"Those are the officers—we elected 'em," he spat toothlessly. "That's Barrett in the floppy hat next to Buttrick. He's the colonel. That young one, the one doin' most of the talkin', is Lieutenant Hosmer. He's got more money than brains and sounds like a bloody Tory. I'm afeared of that one—might be a spy. I dunno. Still, the dumb sons a bitches are fightin' among demselves and about to get us all shot, hung, or taken back to Boston and keel hauled, damn it."

The small cadre of officers stared down the road intently, Buttrick with a brass spyglass. The head with the floppy hat identified as Barrett, with his back to the lines, bobbed as if speaking. The officers nodded among themselves and began descending the hill.

The men were facing east. The sun was now fully above the horizon as the minutemen swaggered into the common, fifes and drums providing an exuberant cadence, probably inspired by fear. The companies on the hill began to move as the officers shouted out orders. Looking east, Brian, a veteran of the United States Army, saw in the distance the impressive military tactical presence of the British regulars, now moving like a drill team with more speed and alacrity—it looked like double time. Now the drums of the regulars, as they drew closer, pounded out a concussive beat like a malevolent metronome, and, combined with the resolute pounding of the marching boots, was heard above all other sounds. The regulars were all business, and Brian knew that would not bode well for the Concordians. The ribbon of red, green, yellow and flashing metal seemed endless. This was no Sunday stroll to frighten the colonists. The militiamen were silent as they hastily descended the hill to the common and began to reform into two lines. Swatches of green that had been approaching in the distance from the southeast, the Lincoln militia, marched into the common and joined the Concord lines. The drum beats grew louder.

Jesus Christ. Here I've been so caught up in being a witness to the living history here that I haven't considered—I could get killed, Brian realized as he glanced over his shoulder at the rapidly advancing column of His Majesty King George III's professional soldiers.

Someone shouted an order to move out, and the formation began to trudge down the road toward the next hill, between the center of Concord and the North Bridge.

※

From the right side of Punkataskett Hill, where Colonel Barrett had ultimately led the companies of minutemen and militiamen on this picturesque mid-April New England morning, overlooking the North Bridge and nearly a mile from the center of town, Brian and the rest of the men, women, children, and barking dogs watched with fascinated curiosity. The gleaming sunlight served an eerie dual purpose this day: It not only melted the shimmering dew from the landscape but also illuminated in blazing brilliance the intimidating highly polished steel and brass of the British Army's swords, bayonets, muskets, gorgets, and other decorative acoutrements as the companies crossed the North Bridge. Two British companies fanned out on their way up the hill and stopped. Four companies kept going.

"They're headed for Barrett's," growled the same old toothless farmer standing at Brian's left. "That's the work of spies. How else did the bastards know where to go?" he added.

"Get these dogs out of here—and women and children as well. There could be ball flying any minute," rang out a voice from somewhere in the rear.

Reinforcements from the surrounding towns continued arriving. Brian recognized that a few units were exceptionally well prepared. The hill began to resemble a battlefield and definitely not a place for anyone other than soldiers.

Colonel Barrett walked past with Major Buttrick and the younger Hosmer. Closer now, Brian saw that Barrett was wearing a leather apron over what looked like a work coat. This was in stark contrast to the uniformed officers and multicolored troops of the king's army that had passed to the right as well as the regular units at the base the hill near the bridge. They surveyed the area silently. Buttrick pointed to the North Bridge, being held by a company that Brian remembered from his knowledge of the history of the battle scene to be the Regular 43rd Foot.

From the hill they could see the balance of the regulars swarming like ants in the town. The defoliated hills reminded Brian of Scotland, and it presented an odd perspective of what was a familiar sight. Absent on either side of the Concord River at the bridge were the monument with Ralph Waldo Emerson's "Concord Hymn" and French's minuteman statue. And the bridge itself was of rough hewn construction in contrast to the sturdier replicas of the modern era.

"And if Revere hadn't made his trips out here recently, the sons a bitches would have captured ALL of our guns and cannon. Damnation those Tory spies," groused the old farmer, continuing a thought and a statement started earlier. Brian had learned that his name was Jake Chamberlain.

"Did you see or meet Revere?" Brian inquired, having been seduced by the incredible history unfolding in front of him and wondering why and how he had gotten here—and how and if he would return to his life some 230 years into the future to describe it.

"Not me, but Samuel here did. Samuel, hey," barked Jake Chamberlain, "come over here."

A short man no taller than five feet—that was another thing Brian noted: most of the men were short, only a few even approaching six feet, which would have been historically correct—Samuel looked over at Chamberlain. Particularly sloppy looking and covered with filth, Samuel leered at the old farmer. "What the hell do you want, you old buzzard?" he snapped back.

"Git over here," ordered Jake. He turned to Brian. "My son-in-law. Pig farmer—smells it too. How my daughter got mixed up with this damnation runt of a fool I'll never know," he muttered. "I think he ruts with the sows."

Despite the feigned surly belligerence, the short man approached.

"You seen Revere. Tell Isaac here."

"Tell him what?" Samuel replied churlishly.

Jake turned to Brian. "What do you want to know?"

"Well, what did he look like? What did his voice sound like? What did he say?"

"Damn. We may all die here, and you want to know that?" said Samuel.

"Just answer him, you damn fool," bristled Jake. "If it ain't pigs, you can't hear nothin'."

"All right. He was a good rider for sure. Handled a horse fine. Spoke softly but quickly. Stocky. Losing his hair. I was on the Committee of Safety, so I met him. Warned us to move our arsenal—spies were everywhere, including ours in the regulars, so's he knew they were probably coming here soon. Came here twice before. Why do you ask?"

"You heard that he made it to Lexington last night?"

"Yup. Heard he was captured, though. That's what young Prescott says. They meant to kill him, and I suspect they did. We should draw and quarter the whole murderous lot."

"Was his voice high, low, or...well, how would you describe it?"

"Normal for a man."

"Thanks," Brian said. He wouldn't divulge that he knew Revere had escaped. And that Major Edward Mitchell, part of an advance unit of officers sent out by General Gage the day before to be positioned along the planned route of the regulars, had threatened Revere with a pistol to Revere's head before he had escaped. Their failed mission had been to intercept the several alarm riders like Revere and William Dawes, therefore maintaining the surprise aspect of the incursion. To have made that known would have aroused enormous suspicion, and rightly so.

"You a spy?" Samuel asked, glaring at Brian.

"Go back to your place, you damn fool. Why would the man be here if he was a spy? You have the brain of a pig. You know as well as I do that the bloody town's full of Tories. Those two strangers what came through last month were spies, and we run 'em out along with that rodent Bliss," roared the father-in-law. The short man retreated to his original position without looking back.

"Isaac, Samuel's nearly an idiot. My apologies," said Jake.

Several in the line who had witnessed the conversation snickered at the comical diversion.

"So, do you have any other family in the militia?" Brian asked.

"Hell, we all do. If you ain't family to no one or t'other, then you probly ain't from these parts. Some here are relations from other places now. Land is a shrinkin', and ya cain't get off the land what ya used to. Pretty much worked out. Now, I know your family is like that too. Your granddaddy Benjamin Monroe's land's been split up just about as much as it can. Same with most of the town founders. Guessin' your boys'll have to move on to make their stake like the rest of 'em at their age. Head north or west, don't make no difference—where there's room, anyhow. Just as well. Real hard scrabble here, and with things the way they been for the last few years, I don't have to tell you its been a struggle to make ends meet."

Brian nodded, but he was gazing up the hill, behind the troops, squinting, concentrating on a small group of women and children, almost too far away to discern. *Where did Mercy go?* he wondered. She had struck a nerve, and he longed to see her again. Remarkably he caught sight of her slight figure in the distance—she was waving to him. She was no longer wearing the bonnet, and her strawberry-auburn hair rested upon her shoulders and wisped in the tender morning breeze. He waved back. She blew him a kiss. *I know that woman as I know myself,* he confessed to himself.

"They're moving," someone shouted. Talking among the assembled militia companies ceased; tension filled the air. The footfalls of some of the regular companies marching and dogs barking at the top of the hill behind them were the only sounds that punctuated the ominous spring air.

"They knew just where to go, didn't they?" the old man growled gutturally. "Went straight to Barrett's. Them sons-a-bastards loyalists. Shoulda tarred and feathered 'em all and run 'em out when we had the chance."

Then the order came, but only after consultation with all of the militia: advance slowly in organized lines, without breaking rank, toward the regulars below, who were guarding the pathway to the bridge for the companies returning from the Barrett farm. The colonists' numbers had grown; they began to edge carefully down the hill.

❊

The militia units had formed a long line facing the bridge. Brian as well as the others could see the town beyond. The regulars had so far retreated from their advances. Brian was edgy—he knew what was going to happen. It had played out dozens of times in books, movies, and re-enactments. But this was different. Despite the fair skies and abundant sunshine, the atmosphere was ominous, uncertain. Eyes darted from side to side, weight shifted from foot to foot, throats were cleared anxiously, nervous coughs hacked quietly, and sweaty palms gripped the stocks of their weapons, mostly heavy muskets, as many thoughts went to family and loved ones.

An unarmed figure broke from the ranks of the militia and walked towards the regulars. He stood talking to the regulars briefly, and then climbed the hill. Someone handed him his musket and he headed back—the regulars let him through, and on his way. Brian knew, as history had recorded it, that this was Lincoln farmer James Nichols, an English immigrant who had no stomach to fight the regulars. He had gone home.

Colonel Barrett, floppy hat pulled down, stood with Major Buttrick and Lieutenant Hosmer, who was wearing a butternut-brown coat. Militia, minutemen, and their officers were indistinguishable by their everyday clothing, some dressed in their Sunday best, should their hasty burials be necessary. They resembled exactly what they were—an eclectic collection of farmers, shopkeepers, and tradesmen, a stark contrast to the majestically uniformed soldiers of the British Empire, the greatest military force in the world.

Suddenly a stream of smoke rose over the town. The officers had moved closer, and Brian overheard Hosmer snarl at his superior officer, Colonel Barrett, "Will you let them burn the town down?"

Captain Smith of the Lincoln militia shouted that his men were prepared to run the regulars from the bridge, and then further down the line Captain Isaac Davis of Acton, sword held high, roared, "I haven't a man who is afraid to go." Brian stared at Davis, father of several small children, knowing he would soon suffer his fate and be forever etched into the history of the American Revolution.

Barrett turned toward the line, took a few steps, and then stopped. "Load ball," he bellowed. Many had done so already. Some double loaded shot into their guns. He began to walk up and down the line, urging the men to hold their fire unless fired upon, but if it happened, to fire back as fast as they could. He glanced back curiously at the regulars holding the bridge and then twisted his head and spat to one side. The billow of smoke rising from in the town had grown.

"Form up. Advance until I say halt." Barrett's voice thundered throughout the valley and echoed across the hill. The men moved forward in double file. Brian watched as the British soldiers responded and began to fall back, their officers glaring up at the colonial resistance with contempt and shouting orders, their clipped voices precise, snapping with authority.

Can Mercy see me now? Is she watching? Brian wondered.

"Well, this is it," growled the old man. He glanced over at Brian and nodded, a twinkle in his clouded eyes. "Godspeed, Isaac Monroe. I hope I live to see my niece marry the man she truly loves."

Brian, concentrating on staying in line, answered perfunctorily, "So do I. Good luck, Jake." They were moving closer to the regulars, who eyed them with the utmost contempt.

"She hasn't taken her eyes off of ya," Jake mumbled. "Back there, on the hill. And don't go gettin' kilt, or she'd never forgive me, either. Mercy, that is." Then he spat again.

Surprised, Brian turned his head quickly and peered at the old man. He stumbled.

"Straighten up and eyes forward, or you might get one betwixt the eyes any second," he heard from behind, the comment obviously directed at him. Regaining his stride, Brian watched as the well-trained and better-equipped Acton militia marched crisply to the front, their child fifer and single drummer playing a lively version of "The White Cockade," a tune that mocked the English monarchy, unquestionably selected to provoke the ire of their adversaries. Minute companies followed the Acton militia, who, Brian now noticed, had bayonets affixed to their muskets like the regulars.

The British companies had now all crossed back over the bridge and looked skittish. As the militia and minutemen companies moved forward, there seemed to be confusion and disarray in the ranks of the regulars.

"Look," someone in the ranks said. "They're pulling up the planks on the bridge."

"Leave our bridge alone," shouted Major Buttrick who was now more personally invested in the fight than anyone as the militia units were standing on his ancestral family land—his house was at the top of the hill behind them: Behind them, where Brian felt the warmth and presence of a woman he had only just met, but somehow knew her and his feelings for her as if he had known her forever.

Suddenly a shot rang out followed by a billow of smoke from the direction of the regulars…then another…then a disorganized volley. Ball whistled overhead as most of the shots were high, but some were not. One of the Acton men, the one who drew his sword, whom Brian knew was the Acton captain Isaac Davis, fell back, deep red blood spurting from his chest and covering the men around him. Near Davis Private Abner Hosmer fell, as did four others, including the young fifer. The militia continued marching forward toward the bridge.

Others were being hit by the British volleys until they stopped, now only about fifty yards from the bridge. Buttrick turned and screamed, "Fire, fellow soldiers, for God's sake, fire!"

Everyone in the ranks began yelling, "Fire."

The regulars were trapped. Brian saw many of the officers fall as well as several of the soldiers. Then, seeing the predicament they were in the, the regulars started running back up the road toward the center of Concord. The militia and the minutemen stopped firing. Brian's ears were ringing from the concussion, and his vision was obliterated from the smoke that now covered the entire area; both sides of the river. He backed up and put the musket butt on the ground. It was a stroke of luck that he'd had experience firing several replica Brown Bess muskets—he was not unfamiliar with powder loading. The barrel was warm. He reloaded. In the turmoil, units and lines had broken apart and pandemonium reigned. Officers ran frantically about, trying to regain order.

Barrett reorganized a force on the muster field above, which included Jake and many of the older men, while the younger militia and minutemen, led by Buttrick and including Brian, crossed the bridge in pursuit of the regulars. Dead and injured regulars littered the area. Wounded and bloodied English soldiers, some grotesque and near death, writhed and screamed and crawled. The scene was splattered with gore.

At the front of the column, Buttrick shouted, "Here they come. Take a position on the hill behind the stone wall." The men scattered, and Brian flopped down next to a young man he judged to be in his mid-teens.

"Hello, Mr. Monroe," the boy said. "I'm Amos Brown."

"Are you a minuteman?" Brian asked.

"Yes, sir. And didn't we show them back there?"

"I suppose we did."

"Oh, look. Here they come. Stopped. Lord, we could pick them officers off like gophers. They didn't even take their dead and wounded with them. Did you see the one with his brains blowed out? They must be comin' back for them now. Oh God, look—there's that Elias Brown right in the center of town. I guess they know he's just crazy. Nobody's botherin' him. Ahh—now they're a goin' back. No stomach for another quarrel."

"Roadkill." Brian snickered despite the fact that he had been repulsed by the scene.

"Huh? What's that mean?"

"Close your gobs, damn you. And hold your fire," hissed a forceful whisper nearby.

Brian looked up, and saw that the four companies of regulars that had been at Barrett's Farm began running. They passed Barrett's men on the hill and then crossed the bridge. No shots were fired. As the redcoats scurried past Brian and the units on the rise above the road, there was chuckling among the militia. It was more of a release born of the realization that they were alive and had overcome fear—their confidence was buttressed and they now had the upper hand. The regulars ran past their dead and struggling wounded, some crying out for help from their fellow soldiers. Not one fleeing regular stopped, as it was clear they knew that their own lives hung by a thread, as if the sword of Damocles dangled above every head. It was certain that if they stopped and tried to take on the militia units on the hill, they would surely be massacred.

"I say we give Tommy his due right now," Amos suggested eagerly. "Kill 'em all."

"Shhh, damn you. Shut your face, Amos. Hold your fire" was repeated, louder this time, and it sounded like Buttrick himself.

After the regulars passed, Buttrick walked behind them. "I want these men to go the back way to Meriam's Corner."

Amos rose quickly, as did Brian. They were included in the sweeping motion that Buttrick was repeating.

Now I'm surely in the middle of it. If I balk now they'll shoot me for treason, Brian concluded. *Jesus, I like history just as much as the next guy, but how and why the hell did I get right in the middle of it? Better yet, how the hell do I get out of this predicament?*

"Mr. Monroe, why didn't you join the Minute Company?" the young soldier asked as they staggered along the crest of the hill.

"Not sure. Too old, I guess," Brian answered, becoming winded alongside the younger man, though he was not much younger than the person Brian had seen in the mirror earlier at Dr. Minot's.

"Ha…too old. My brothers are older than you." The boy sniggered.

"I suppose I'm more of a militiaman, then. Call me Isaac, please!"

"That must be it. I'll bet we're in for a real fight at Meriam's, Isaac." The boy smiled appreciably at the acknowledgement of his accepted equality and familiarity.

"I reckon so," Brian heard himself saying, a phrase he could not remember ever saying before. He looked back toward Punkataskett Hill and saw tiny objects moving around just above Barrett's militia forces on the muster field in front of Buttrick's house. He knew that one of them was Mercy—and he knew not why, but he longed to get back to her. He suspected there would be more danger ahead before he could.

"Say, Isaac," asked Amos. "Where did you git that accent? I know you're from around here, and I never talked to you before, but it sure ain't nothin' I ever heard before."

⚔

What cover there was around Concord center was mostly quiet, as the ground was springtime soft. Smaller units skirted the outskirts of the town in large concentric circles, moving cautiously, wary of British patrols and flanking parties. Brian and his new young friend, their heavy, primed muskets in their hands at their sides, broke off as their unit sought higher ground. As they reached the rise of each hill, climbing higher, to their right they could make out the center of Concord. Whatever was burning before was out, and the town was spared for the most part, although from where they were they could see a lot of debris everywhere, as if a good deal of ransacking had occurred.

"I wonder what the time is," Brian posed, basically a rhetorical question.

"Oh, it's about midday, Isaac," the young Amos stated confidently. "The sun is just about where it should be right now. Noon. Hey, look," he suddenly announced excitedly. He pointed to the Boston Road off in the far distance. A ribbon of regular soldiers were advancing away from Concord.

"They're leaving," Brian confirmed. Without saying so he recognized the corpulent Lieutenant Colonel Francis Smith on horseback at the front of the column. Historically that was accurate.

"Look," Amos said, poking Brian's arm and pointing northwestward. Several companies of militia streamed across the terrain toward Meriam's Corner, like ants on a warm spring day. "Now they're in for a real spanking," he gloated.

Suddenly, a split second after several loud reports from nearby muskets, Brian felt a thud against his back and was knocked forward with an excruciating pain just under his shoulder blade. Just as he fell, he turned his head to his left and saw Amos running away in the opposite direction of the shots. Two more shots were fired, and Brian heard a voice with a noticeable Cockney accent say, "Well, we got one of the bloody devils—let's finish him off with the bayonets."

God damn it. A flanking party. Didn't see or hear them. They must have snuck up behind us. Shit. Now I'm done for. Brian's heart was racing, and the pain was numbing.

"Move on. Leave him. He'll bleed out anyway. Take his gun. Look at them over there on those hills and meadows. He'll not be of concern to us, but they most assuredly will. Besides, someone was sure to have heard the shots. Let's get out of here—quickly," said an authoritative voice with a more refined enunciation of the king's English, the speaker unseen by Brian. His entire right side was now in agony, throbbing, and he knew he was losing blood. Heavy boots shuffled around him. He laid still, even slowed his breathing down as best he could, hoping that the movement was imperceptible and he would be left for dead. He coughed.

"C'mon, Captain. Just let me run the bugger through once or twice and finish him off," the possessor of the Cockney brogue entreated.

"Leave him to die on his own time, not ours," another voice responded. "We'll soon suffer his fate if we don't move fast—that bayonet will have a need for fresh blood before you know it."

Then Brian heard the soldiers moving away quickly. When the footsteps had faded, he tried to stand but fell forward on his face. He was now wracked with pain, nauseous, and thirsty. Another set of footsteps approached. He tried to see but realized he had lost his glasses.

"He's badly wounded. You two men there, get him to town to Dr. Minot's. Then head for Meriam's Corner. You can join the party there."

In the distance an explosion of musket fire erupted. Brian felt four hands lifting him to his feet.

"Like I said, you can join the party at Meriam's Corner, gentlemen."

"He's got hit from behind in his back," said one of the men holding Brian.

"Can you walk, lad?" a hearty voice cried in his ear.

Brian tried to speak but only managed a dry-throated gasp.

"We have you. We have your spectacles as well. Do your best, friend."

On each side a strong man hurried him down in the direction of the town while his legs, shaky and unable to support him, pedaled uselessly. With each step that his rescuers took, pain shot through his upper right side, as if he were being stabbed repeatedly.

My God, if I die here, what of Meredith and my family? They're in another century right now, for Christ's sake, he pondered. *And all along I thought I was in a dream. This doesn't feel like a dream. And Mercy, what is the mystery of her?*

Brian was losing strength as they reached the square. Both men, breathing heavily and soaked with perspiration, looked ahead and began dragging Brian across the square. Almost immediately several others, men and women, came to their assistance, picking up Brian's feet and supporting his midsection.

"Here—set him down and put him on this plank," one of the volunteers exclaimed.

Once laid on the broken section of what seemed to be a door, Brian, barely conscious, rolled his head and saw the smoldering remains of the Liberty Pole and some of the scattered debris left behind by the marauding regulars.

"Thank you, kind sirs. We must get on and rejoin our unit," said one of the militiamen who had carried Brian into town. "A drink would be much appreciated—"

"The tavern is open, never closed," stated a woman, her voice hoarse and strained, with a muffled backdrop of uninterrupted musket fire in the distance.

"One, two—that's it, up with ya."

Brian was hoisted up. He was beginning to fade in and out but heard the voices around him.

"Let's get him to Dr. Minot's."

"Isaac, Isaac." He recognized Mercy's shrieks. Suddenly Brian realized that she was beside him, squeezing his hand and stroking his hair. "Oh, my dear Isaac, I knew there was grave danger for you. Oh, Isaac, my love," she wailed desperately.

"Now, ma'am, it's best for us to get through and get him help from the doc."

"Oh, yes, I know. Please, stop for just a moment and let me kiss him."

Brian could feel her soft face close to his and opened his eyes. Her hair draped over him, and he felt a warm tear on his cheek as she kissed him. Then she nuzzled her mouth next to his ear, and he felt her warm, moist breath as she whispered, "Oh, Isaac. I love you so. God will save you for me and our child. My dear, dear love, our souls are bonded in love. No matter what happens, know that we will seek each other out in the hereafter or another life. I will be with you forever. I will feel the warmth of your heart in every ray of sunshine."

He tried to speak as she pulled away, but his mouth was as arid as a desert, his jaw locked. Despite his growing delirium, her last sentence was one that echoed in his head—it was a phrase that was not unfamiliar to him.

"Someone give him a drink...please," Mercy pleaded.

Brian was suddenly aware that he was inside the foyer of Dr. Minot's. A goblet was placed to his lips, and he tried to sit up but had no strength. Mercy stood beside him, silhouetted by the light of the windows behind her.

"Up to the table upstairs in the operating room," shouted Minot, standing near the door.

As the men struggled up the stairs, Brian began to lose consciousness.

"Mercy…" he called out weakly, incoherently. He closed his hand, but she was gone. There were no longer the warm, soft fingers to touch and hold.

The door to the room was opened abruptly, and, though failing, he realized it was the room he had slept in the night before—room twenty-four.

"Step over these dearly departed redcoats and lay him on the table. I may be able to do something for him if it's not too late," entreated Dr. Minot. The two men awkwardly held the board next to the table and maneuvered themselves to move Brian. Another man came into the room and, with Minot, picked Brian up. One man lost his hold, and Brian came down onto the table with a jarring thud.

⚔

Brian Winslow was jolted awake. Peering through tiny slits, his eyes began to focus. Glancing from side to side, he saw that he was lying on his back lengthwise across the double bed in his room—at the Concord Inn, in room twenty-four. He was sweating profusely. The men had disappeared. There was light in the room, a pale-gray glow filtered through white curtains. But there was something else—a dancing, changing glow from a TV screen, still on but nothing that he could now see and could only barely hear. As he propped himself up on his elbows, a sharp pain pinched him just under his right shoulder blade. He winced, and it was gone as quickly as it had come on.

There was a faint odor in the room—an aroma that seemed to be a mixture of repugnant rotten grass and the sickly sweet smoke from gunpowder. Rain pelted the windows facing the east, and an unforgiving wind whistled and pummeled the outside walls like glancing blows from a heavyweight boxer. He realized that he was fully dressed and lying on top of the bedspread. The bed had never been turned down.

Cautiously he rolled over and rose to his knees. He rotated his right shoulder—it seemed normal, no pain. Squinting, he espied the room. There it was—the TV, still on.

The TV...What has happened? The bathroom is there. My God. Was that all a dream?

He jumped off of the bed, and as he put his feet down his right ankle twisted, and he began to fall but grabbed the side of the bed. Looking down he saw that he had stepped on his replica buckle shoes. *I don't remember leaving them there*, he thought as he repositioned his feet and stood. Looking to his right, he noticed his glasses and cell phone on the table next to the chair in front of the television. He walked over to the bathroom without turning on any lights. He splashed cold water on his face. Grabbing a face cloth, he held it under the water and then, after wringing it out, pressed it against the back of his neck with his right hand as he leaned on the counter with his left elbow.

"Jesus Christ, I feel like I haven't slept at all. I'm exhausted," he mumbled as he reached for the light switch and flipped it upward in one long, sweeping motion. The sudden harshness of the light made him recoil, squinting. He threw the facecloth in the sink and straightened up. Then he began removing his clothes. Reaching down, he pulled the plastic shower curtain open, momentarily breathless until seeing that there were no surprises to startle him in the shower—surprises that one might come to expect in a room with such a legendary and notorious history.

As soon as he dressed, Brian Winslow was ready to leave. He quickly packed. Picking up his garment bag, he noticed it was unzipped and quickly stopped, slipped the strap of his duffel suitcase off his shoulder, and set the bag down. The zipper was stuck, and, lacking any resolve to wrestle with it, he picked up the strap from his bag and for a second time dipped down and slid it onto his shoulder. He then grasped the hanger hooks sticking out of the garment bag and flung it over his other shoulder. Quickly he glanced around the room one last time looking for forgotten or overlooked items. The storm was still gnawing and grasping at the outside walls.

Brian proceeded into the creaky hallway and down the even creakier stairs on his way to breakfast and checkout.

"So, Mr. Winslow, how was your evening? Restful, I hope," a voice from behind inquired. It was Joel Meyer, the manager, following him down a second set of the stairs off of a section of the lobby.

Brian stopped and turned carefully, his bag bouncing gently off of the wall.

"Quite a night," he answered.

"I certainly hope it was everything you hoped for," Joel offered, smiling cleverly with a twinkle in his eye—an expression Brian did not see but heard, having turned back around.

"All and then some," Brian shot back hurriedly over his shoulder as he rumbled clumsily down the narrower of the two staircases.

⊰⊱

As he swung into his driveway, windshield wipers scraping across the glass, he realized that he hadn't turned on the radio. That was totally unlike him—he had been addicted to XM radio ever since it came as an option in a new Buick several years before. But not to have even listened to a CD or plugged in his MP3 player was a rarity. His mind had been preoccupied with the events of the night before. It had seemed so vivid and real.

The rain was still falling, however most of the wind had abated. After hauling his bags out of the Escalade, he ambled like a Sherpa toward the breezeway door of his house, a fairly good-sized garrison colonial. A small roof held up by three white posts supported with braces at the top, forming a Y, covered a patio area in front of the white door next to the garage at the end of a winding flagstone walkway.

Just as he arrived and stepped up onto the patio, the storm door swung open, and Meredith stood before him. She wore a sweatshirt emblazoned with "UMass Minutemen" on the front and jeans that clung tightly to her slender hips. Her short-clipped dirty-blond hair was uncombed and looked very appealing in a wild sort of way. She was barefoot and had one hand on her hip.

She looks striking. Oh, how I love this woman, he thought. Struggling, he turned and plopped the garment bag onto one of the rattan chairs.

"My hero back from the war," she teased. She stepped down and wrapped her arms around his neck. The strap from the bag slipped off, and the duffel fell to the patio, into a puddle.

"I have come to claim my queen—the spoils of war," he announced regally. They kissed.

"Spoils of war?" she asked dolefully, pouting.

"Ahh...Your knight has misspoken, milady—just an expression, really. REWARDS of war is a better choice of words, for a finer lass is not to be found in this or any other kingdom," he declared as he pulled away and looked into her eyes. His knees buckled slightly. These were the eyes...the same eyes that he had seen only hours before...maybe centuries before. They were Mercy's eyes. He was sure of it.

God, that took me by surprise. But that would make perfect sense if it were a dream, that it would be Meredith and not someone else last night. But she looked different...And the voice—that was also Meredith, he reasoned.

"Oh, dear. I am but a defenseless conquered queen, and alone in this castle. If I am to survive, I must submit to everything you command of me," she said, whimpering breathlessly while adding a salacious wink for good measure. They moved inside together.

"Hmm...Well, I think we are in the wrong century here, but I know this castle has a Lords and Ladies Chamber—by the way, there was no mention of shining armor, thank God. Wait, I do have some shining amour," he said.

"How do you know it's the wrong century?" she murmured softly. Meredith giggled as he pushed the door closed behind him, and she gently leaned forward against him.

"Because I am coming from representing—or rather was to represent—eighteenth-century America. Colonial times. There were no knights or castles there. Well, I suppose we were *fighting* a king and knights and earls. That being said, I have every intention of consummating these spoils of war—I mean delights of war—right now," he stated demonstratively, with a flourish.

Meredith's upper lip quivered and then she moved her head forward, and their mouths joined in a rapacious, smoldering kiss.

"I have to get the stuff off of the patio," he said out of one side of his mouth. Meredith pulled away. "Queen, prepare thyself to be ravaged in thy royal boudoir, that is if we have time.

"We have time, oh handsome knight. I will be waiting and must confess that my anticipation will be long and cold until you arrive. And I have a secret."

"A secret?"

She smirked with steamy sensuality. "I fear your dear conquered queen is not wearing her chastity belt, my lord, or anything else under these commoner's denim britches."

"Oh, boy—I mean yes, my queen. Wow. Now I really have to hurry. Yikes! I hope I can walk." He turned, opened the door, and stepped down to grab the duffel and garment bag quickly. "I'm coming very, very quickly, my dear, or whatever," he muttered, moving in darting motions. The storm door banged against him as he scurried.

"I see my knight has suddenly become most interested—as if he has something very pressing on his mind," she purred.

"Your knight," he began, grunting, "is...wait...get to your boudoir at once, you royal coquette," he ordered, fumbling with his luggage. "And extricate thee or thyself or whatever from your attire."

At that moment, the sun, peeking from behind a lone, puffy white cloud, bathed the entire neighborhood with brilliant sunlight.

Meredith turned to go. "Oh, I shall my lord, gladly, and will not fear the cold until you arrive for I know that I will feel the warmth of your heart in every ray of sunshine."

"What?" Brian barked, his eyes flashing and heart nearly jumping out of his chest. His garment bag fell onto the floor, the contents spilling as a result of the broken zipper. He ignored it and looked Meredith straight in the eyes. "What did you say?"

"I said I will feel the warmth of your heart in every ray of sunshine."

"But what made you say that?"

"Oh, I don't know," she answered, somewhat perplexed. "No particular reason—it just came to me. Shouldn't I have said that?"

"No, no—hell no," Brian spluttered. She glanced down at the garment bag. "It's just that—"

"Oh," she gasped, staring intently at the bag, her sudden exclamation cutting off his words. She paused, and then he watched her ease into a gentle calm.

"So now you know."

"Know what?" he asked, bewildered.

Brian followed her eyes downward. He felt a wave of incredulity flow through his entire being. His navy-blue waistcoat lay sprawled on the hardwood floor with a large hole in the back, just below the armpit—about the size of a musket ball.

Their eyes met again.

"So now you know," she whispered.

Now he understood exactly what she meant.

"So it has been centuries after all, hasn't it, Mer?"

"Yes…And we will always find each other, my love. It wasn't easy at first—took a couple of lifetimes to finally accept that which we couldn't deny, but once we did…"

Then Meredith knelt down on one knee and slid two fingers inside the right pocket of the waistcoat and carefully removed an object. She looked up at him and smiled softly, lovingly—an eternal smile that spanned hundreds of springs, summers, autumns, winters, and births. Slowly, she opened her hand. Resting in the middle of her palm was a small, silver cross.

TIES

I t could have been anyone lying in the coffin.

She looks like a wax figure, I irreverently proclaimed to myself. It didn't look like Mrs. Adams, certainly not the Mrs. Adams I had known. And it wasn't necessarily that she looked so much older than the last time I had seen her alive—three or four years ago, perhaps. I had known her since I was old enough to know anyone, which was more than fifty years. And while I was growing up, Mrs. Adams was a fixture in the neighborhood, that being a tidy cluster of twenty-four modest post–Second World War capes on either side of an eighth of a mile strip of asphalt in a small New England community. OK, not all capes. There were a few mavericks built by their original owners.

The street had a cul de sac known to the residents there as "the circle," surrounded by three houses that separated the neighborhood from a vast, woodsy wetland referred to as "the swamp." In the middle of the circle was a grassy island—by midsummer it was comprised mostly of spiky crabgrass, but at least it was green; the rest was brown like most of the lawns on the street. Through the years it had been adorned with a single balsam—several in succession actually. They would start out small and, being firs, would grow quickly and become unwieldy and dangerous, only to be cut down and be replaced with another sapling.

The actual street itself started at the foot of a sloping incline off of Elm Street—a busy thoroughfare whose inception corresponded with the settlement of the town in the seventeenth century. Named in deference to the American elm, gracious deciduous giants that formed a natural archway over many a roadway, the reason for the name was no longer obvious or relevant. In the 1930s, '40s, and '50s, Dutch elm disease, a European import, decimated most of the elm trees in New England, putting an end to their majestic reign.

A "no exit" sign stood in relative obscurity on the western corner at the beginning of the street off of Elm (that part of the street was not squared but flared like the lower portion of a pair of bell-bottom trousers); on the opposite side was a six-foot galvanized metal pole upon which rested a long, rectangular street sign emblazoned with bright-silver letters, against a green reflective background, that said "Woody Knoll Drive."

The aforementioned entrance of the street had been purposely made that way—widened to permit an adequate field of vision in both directions for safer egress onto the busier main road. One of the corners, the one with the "no exit" sign, also served as the school-bus stop for all of us who attended public schools in town during the 1950s and '60s: only one or two went to private schools, later. At one time there had been a small island in the middle of the street at the base of "the hill," as the incline that led to Elm Street was known in the vernacular of the residents. It had been removed after a very short tenure, having quickly become a hazard during the winter months.

Before the days of front- and all-wheel-drive vehicles, the town Department of Public Works had left a large, green wooden box full of sand and a shovel near the bottom of the hill. Many a rear-wheel-drive car with chainless tires would get stuck in the snow and ice and need to be pushed or abandoned—going uphill in reverse seemed most practicable. The inherent danger of that particular exercise paled in comparison to an uncontrolled slide coming down the hill—the road was downright treacherous. Then, as one might expect, many a runaway vehicle would be picked off by the island, some ending up in the middle, wheels dangling and useless, or on the other side of Elm Street sans important equipment from the underside that had been torn away and remained on the island. It was messy business.

One day the island was gone. It had disappeared. That may have been shortsighted, as it had, at the very least, prevented some vehicles from careening out into the busy street. We suspected that the real reason was too many mothers had careened over it and ripped off exhaust pipes under perfectly fair meteorological driving conditions, and then had to explain to hubby why the car sounded like a Mack truck. Few families had more than one vehicle. Oh well—we didn't miss the island after two weeks.

Climbing the hill in more pleasant weather, one would see houses and lawns that were adequately maintained, for the most part. There were no real standouts—green was sufficient for the lawns, except for those with large oaks where grass wouldn't grow. As mentioned before, by August most lawns were brown anyway—no one had in-ground sprinkler systems, and few bothered with other than token watering. It dawned on me years later, as an adult with my own home, that no one had obsessed over their lawn: there were other priorities then. Fertilizer and other "necessary" lawn maintenance products hadn't yet become a Madison Avenue bonanza. There were a few years where drought conditions had limited watering in town, but that wasn't particularly an issue on Woody Knoll. I think we still ran through the sprinklers in our back yards on hot summer days. I don't remember anyone having air conditioning, either, until the mid '60s.

Coming up the hill from Elm Street, behind the backyards of the houses on the right side and unseen from the street, was a chicken farm replete with its appurtenant summer flies; ripe, noxious ammonia odor; and grain-loving rats. Everyone soon learned that the hotter the temperature, the more repulsive the fragrance, as the manure cooked inside the larger coops where, on a sunny summer day, the temperature could easily hit 125 degrees Fahrenheit. The proprietor of the chicken farm was a friendly, hardworking man whom everyone liked, and the fresh eggs, fertilizer value for gardens, and employment for some of us kids were boons to the neighborhood. Working at the chicken farm was a real character builder.

Past the dilapidated barn and four very large commercial chicken coops were two large fields rented by local farmers who raised vegetables. Some of us worked there, too. Those five or so acres abutted the aforementioned swampy woods, which curled back around behind the houses on the circle. Natural springs, known only to the kids on Woody Knoll as "Bubbling Springs," fed the swamp and created meandering, woodsy streams that were full of aquatic wildlife. The origin of the name Bubbling Springs was unknown. The whole area was a natural wonderland for us kids.

On the left side of street, the backyards ran into a small spinney that rimmed a deep, rock-strewn manmade amphitheater—a construction company was headquartered at the base of a steep incline. The stuff left in the construction company yard left lots of opportunities for kids to get into trouble when no one was around.

Most of the stones on "the cliff," as we called it, were shards of brownstone and red stone, once the staple industry of the town that, except for one small stone company still operating near the center of town, had pretty much faded away seventy years prior. In the beginning the town had been largely agrarian, but eventually the economy was fueled by the output of its world-famous stone quarries. Until late in the nineteenth century, the stone industry was thriving, as evidenced by brownstone buildings throughout the northeast. Hardpan red clay just beneath the topsoil throughout the town provided little drainage. That combined with a plethora of natural springs left most of the basements in town damp or downright wet. The young families who settled into the new development in 1951 and 1952 soon discovered that, to their collective consternation, Woody Knoll was no exception despite being on somewhat higher ground. Even sump pumps couldn't entirely hold off that which nature had sometimes wrought, or rather brought.

Going along the left side of the street as it continued over the crest of the hill on an unwavering straight line toward the cul de sac, treed copses bordered backyards and formed a natural barrier to the cliff, and just beyond were railroad tracks—a small service line of the New York New Haven Railroad. The thirty miles of single tracks connected East Hartford, Connecticut, to Springfield, Massachusetts, and served businesses with spurs along the way. At the turn of the nineteenth century, it had also been a bustling freight and passenger line. Later it became an attractive hazard for kids from the street predisposed to hopping the freight trains as they passed through. We likened ourselves to hobos and knew most of the train crews. We even got to ride in the caboose occasionally. However, the first Friday of the month was taboo—the trainmen had tipped us off. We had to stay away because the big boss was onboard.

The street itself was perched on a natural wooded knoll, hence the name Woody Knoll, and had once been part of a large orchard. The entire street was isolated not only from other neighborhoods, but also from the rest of the community. A very unique and eclectic group of postwar baby boomer families had moved in during the first decade of its existence, the early 1950s, and the majority stayed for decades. Most of the parents and kids coalesced into a delightful camaraderie. There were exceptions…those who chose to stay somewhat aloof or were socially more involved elsewhere, but they were a very small minority. We all had bikes of varying shapes, sizes and ages. Some of us played endless games of whiffle ball, touch football in the street, and hockey or other sports on town teams. In winter we skated on the swamp or a small pond, and sledded on the cliff.

We had an annual street picnic, a block party that was hosted by alternating groups of families each year, and the fathers, aided by kids, would transport picnic tables upside down on wagons all Saturday morning. It was an exciting day and weekend for kids. There would be entertainment, games, prizes, unlimited soda and hamburgers for the kids, kegs of beer for the dads, and just wilding fun. It generally lasted well into the night, and the festive atmosphere would continue into Sunday. We kids could stay up late and gorge ourselves on limitless hamburgers and soda.

The kids on Woody Knoll anticipated the street picnics every bit as much as they did Christmas (all the families were Christians). Returning the picnic tables afterward to their rightful owners was akin to taking down Christmas decorations—a bummer. Still, the kid friendships and teeny bopper romances forged in the moonlight hidden from the lights strung among the tables as well as the stories of tipsy fathers singing old silly songs were still fresh in our minds. One or two dads were almost always were locked out in the wee hours, on purpose, and forced to spend what was left of the night on the porch sleeping it off.

The block party had its origins in the first year of the street's existence. It seems the developer had left a sign at the foot of the hill that was appropriated by several picnicking fathers (who were in really good *spirits*). They proceeded to march up and down the street, singing and stopping only to take on further liquid refreshment. From that evolved the name The Woody Knoll Chowder and Marching Society. It stuck, and forever the moniker would be the call to arms for every annual picnic thereafter, as different groups of families would host the event each year and continue the tradition and the life of the Chowder and Marching Society. Years later, as a testament to the collective sense of humor the parents had, several obituaries of still-current and some former residents referred to the deceased as being charter members of the Woody Knoll Chowder and Marching Society. Great stuff!

Unquestionably Woody Knoll had the feel of a small, cloistered village, and that was exactly what it was in the '50s and '60s. Visitors to the street would often marvel at our cohesiveness—the closeness of the neighbors and their kids. Around our small town Woody Knoll was not only somewhere to be from, but it had also become an adjective with its own very distinct feel and connotation. It gave us a unique identity—not necessarily notorious but of being from somewhere special. None of us kids would realize how very fortunate we were until we became adults, and the magic of our very fortunate collective childhoods had faded well into the past. My friends and I were the Tom Sawyers and Huckleberry Finns of the boomer generation.

The town changed after we grew up, went to college, and then moved away. Suddenly one day—just like the railroad—that life as we had known it was gone. And not just because we had our own lives and were no longer kids, like Wendy, Michael, and John in Sir James Barrie's classic *Peter Pan* but because the town, the street, and the world had changed as well. Later visits in the '70s, '80s, and even into the '90s became not much more than fond recollections. A whole new dimension had enveloped us as adults—we had families of our own and relationships had changed. It's a shock to grow up!

We suddenly found ourselves becoming fast friends with the parents of our peers with whom we had shared the idyllic kid life. It was very odd, at first, to have become friends with them, later dubbed in the media as the "Greatest Generation." Eventually those changed relationships actually genuinely added to the charm and memory of it all. That was also when we found out exactly what they thought of each of us as kids—and that we really didn't get away with much that they didn't know about. They became awfully smart in those intervening years. Now, sadly, we were losing them one by one. Time waits for no man or woman.

As I progressed through childhood and adolescence, Ester Adams had always been there, silently peering from behind the drapes in her bay window, watching the comings and goings on the street. She never said very much, at least around us kids, but we all surmised that she knew a lot. Later I learned that she was quite voluable around the other adults. We all suspected that she spread the word discreetly to our parents, but most of the time she struck me as someone who simply had a compulsive voyeuristic urge to supplement a fairly large dose of suburban ennui. But what did I know? We all have our foibles. She was the parent of a peer, and she was always pleasant to me, and I was polite to her. And she, of anyone on the street, knew I was the premier mischief maker.

My friends and I were the hooligans of the street. Maybe that's a little strong—more like rascals. Everyone who lived on Woody Knoll knew that Ester didn't miss a trick, including what we did. My adolescent cohorts and I used to posture occasionally, deliberately acting up for her ever-observant eyes, late at night drinking beer (yes, we were considerably underage) and then, under a streetlight cleverly, at least we thought so, writing our names in pee on the street. Of course the group I am referring to now consisted entirely of boys. We would all be back early the next morning to admire and critique our "penmanship." It would have made much more sense to use noms de plume, but then we really didn't care. We lacked sense as well. Kids can be really dumb! The strangest thing was that our written names, in cursive on the street, looked just like our actual handwriting. Go figure!

Mrs. Adams's obituary had caught me by surprise. Although somewhat disconnected from the street since I had sold the family homestead—my widowed mother had moved to assisted living nearly five years before—I had still maintained contact with some of surviving and now elderly parents of friends who still clung to their homes there. I moved away, for the last time, twenty-nine years before. That was the second time: after my divorce. My folks wintered in Florida after my father retired in 1974. In the late '70s, I had stayed at their house on the street for a short while. It was convenient and cheap but only a sojourn until I found an apartment. I did store stuff there—isn't that what kids are for?

Still, the old place was never the same after high school. Certainly not the house next door for sure. That was where Molly Buckley lived. Molly was special. Her smile could send a glacier melting in retreat. I silently, secretly longed to see her and hoped she would show at the wake. The Buckleys had moved away in 1972. Molly married a nice guy—we were all so very happy for her. I was at their wedding with my parents. I was married the same year. Her first marriage had endured the test of time. I never figured out why my then fiancée and now ex-wife wasn't with me at Molly's wedding. That being said, I don't care either. Perhaps a harbinger, as many other signs back then should have been.

So there I was, staring at a corpse I didn't recognize. If it used to be Mrs. Adams, so be it. *What's the point of this?* I pondered. Much to my liking, my father's family hadn't displayed a dead body in a box for over forty years— that was my paternal grandmother. That was enough for me. I'll never forget that. Better to remember through pictures and memories of when they were living, I believe. My other grandmother was Catholic and believed in opoen caskets—more about that later.

The truth be known, my motives for being at the wake were only partly malevolent. Sure, I was being compassionate and respectful for old friends and neighbors, but I was also being opportunistic. Curiously, Molly Buckley had lingered in my psyche since childhood—we were best of friends since she and her family, which then consisted of two parents and two brothers, moved next door when both Molly and I were six years old. I didn't realize it at the time, but she was my first real "girl" friend. That's not a typo—the words *should* be separated. It was the beginning of a relationship that was new and would evolve into something totally different from any before, then, or after. It would take years and years to define and fully understand. Particularly in the era in which we grew up.

Molly and I went through twelve years of school together. Since our last names were so close in spelling, and our world back then was almost completely alphabetical, we were destined to share the joy and suffering of the same school-life experiences throughout our most impressionable pre- and postpubescent years. It was a most unique friendship, and we bonded quickly as youngsters. There was no one ever nicer than Molly, and in all honesty my primary reason for being there on a Thursday afternoon during my busiest time of the year at work was probably, subconsciously, with the express intention of hopefully seeing Molly again. Carrie Adams—daughter of the aforementioned and now deceased Ester—and Molly had always been close friends, and I had suspected—no, I knew that Molly would be there.

I shuffled away slowly from in front of the coffin, having respectfully mumbled some sort of obligatory final respects, some mumbo-jumbo excuse for a prayer, and then crept contritely toward the lineup of bereaved family members, carefully shifting my weight from one foot to the other. I'm not Catholic—they have preplanned things to say when they kneel down. We Protestants stand and stare, thinking, *What do I do now? Yup, that person sure looks dead.* And Jews handle death completely different. No wakes, at least their version is after funeral services and burial. Probably better.

Then, it's time to console the survivors. Unfortunately these rituals, as a matter of course in human existence if one survives long enough, become so commonplace that we tend to compartmentalize and sanitize the grief to insulate ourselves. Our reactions become mechanical, automatic, and predictable. Even the words are the same every time, practiced and deliberate: comfortable. That is for those who are not close to the deceased, I suppose. We have scripts in our heads. We say the same rehearsed few words. We do not want to appear clumsy or say the wrong thing.

Young people are always devastated—we know they will be like us some-day, as death becomes much more familiar, repetitious. I know I shouldn't, but I find that young people tend to be way too generous and gracious to dead people just because they are dead. I cringe every time I hear a teenage patently shallow and patronizingly predictable description of the dead person as being "amazing" or "awesome." Besides, there are more words in the English lan-guage—come on, kids, check out a thesaurus. And let's face it; people don't become amazing and awesome just because they are dead. But that's life, I guess. A little irony there!

Anyway, it seems that at every wake or funeral for parents of someone my age—midfifties, let's say—the same morose statement is to be heard: "Well, we're next."

"Not so fast," I often implore, "I have older brothers," which of course means no ill will toward them but just injects an element of false deferral in my own head. Which leads me to this—I often spout what I think are funny quips in the face of serious or sad settings. It's a coping mechanism. My wife hates it about me. I have always been a huge proponent of the proposition that it is better to laugh than cry when one has the option. That has gotten me many laughs through the years and in big trouble on occasion as well. After all, no one bats one thousand—there have been a few embarrassing and re-gretful bloopers! Then I have to try to fix it later on if I really care about the afflicted person. That may sound rather crass and cold, but that's my nature.

I found myself next in line to express my condolences to Carrie, née Adams. As a kid she had been a nice girl—demure, never particularly ex-troverted, but commanded a consistently pleasant countenance. Carrie and Molly had been inseparable from junior high school. Carrie had been com-fortably quiet—when she and Molly laughed, you heard Molly. I'd never talk-ed to Carrie a whole lot, but still we enjoyed each other's company. I liked her, and I think she tolerated me. I got to know her husband, Rick, as we crossed paths at various times in our lives. He's a solid guy. A real kidder, too. Birds of a feather…

Carrie was first in the receiving line, if that's what it is called at a wake. Her dad had passed away a few years before. Now I waited for the heavy woman who was bulging unflatteringly out of several places of a black dress in front of me to disengage. She kept hugging Carrie. Three, four, five times—way overdone. A hugger. God Almighty…Maybe she was trying to get closer but couldn't. The hugger's auburn hair was cut short, and her skin was pasty. The lights seemed harsh, and I became aware of the pungent fragrance that emanated from the floral displays that splayed out to either side of Mrs. Adams's bier.

I was queued for Carrie's waiting embrace. It was genuine. I knew how Carrie felt, having lost my parents in the same order. When your mom is left and then she goes, that's a strange feeling. It's not so much grief as inevitability, mortality: finality. Time has finally caught up with you. You thought you could outrun it and beat it forever. As kids, life is forever.

Carrie is a few inches shorter than I am and her blond-highlighted hair was pulled behind her ears. She had her father's pointy nose and chin.

"Carrie, I'm so sorry about your mom," I whispered sincerely, my face brushing past her hair, still mostly brown on the side of her head. I caught a whiff of her indistinguishable perfume and hoped I wouldn't sneeze. I have a serious allergy to that stuff, however slightly applied.

"Thank you, Joe. It's so nice of you to come," she replied.

Then, for a split second, I realized I hadn't planned to say anything past my first consoling remark, and I panicked.

"I didn't know that your mom was sick," I quickly added, drawing away and looking into her eyes, remembering that they were earnest and honest eyes—there was never a hint of malice or pretentiousness lingering anywhere in her soul.

"She had a massive stroke. Only lasted a day or two," she explained sadly but not morosely. "It was peaceful in the end," she added dolefully, calmly. She seemed satisfied that her mother had passed painlessly.

"I am so sorry," I added reassuringly. Then I realized why her mother didn't look just right. I had seen it many times before. *There must be a physical reason. Maybe the muscles are affected, and the musculature of the face contorts or something*, I instantly reasoned. I recalled many years before my own grand-father—my mother's dad, with whom I'd had a very close relationship—was the same way after dying from a massive stroke. My grandmother, a devout Catholic, insisted on an open casket. I hadn't recognized him either. That sucked—it was then I vowed that if I never saw another open casket it would be just fine. And of course I still have that picture in my mind. Argh.

I suppose we all secretly wish that in these situations our words are so pro-foundly beneficent and expressed with such feeling and inflection that we will be remembered as the one who provided real comfort and consolation to the mourner. In reality, having been there, you remember the people but not neces-sarily the words—it's all a blur at the time. That in and of itself is good therapy, I suppose. Better not to have a clear recollection of grief's savage and grisly details.

"There's someone in the back of the room who is anxious to see you," Carrie said, smirking. She caught me completely off guard. I glanced over her shoulder and was instantly mortified—a bashful schoolboy once again. There, sitting alone, was Molly, just as resplendent as ever. She was like a beacon. Molly was looking at me and smiling broadly, and I quickly looked back at Carrie shyly and smiled weakly. I felt my pulse racing—my knees were trembling. My heart was pounding away in my chest, and I felt my sweat glands charging into action.

"Molly?" I asked weakly, my voice wavering.

Carrie didn't hear me—she had already moved on to the next person fol-lowing me in line. Next was Rick. We joked about something, quickly. Then came Carrie's older brother, her only other sibling.

"I'm sorry about your mom, Ed," I offered as I grasped his hand in a shake.

"I didn't catch the name," Ed, his curly hair combed straight back, de-clared with a puzzled look. He was retired from the gas company or something.

"Joe Bradford, Ed. After all of those years playing baseball and touch football in the street? I hope we still have the Mets in common," I responded with a grin.

"Joe. Wow, I'm sorry. I didn't recognize you—your hair migrated from your head to your face," he quipped with a sneer. It didn't bother me—I was distracted anyway. Molly Buckley, now Campisi, was sitting in the back of the room, not thirty feet from where I was standing. I had felt this way around her ever since she'd gotten married, though I wasn't exactly certain why. It was this overwhelming sense of guilt that I should desire to see another woman who, like me, was married to someone else. Especially a woman for whom I had such strong feelings. And those feelings of guilt had remained unclear—confused for so long. We had been the best of friends growing up. She had been so important to me, and I to her, that we had gone to our junior prom together. I'd had a girlfriend at the time but decided on Molly for such an important occasion. She said yes. Obviously the girlfriend did not understand and summarily severed that relationship. Oh, well. But then Molly was so much more special. Cad!

I wore a white tuxedo jacket and she a most exquisitely filled out, lovely snowy-white gown. Molly was very ladylike and quite mature for her tender years. I had escorted her to a small, very cozy Italian restaurant. We came away unscathed. I still don't know how we did it. We both had spaghetti and meatballs, I think. That was a miracle for both of us—we had always both been habitual spillers. I'm sure we laughed all night—we always had so much fun together.

Now I swept through the rest of line as quickly as I could—the grandkids and their spouses. Blah, blah, blah. I have no idea what I said, and didn't particularly care. I'm sure it was consoling. Right! The memory of Molly and our teenage fling wafted across my mind. It wasn't anything more than a couple of dates and some necking at a drive-in movie a few weeks after the prom. I think we both felt compelled to start dating officially—that was the expectation and perception in the '50s and '60s. When you like a girl, you date her, and she becomes your girlfriend. *Especially* if you took her to the prom. One-word girlfriend, that is. Except Molly. We both soon learned that the relationship we shared was like no other. I really, *really* liked her. Kissing her romantically was awkward and, as the old cliché says, like kissing your sister. Indubitably. We ended up laughing at ourselves. We much preferred smoking cigarettes and talking. Friendship was what we were all about. We were destined to always be those two six-year-olds who immediately bonded when we first met—a decade before gender meant anything to us. Don't get me wrong, Molly is a very beautiful woman with a personality that is magnetic and a smile that can light up a room. Any guy would have done somersaults to be with her. Apparently her husband of thirty-five years did just that or at least caught her fancy. Molly is a peach.

But to me Molly was a special friend to whom I could confide and talk to about everything and anything. I couldn't even talk to my mother about some of the things we talked about—back then she was the only other woman in my life with whom I could confide, without limitations. Molly and I talked endlessly across our driveways, out of our bedroom windows, until one of us would realize that the other had stopped responding and had fallen asleep. Our houses were close. I had two brothers—so did she. One of her brothers was one of my best friends growing up. Our parents were close. Unknowingly, Molly became my surrogate sister. And I loved her that way. I never had a sister—Molly was it.

We hadn't really seen each other alone or talked for decades, and there were times in the interim when I thought of her and had wanted to talk to her and get her advice or just tell her how I felt about her—how valuable a friend she had always been. I had all but resigned myself to the fact that my unrequited—well, yes…love…was destined to be a silent yearning I would have to endure for the rest of my days. After all, I was a guy and she a woman. We were both now happily married for years. I was afraid that if I ever expressed my true feelings, my intentions could be interpreted the wrong way and misconstrued as improper. I wasn't sure how she, her husband, my wife, or anyone else for that matter would react to my seemingly sudden confession of deep affection and admiration. Not romantic love but a deep and sincere friendship. Rare for my generation or any men I have known. It was a conundrum. Yet there she was again. And, as always when I was in her presence, I was nervous and extremely excited.

As I left the end of the line, I saw out of the corner of my eye that she was sitting alone and still watching me, smiling. I took a detour to the right to greet an old friend from my older boys' baseball days nearly twenty years before. Jack was a great coach and had the best interests of the kids at heart. And he knew baseball. I quickly made the connection. He sold medical supplies to hospitals—he had dropped in to see me after I had an operation. I figured talking briefly to him would give me a chance to catch my breath and calm down a little. I had my back to Molly. Jack and I had an amiable, animated conversation, and as soon as I got my sea legs back I cordially extricated myself and turned around. That was when our eyes met.

Everybody has moments in their lives when something so unforgettable strikes them, and they are suddenly aware of being in a defining moment. You know at the instant that it happens that the sights, the sounds, the smells, the tastes, or the feeling will be indelibly etched into your memory, your psyche, your soul—that something has abruptly changed your world. So it was then with Molly. I immediately saw in her eyes what she unquestionably must have seen in mine—and we both smiled broadly, warmly, lovingly. Old friends. I practically ran over to her, and if she had hugged me any tighter I would have been asphyxiated. I went to kiss her cheek, but she would have none of that—she grabbed my face in the palms of her hands and planted a real smacker right on my lips. Then we hugged tightly again.

"Molly," I whispered, grinning widely as we pulled away to arm's length to get a good look at one another. I had a tear in my eye.

"Joe, how the hell are you?" she bubbled happily. Her voice reached my soul.

"It is so great to see you. You look fantastic," I gushed, sounding somewhat trite but with absolute sincerity. She had a wonderful creamy complexion and hardly a wrinkle on her face. Her thin eyebrows darted expressively as she talked and accentuated the emotion of every statement.

"So do you. It is really fantastic to see you. I like the beard," she said with eager enthusiasm and reached up and tugged playfully on the whiskers on my chin with her right hand.

"I'll bet you used to do that to Santa Claus," I joked.

"You bet I did—got into a lot of trouble with my dad too!" she beamed.

Our eyes remained locked as we sat down. We were both smiling so broadly that we could have easily pulled some muscles in our faces.

"Molly, first of all I want to say how very sorry I am that I couldn't be at your father's funeral. I had desperately wanted to be there, but a professional seminar in Boston could not be missed. Try as I may I couldn't get out of it—I needed the course to renew my license to practice. I had a deadline for continuing education requirements," I blathered quickly. It had been a major disappointment for me—the family had decided against calling hours, and the service was at the other end of the state. I felt terrible that I wasn't there to pay my respects and to see Molly and her brothers. Her mom had passed away years before.

"Oh, Joe, I understand. Hey, the tribute you wrote online was wonderful. I immediately called my brothers and told them to read it. It was perfect—and so thoughtful of you. And your card—what you wrote to me was so touching and personal. I really appreciated it. So don't feel as though you need to apologize—"

"Molly, I will never forget seeing your face at my mom's wake, when you were there with Dusty and your dad. It meant so much to me. You being there for me made everything OK. I mean that."

"You didn't think for a minute that we wouldn't be there for you. Listen, our arrangements for my Dad were not convenient for everyone, we knew that. It had to work for both of my brothers—one was coming from Indiana, the other California. We had a limited window of time. We were able to make your mom's because it was more convenient. I understand. Still, what you wrote was special, and we all appreciated your kind thoughts. We did have a laugh as well," Molly explained tenderly as she rested her hand gently atop mine on my leg. It was warm, soft, and empathetic. I'd always trusted her and our friendship.

"I felt really, really bad. I was lucky to get to know your father as an adult; we had Kiwanis in common. He was a great man, and I really liked him. There are so many stories from when we were kids. I'll never forget the way he smiled at me at my mother's wake. He was standing behind you guys and kind of peeked between you—that Irish grin. He mentioned how he distinctly remembered how much mischief I had gotten into and that now he could just chuckle with the memory. He said I was 'all boy.' I took that as a compliment," I said.

"We'll have to stop meeting like this, Joe. Wakes and funerals. Ugh." Molly smirked.

"Well, we are at that age," I retorted matter-of-factly and received a delightful squeeze of the hand as she straightened up in her chair. Molly has always had those squared shoulders and excellent posture, an inch or two taller than me as well. She was always down to earth—no airs, genuine and extremely modest. Molly Buckley was unselfishly considerate and thoughtful and possessed impeccable character. Even as a youngster, her presence demanded certain decorum—I never saw or heard any improprieties or disrespectful behavior in her company. She wasn't a prude or prissy either. Molly was truly a lady, and, just like with her mother, everyone knew and respected her for it, especially me.

We talked and laughed for nearly an hour, as if we were alone in the funeral parlor. It was remarkable. We hit upon every relevant subject and updated each other: our spouses and marriages, our kids (now all in their thirties), our grandkids. Molly had a photograph of her oldest grandson: a darling little sprite, nine years old. We bragged about our kids' achievements, and pondered some of the bad decisions our kids had made through the intervening years. I was quick to point out that flawed judgment was common to every generation, especially ours. She laughed. Molly's the one who'd had trepidations about my ex-wife when she was my girlfriend. She knew me well and is a great judge of character—Molly is very perceptive.

Carrie had broken away from the receiving line and was meandering over to visit with us. Molly and I were sitting in the first two seats of a row of chairs toward the back. Carrie arrived and stood before us. She looked down at me and immediately spilled the beans. "So, how's your book coming?"

Molly turned to me with an incredulous look, her mouth agape. "You're writing a book?" she said demonstratively.

Molly was staring at me with her left eyebrow raised—she could always move that left eyebrow so expressively, which I had always attributed to much practice in the mirror. It was so very effective. I squirmed uneasily. I'll bet her kids had their fair share of angst when they were younger and the eyebrow was askew.

"Ah…yeah," I responded somewhat sheepishly, not wanting to appear immodest yet for some reason expecting Molly to be just a tad envious that Carrie had known this about me before *she* did. *Envious* is the wrong word; too strong perhaps, and there was never a trace of envy or petty jealousy in Molly Buckley's body ever. Rather, I might have detected a somewhat more proprietary sentiment or even disappointment at having found out something so significant about *me* from someone else, secondhand. I would have felt the same if the tables were turned. But then we had been talking for only about twenty minutes. In the scheme of things between Molly and me talking, twenty seconds is a millisecond.

I paused for a moment and then added carefully, "I'm actually almost finished with my second novel."

Her brown eyes danced back and forth as she gazed into my eyes, searching for more information. I sensed that she wanted to know everything about my writing as quickly as she could, by osmosis or some instantaneous download if possible. Looking into those eyes, it suddenly dawned on me that she was experiencing the same thing I was—the sensation swept over me like the warmth of the sun coming out from behind a cloud on a cool spring day. We *had* been seeking, searching for one another—it was as if this time and place had been predestined and that we were finally, at last, together again. Old friends finally reunited. I shifted excitedly in my chair, unable to stay still, and switched my crossed legs rather clumsily. My left leg is no longer as flexible as it was, nor does it have the range of motion it once had. A familiar memory, that of the Simon and Garfunkel song "Old Friends," instantly wafted through my mind.

"Your second?" she gasped, appearing even more surprised than before. By now both eyebrows had flattened, and her forehead was slightly furrowed. She had the same nose I remembered—not exactly turned up, sort of a smaller version of mine, somewhat rounded on the end, nonetheless perfectly suited for her face. Again I couldn't help notice that her complexion was extraordinarily smooth, and other than a few obligatory crow's feet at the outside corners of her eyes that one would expect to see on a fifty-six-year-old, her face was markedly wrinkle free. She wore only a trace of makeup—not particularly noticeable. Her darkish-red brown hair was fairly short: It covered her ears and stopped unevenly about halfway down her neck. She used to wear it short as a kid, mostly tucked behind her ears and very cute. Her face was roundish, and her eyes sort of almond shaped; she had generous cheeks, full lips, and a delicate chin. Molly was neither glamorous nor plain—she was most definitely wholesomely attractive. For fear of sounding trite or inane, she was the epitome of the girl next door. But when she smiled, she beamed, and her eyes twinkled—that Irish gleam inherited from her father. A pretty girl, yet it was her persona that exuded beauty. And that persona manifested itself in a wonderful friendship.

"My second," I answered confidently. I could now feel the timorousness that I had experienced those precious few times I had been around Molly in the last thirty-five years melting away.

"So when do we get to read the first one? Has it been published yet?" Carrie, still standing in front of us and almost forgotten, chimed in, reminding both Molly and me that we were not alone.

"Not yet," I stated, hoping not to disclose my exasperation while sounding upbeat and positive.

"Why not? It's done, isn't it?" Carrie pursued doggedly, more inquisitive than inexorable. I could sense that she was just being curious, not insistent, though.

"It's a long process. Right now it's on hold. My literary agent has shopped it a bit but is now interested in getting number two into the pipeline. I'll be working to revise the first one this summer," I said.

"You have a literary agent?" Molly quizzed. "Where?"

Her tone was more interrogative. As good a friend as Carrie was, I sensed that Molly now had a yearning to be the first to learn these more intimate and exclusive facts about me. I wondered why I hadn't called or written her to tell her all of this. Then I remembered how intimidated I had been all of those years, thinking that any ovations on my part toward Molly might have been misinterpreted. *Who would have known she was like a sister to me?* I reasoned.

"*She* is in New York City. I'm under contract with her agency," I answered, trying to sound as modest as I could. I was delighted to be telling Molly this. I knew she would be proud of me and would want to give anything I had written an honest read.

Molly's eyes widened, and the corners of her mouth curled upward with the beginnings of a wide grin. "My, my. Local boy makes good. I am not at all surprised," she announced. "Good for you. What's it about? I mean the first one."

"They're both romances," I replied confidently yet preparing myself defensively for Molly's reaction. "Historical fiction," I added to complete the description.

"Romances?" she said softly, as if repeating the word to herself. "Historical fiction. Hmmm."

"There is some action and intrigue and other more serious issues involved—I don't like just fluff, or popcorn, as it is referred to in the trade. The first one was set during World War One, the second in the thirties," I explained quickly. "But the underlying themes are basically love stories."

"You always were a sensitive, imaginative guy," Molly offered softly, smiling gently. "Yeah. That makes sense. Yup. Beneath that *all-boy* rough and ready exterior, as my dad said, to coin a phrase, you have always been a romantic. Romantic in many ways—I mean more like having a real affinity for people and their emotions, yet adveturesome, like a swashbuckler. A keen observer too. Combine that with an interest in history and your imagination, and it makes perfect sense to me," she offered with a confirmative nod of her head. Carrie nodded as well but with a less assured expression of concurrence, as she hadn't been close enough to me to ever have been familiar with that side of my personality. I'm certain she agreed with Molly's observation, knowing that Molly knew me so well.

"I should get back," Carrie stated abruptly. Glancing over I noticed her brother looking in our direction. We were probably being a little too boisterous and jocular, considering the solemn circumstances. Molly and I glanced at one another and shared discreet grins, having both noticed that Carrie's brother was now glaring across the room with increased intensity.

"I'll see you before I go," Molly conceded as her friend turned and reciprocated with an easy smile, and then Carrie walked away. I suspected that as much as she felt an obligation to react to her brother's guilt-inducing, steely glare, she was also cognizant of the dynamic that was occurring between two old and very close friends. Here, at her mother's wake, amid a crowd of mourners and final respect payers, a very special bond was being reconnected. I was sure Carrie had seen it in the way Molly and I looked at each other and were interacting: She knew how close we had been as kids all those years ago. We were probably as close as they were yet very different for obvious reasons—I was a boy and she was a girl.

I then initiated the resumption of our private conversation. "My first novel is based on a true story," I pronounced somewhat plaintively. "Actually both stories contain some actual history. I do tend to ascribe to the use of metaphors, and many times I reach back into my own private museum for examples of life imitating art. In any case one of those artifacts I frequent relates to a couple of very serious relationships I had many years ago," I explained.

"I vaguely remember hearing about some of that stuff," Molly said, squinting and wrinkling her nose slightly, as if trying to focus more clearly on a mental image. I was suddenly nervous again, as if I had struck a discordant nerve within my own psyche.

"One was very serious…and ended badly," I added spontaneously, without thinking. I diverted my eyes and stared at the floor. I heard Molly move, not uncomfortably, and she cleared her throat easily. There was a pause. I had divulged a secret to her of which very few were aware.

"But I digress," I said suddenly. "So how's Dusty?" I said in a desperate attempt at diversion. Dusty was Molly's older brother by two years.

"Dusty is Dusty—six kids and all," Molly answered obligingly, obviously understanding that I might have inadvertently journeyed off course from my emotional comfort zone. She then gave me an update on Dusty as well as her other sibling, Arthur. I breathed easier. Leave it to Molly—she read me well even after all of those years. Once again she made me feel comfortable and at ease. I also knew, as did she, that I would fill in the details of the parts of my life that she had missed, and she would do the same for herself in the near future. Neither of us was going to let go this time—time was too valuable and our friendship too precious.

Finally it became time for me to get back to work. Molly had come directly to the funeral parlor after finishing the school day with her fourth-grade class. We exchanged all of our phone numbers, home addresses, and, of course e-mail addresses—and set a tentative date for lunch. Then we kissed and hugged, and I scooted, but not before a final wave as I headed out the door.

I couldn't stop thinking about how serendipitous our meeting was but that it really wasn't by chance. In fact for me and, as I would find out in a flurry of e-mails for months afterward, not for her either, as that was the subliminal hope that accompanied a well-intended dose of sympathy for another friend. Our meeting, as Molly and I confessed later, was thrilling and hoped for.

When I arrived home that night, I was thinking about Molly and her family, particularly her dad. For some reason he was on my mind. A World War Two veteran, having been stationed in England, he had been a bombardier on a B-25. He had seen his share of action. He had been, understandably, very tight lipped about the horrors of war that he had experienced. I will always remember him at the street picnics parties singing "Lil Marlene" in French and getting everyone to learn the lyrics and join in.

Nevertheless, despite my youthful exuberance and capacity for mischief as a kid, I always had a feeling that he liked me, as did Molly's mom. And getting to know him as an adult was a real pleasure. We swapped many stories one day at a Kiwanis meeting in Worcester—we were both enlightened, to say the least.

Sean Buckley had been an executive for a large regional electrical-equipment manufacturing company. In my reverie I recalled that they had many promotional items with their logo on them, which consisted of a little man nicknamed Andy Amp holding a bolt of electricity. Of course, living next door, I nearly always was the recipient of at least one of those promotional trinkets, which, being a kid, I promptly lost or misplaced. My dad also brought home similar knickknacks, which I no doubt shared with Molly and her brother. In fact I remember a lot of that in the neighborhood—someone's dad always had a handful of trinkets. Though not an affluent neighborhood by any stretch of the imagination—probably best described as modest middle class for the 1950s and '60s—most of the mothers did not work or worked part time.

I recalled fondly the night that Molly, I, and a couple of other kids were sitting on their breezeway, and I had my guitar. Nothing fabulous—a cheap imitation folk model. I was playing, and we were all singing "Last Time" by the Rolling Stones, as I remember, quite loudly. It was a popular song at the time. Suddenly Mr. Buckley burst through the kitchen doorway and said, not in a loud voice but firm and with his measured authority, "This *WILL* be the last time if you don't knock it off." It was late at night during summer vacation. We were young kids. I stopped. That was that. It WAS the last time. When he was a safe distance back inside the house, and the back door closed, we all nearly chocked stifling our guffaws—we laughed about it for years.

So, after reconnecting with Molly, I couldn't wait to talk to her again and start e-mailing. I was about ready to burst with anticipation. I suppose my wife wondered what was going on. I did tell her the whole story, which she had heard more than once over the years, especially about the Italian restaurant before the prom. Getting ready for bed that night, I wondered if I had any of the trinkets left over from all those years ago and went into the top drawer of my dark-maple dresser.

I located my special box that contained dozens of keepsakes and bits and pieces of a lifetime. The vinyl-covered box was crammed full of over fifty years of stuff. I noticed the box was stuck—and the top was ajar. Something was wrong. I reached in and noticed that something was wedged between the top and the case, inhibiting its opening.

It was only partially visible; I tried to pry whatever it was, but it was not going to move without a fight. Now I was nervous that if I used more force, I would break the top right off of the box. *Damn it. If only I can get something behind the thing back there*, I thought. I held the box up and heard everything inside slide—if the box opened now the contents would be all over the bedroom floor. I decided to hold it halfway inside the drawer.

Using a pen I pried very carefully, slowly. It was small, and as it moved I worked it back and forth with my thumb and forefinger until the object that had been jammed in the hinge suddenly fell into the palm of my right hand.

I drew my hand out of the drawer and was ready to throw the obstruction onto the polished dresser and proceed with my search, but I stopped. I looked at the object. Then I thought about how that box and the priceless memories it contained had been through a marriage, a divorce, several moves, another marriage, another two moves, and now to this point in time—rarely opened and certainly never organized in any logical fashion. And, never before stuck. Inexplicably, tonight the object that had brought attention to itself in a most demonstrative fashion after nearly fifty years of being dormant and insignificant seemed to affirm a destiny—one which may have been guided by sources unknown and unknowable to me or anyone. I truly think it was not some bizarre coincidence: I believe it was kismet.

Yes, there it was: a tie tack.

A definition flashed through my mind: *Ties, by definition—connections or links.*

Why it was where it was at that time I will never know or understand. I just smiled.

There was Andy Amp, holding that bolt of electricity and grinning at me.

WALLPAPER

...Well, I say no: and therefore for assurance
Let's each one send unto his wife;
And he whose wife is most obedient
To come at first when he doth send for her,
Shall win the wager which we will propose.

—WILLIAM SHAKESPEARE, THE TAMING OF THE SHREW

"...And Welker makes a sensational diving catch of another Brady toss. The Patriots continue to move the chains against the Jets..." barked the voice of announcer Gil Santos through the speakers of the silver Panasonic portable stereo perched atop the lone piece of furniture in the twelve-by-sixteen room—a maple bureau against the wall closest to the door, covered by a blue tarpaulin. The room had three windows—two on one wall facing west, the other on the north side of the two-story garrison colonial. Indirect sunlight illuminated the room with a soft glow on this sunny afternoon in early October.

Tom Arnett hunched his forty-six-year-old, athletic, five-foot ten-inch frame over a long aluminum table, spreading out a length of wallpaper from a roll. The pattern was face down and had a plain maize background dotted randomly with light-blue speckles.

Thank God I don't have to match a pattern, he thought as he steadied the paper with one hand and then picked up his X-Acto knife with the other.

"Shit," he muttered as the wallpaper began to slide on the table.

"...Fumble. Fumble...the Jets have it..." bellowed the excited voice from the top of the bureau.

"Damn." Tom reached over, nudged the paper closer with his right fore-arm, and quickly drew the razor-sharp blade across, slicing along the thin pencil line made moments ago after careful measurement. He moved the blade swiftly yet carefully to avoid ripping the paper. His lower back was singing with pain—these jobs used to be much easier when he was in his twenties and thirties, but years of playing sports, coaching kids' teams, skiing, and just father time had begun to take their middle-aged toll.

Most of the furniture that had occupied the room—the upstairs guest room of the house—had been moved into the hallway just outside the door. The light-maple twin beds were taken apart, and the mattresses rested against the hallway door just outside the boys' bedroom. The other bureau, the smaller four footer, and the bedside table were stuffed precariously into Tom's teenage daughter Carrie's bedroom—not without objection, of course. She protested just about everything these days.

The lone bureau in the room that now provided a surface for the radio and tools was one of two ordinarily in the room. They didn't match. They were part of an eclectic collection of furniture inherited from both sides of the family. Some were valuable antiques, most not.

Two windows were open, one on the west side, and a cool afternoon autumn breeze filtered unnoticeably through the screens from time to time. The curtains and shades had been removed weeks before the work start-ed in earnest—sort of the first real commitment to begin the project. New curtains, matching the colors of the new wallpaper, would soon adorn the windows.

Tom held the end of the long piece of wallpaper with his left hand and used a heavy yardstick to prevent the other end from sliding errantly on the table. First he smoothed the surface with a large, flat wallpaper brush and then quickly slathered paste onto the paper with a smaller brush saturated with the sticky substance. The smell of the paste always inspired memories of kindergarten arts-and-crafts projects with Tom for some reason.

"Man...why did I let Janice pick out this crap? We should have bought the prepasted stuff—a lot less mess and headache," he mumbled for no one to hear but himself.

He heard someone call out from somewhere fairly close in the house, presumably for him.

"What?" he answered, unable to discern exactly what was said or by whom.

"Mom wants to know if you want something to eat."

It was Carrie shouting from her room, where, Tom knew, she spent an inordinate amount of time blathering endlessly on her cell phone. Expressing his opinion about her behavior and habits was precarious at best—Carrie was in teenage denial and combative. The door to her room was always closed when she was in there, of course, which was nearly all the time when she was home. Her brothers, in her much less than humble opinion, were geeks and pests, having been brought into this world only to annoy and harass her—a pestilence like the plague.

Tom had learned that trying to figure out a teenage girl is akin to understanding Einstein's theory of relativity—so he gave up long ago. He was once delusional and thought he did have editorial privilege on her actions and conduct. Thought, that was. Then her mother was also at wits' end, but he presumed she had a more enlightened perspective, having been one of those *things* herself. Therefore the assumption was that Mom understood Carrie better than he. Partly true. As it turned out, it had as much to do with being a teenager and having a serious hormonal hurricane raging inside as it did gender attributes.

Wrestling with the piece of wallpaper covered with paste, he dragged it face down, paste side up, to the stepladder in the corner.

"Please. Peanut butter and jelly on rye," he shouted as the paper twisted and yawed in his grip, causing him to turn involuntarily. Some fancy footwork was required, as if accommodating an unpredictable dance partner to avoid the potential disaster of having the whole thing stick together like an uncooperative piece of Saran wrap.

"Eww…how can you eat that stuff?" came a reply from somewhere in the hallway, accompanied by sounds of faux regurgitation.

Carrie outside her bedroom in the daylight? How rare, Tom thought.

Straining, he held up the burdening wallpaper and grunted an answer. "Never mind the puking noises…just tell Mom that's what I want. I'm eating it—not you."

"Blah, blah, blah. That's soooo gross…" he heard her groan, mockingly loud enough to be heard over the radio commercial for Lumber Liquidators but then falling away down the carpeted staircase. The guest room door was three-quarters closed.

For a split second, he envisioned a petite seven-year-old in pink Dr. Denton's adorned with images of the Little Mermaid cozying up beside him on a couch, clutching a copy of *Alice's Adventures in Wonderland; a* dead-of-winter evening crackling fire casting a warm amber hue upon her soft skin and shimmering, shoulder-length, platinum-blond hair. Tom smiled affectionately at his muse.

Who took my sweet little cutie away from me? he wondered. *And where did she ever acquire a penchant for deep-blue eyeshadow, tawdry clothing, a cloistered monistic existence, and a supercilious, superior attitude?*

The last piece. Hallelujah! he rejoiced silently while stepping carefully to the next rung of the ladder. He steadied himself and then hoisted the heavy wallpaper, sodden with paste. His arms and shoulders quivered—he was arm weary. He had started papering yesterday. That was after three weeks of stripping four layers of ancient wallpaper down to the plaster of the 150 year-old house then repairing and skim coating all four of the plaster walls and ceiling.

He carefully pressed the paper into the angle where the moulding met the ceiling with his fingertips, leaving about one inch of paper above the moulding to spare. Then, lining the paper up, he slowly stepped down the ladder, smoothing from the middle toward the edges of the piece with the long, blond-handled flat brush with the straw-colored bristles— the same brush he had used minutes before to flatten the paper on the worktable. He stepped from the bottom rung onto the floor and pulled the ladder out of the way to the side and brushed the lower portion of the wallpaper. The sizing applied to the wall the previous weekend had grabbed the paper and immediately bonded with the paste. He remembered to climb up and press the top edge with the flat brush so the paper was flush between the moulding and the wall.

Back down the ladder to the floor, he searched for imperfections—mostly bubbles or unevenness. With a sweeping motion here and a whisk there, he gave it a finishing touch. Then he placed the brush on the bureau and searched for the seam roller. With a damp rag in his left hand, he rolled the matched edges with his right hand, wiping off any excess paste that may have seeped out from the pressure of the roller.

"...Brady is sacked..."

"Jesus H. Christ," Tom muttered with disgust and shaking his head. Not uncharacteristically the Patriots had been dominated in the first half by their nemesis, the New York Jets. *They are a second-half team...I hope they get their butts in gear*, he thought.

Stepping back, he admired his work. *All that's left is the finish work, cutting the excess at the moulding and baseboard and then cleanup. I might be able to watch the last ten minutes of the fourth quarter*, he considered. Tom turned down the volume on the radio. The room was suddenly quiet.

He heard the muffled sound of footsteps on the carpeted stairs—they become louder as they approached the hallway. He knew the boys—Tom, Jr., who had just celebrated his fourteenth birthday; and Mark, twelve—were out somewhere in the neighborhood, probably down the street playing street hockey at the Johnsons' in their double driveway. It wouldn't be Carrie; she pounded her feet as if she were a three-hundred-pound Sumo wrestler. Besides, Carrie had no doubt retreated into her cave. Carrie was all about Carrie—she might yell out a lunch order, but help out? Hardly.

Now on the landing at the top of the stairs, the footfalls became louder as they came down the hallway. With the door mostly closed, Tom, distracted as he turned up the volume on the radio again, was not paying particular attention.

"...Interception. The Patriots have the ball on the Jets' thirty-five."

"Yes," he hissed and pumped his fist.

In anticipation of a late lunch arrival moments away, Tom took the long-stale Juicy Fruit gum from his mouth and threw it into the wastebasket full of paper cuttings and other trash. Instinctively he perceived that in a moment, the former Janice Babcock, his wife of twenty years or so—he never remembered exactly—would be coming through the doorway, which his back was facing.

He and Janice had met one glorious weekend in Maine on a chartered schooner—he had been alone and she with a friend. Originally Tom was attracted to her friend, a college roommate with whom she was reconnecting with after several years, but it was Janice who eventually prevailed and won his affections. By the end of the three-day chartered sail, he and Janice had pretty much sealed the deal. Janice's friend was the odd girl out. The rest, as they say, is history.

He sensed her presence; the door hinges made a slight squeaking sound as she pushed the door open. He made a mental note to oil them.

"It looks like you're pretty much done," a voice said. "But I'm not sure I like the paper now."

Tom Arnett froze. Suddenly pangs of hunger were eclipsed by a jolt of shocking surprise—a totally unexpected voice that he hadn't heard in decades. He felt his body stiffen, and his already-sweaty extremities began to pump newly stunned perspiration. He thought he felt his heart skip a beat: It was a dull thud in his chest. He recognized the speaker; at least he thought he did. There was no mistaking the deeper resonance—a throaty mezzo-soprano tonal quality and very sexy.

"Well, if you're too busy I'll just set it up here with the rest of the things on the bureau. I hope the bureau is not getting scratched." The tone was somewhat more admonishing than not. He heard the plate being placed on the tarp and thought he smelled the peanut butter.

He dropped his hands to his side and turned slowly to face the speaker, who he had expected would be Janice. But that was not Janice's voice. His entire body quaked. *It is her. How could it be, and what is she doing here?*

"M…Myra?" he asked sheepishly.

"You were expecting someone else?" Myra asked.

"Wah…well…well…what are you doing here?" he stammered.

"Tommy. Are you feeling all right?" she asked.

"*Touchdown Patriots. Brady on the keeper…*"

He leaned over and shut the radio off. The game was suddenly irrelevant.

The dark-brunette, almost raven-haired Myra Winkler had been the first real love of his life, and she had adored him. But they had gone their separate ways after college—though she was a year behind him, they had met at the University of Rhode Island and were inseparable for nearly three years. He was from Westerly, Rhode Island, and she Garden City, New Jersey. Surreptitiously she had moved into his dorm room and then to an off-campus apartment with him in his junior, her sophomore year. They worked together during the summers at a resort hotel in Watch Hill, Rhode Island.

But after graduating and taking his first job in New York City, Tom believed he wanted his freedom and broke off the relationship. She was devastated and would not accept the finality for months—she showed up at his New York apartment several times and went so far as to lobby his parents in an unsuccessful effort to win him back. And, although she was the jilted party, he ultimately realized that the cost of his freedom was far greater than that for which he had bargained. But timing is everything in life—she wanted to get married, he didn't. There were still oats to be sowed, or so he thought, for him to be happy.

Through the intervening years, his memory had quite often drifted back to sweet Myra and her easy ways. Now there she was in the flesh, looking older but much better than he had imagined she should have considering the twenty-five years that had passed since he had last seen her in person. Her once-wispy figure was a bit chunkier but pleasingly so, her hair with hints of gray, and there were gentle crow's feet tugging sagely at the corners of her eyes. In relative terms, she had aged well. Tom had heard that she had married an attorney who was also Jewish, which was sure to have made her mother very happy (he never thought her mother cared for him because he wasn't Jewish, but he got along famously with her father, who he considered to be a great guy and uxorious), had a couple of kids, and was happy. Admittedly, though he was happily married himself, fond memories of her had wafted through his reveries from time to time. In fact just this morning he had mused about what might have transpired between them had he not ended it all so abruptly after having developed what were eventually only fleeting infatuations, one with an NYU graduate student from White Plains, and another with a debutante from Great Neck. Also, as he learned from his early to midtwenties mild Don Juan syndrome, no woman he had ever been with could come close to Myra in bed. He often credited that to their total and complete surrender to each other. In college both had trusted that it was unimaginable there could ever be other lovers in their lives: there was no reason not to think that they would be together and deeply in love forever.

"Yeah. I feel fine. How have you been?" he asked, answering as though she had walked in on him at a college reunion. He was momentarily distracted by a gust of wind outside that sharply rustled the rigid russet oak leaves, the last hanging—procrastinating, refusing to surrender—the very last to let go of their mother tree, just outside the front windows.

"Huh? What is that supposed to mean?" she responded with a puzzled look on her face. "I'm your wife, for goodness' sake."

This time Tom nearly jumped out of his skin. Her words rocked him to the core: His body became numb. He stared into her long dreamed about and missed hazel eyes, and his mind blanked. He searched for something, anything to say. He couldn't find his voice.

"I...I...I mean, you are?" he blathered apprehensively.

"Tommy, why don't you come downstairs and lie on the couch for a few minutes? I think you've been breathing too much of that glue," she urged.

"Paste," he immediately corrected.

"I don't care...paste, glue, whatever. I think it's scrambling your brain," she said.

"Come on, what's the gag?" he asked, regaining his composure a bit. "I don't know what's going on here, but I might add that it's fantastic to see you again," he said.

"Oh, boy. Let's go, honey," she ordered, picking up the plate she had earlier placed on top of the bureau. "Come on."

I suppose I should cooperate and go along with this—there are probably people downstairs who are going to have a hell of a laugh at my expense, he surmised.

She reached out her hand, and he grasped it firmly; he felt a sensation that he hadn't known in decades. It was Myra's hand...blindfolded he would know the feel: they had held hands habitually for nearly three years. He stepped over some rubble on the floor and came close to her. She watched him carefully.

It's her. I remember the perfume she used to wear...can't think of the name, but I smell it.

She walked ahead of him into the hallway.

My God, she looks sensational, he thought, getting a full view of her—white blouse with violets trimming the collar and sleeves and well-fitting black slacks.

Where is Janice? This has got to be a setup, he concluded, but he was afraid to verbalize it at this point. His apprehension was a blend of being slightly disoriented and fear of repercussions if he was too friendly or drawn to a woman Janice knew was a long-lost love from his past.

"Now, be careful on the stairs, Tommy," she warned.

"What's the matter?" asked a young woman's voice, this one coming up the stairs. Tom looked down and saw a pretty teenage girl with lightly tanned skin and short-cropped blond hair. Her University of Rhode Island sweatshirt was tight and revealed a mature woman's bosom. The sleeves were rolled up just shy of the elbows; she wore khaki shorts and was barefoot.

"Dad's been sniffing too much glue, Courtney," Myra stated, followed by a whimsical chortle.

"Courtney?" Tom asked, puzzled. "Where's Carrie?"

"Who's Carrie?" asked Courtney furrowing her brow. "Mom, do you want to take him to the emergency room?"

"Don't mind him; he's just a little confused right now."

Tom stared at the teenager and then glanced back at Myra. *Like mother, like daughter. She is a knockout. Except where does she get blond hair like mine used to look?*

"Daddy, it's me. You act like you've never seen me before."

"I'm sorry, Courtney, if that's your name, but I'm onto the joke. Where are the other people?"

"Whoa. Are you sure we shouldn't call the EMTs, Mom?"

"No, let's wait a few minutes. Dad's just been shut up in that room too long. Maybe a little fresh air might help. Tommy, take a walk with Courtney, will you please?"

"Mom," the girl whined. "Why me?"

"Just do it," Myra snapped back.

The teenager responded with a loud but compliant cluck despite the steely glare of her mother.

"Where are the boys?" Tom asked.

"Boys? What boys? Do you mean Noah and his friends?" Courtney inquired. "In jail, I hope."

"Courtney Sarah Arnett," Myra snarled brusquely.

"Who's Noah?" Tom mumbled.

"Wow. Come on, Daddy. Your son. You know, the kid who is going to have his Bar Mitzvah next Saturday. Which is a joke in and of itself."

"He is?" Tom's voice squeaked. "I mean having his Bar Mitzvah next week? Where is he, then?"

"You're the one who said he could go to Six Flags with the Sambergs. I was there," Courtney answered, staring cautiously at Tom.

"That's right, honey," Myra cut in. "And the guest room had to be done because my parents are coming on Friday morning. Remember?"

"Never mind." Tom's head was spinning. *The kids are Jewish. This whole thing is stupid but would make sense if Myra is their mother. God, I recall talking about that when we were going together in college—lots of discussions about religion and kids. I never had a problem with that, though my parents were... Hold it...It sounds like I've already bought into all of this nonsense. Damn it all.*

Reaching the bottom of the stairs, he saw there was no one else in the house, at least not in the immediate vicinity. Myra broke off toward the kitchen with the plate and sandwich while Courtney threaded her arm in his and pressed tightly against him.

"Hey, Myra," he called after her, "I never said I wasn't hungry." There was no reply. He felt Courtney press against him in an attempt to direct him in the direction of the front door.

Feeling a tad uncomfortable with being this intimate with a young lady with whom he was not acquainted, he pulled away carefully.

"I'm fine, Courtney. I can walk on my own. I'm not dizzy or anything. Besides, I'm still hungry."

"Right. OK, let's hit the bricks, Daddy. You can eat when we get back. We're not going to run a marathon or anything."

Looking around, he noticed that the furniture was totally unfamiliar—but the style and colors vaguely reminded him of Myra's parents' house. As they approached the front door, he kept waiting for the other shoe to fall—for people to spring out of the closets, the basement, or the dining room. *That's it, they're waiting outside on the front lawn. Now I get it*, he speculated.

But as Courtney swung the half-leaded stained-glass door open, he could see through the glass storm door that it was obvious they were going to be alone outside.

"Be home in fifteen minutes." Myra said. She had silently traversed the living room carpet and now stood behind them.

Tom spun around and looked at her again, still disbelieving yet enjoying her presence. *Whatever this is, I better be careful—she's still a lovely married woman, and Janice is my wife.* He noticed her polished fingernails and toenails as well. She was wearing open-toed pumps. *Janice never has her nails done like that.*

"Do you have your cell, Court?" asked Myra.

"Yes, Mom," she said as she and Tom ventured outside. Courtney held the storm door open.

Now that is really odd. First of all no one would ever ask Carrie if she had her cell phone. It was attached to her hand, Tom considered. *Second, Carrie would wait for someone else to hold a door. Lastly, she would only grunt barely discernible responses*, he reasoned.

Then, with Courtney pulling at his right arm, they were off, down the brick stairs and up the flagstone walkway. The October air caressed him, and the rich fall fragrance enticed him. As they cornered onto the concrete sidewalk, he glanced back at the house and not only saw Myra standing in the door but was suddenly aghast at the color of the house.

Holy shit, that's putrid. Lavender shutters or whatever that is? That sucks. Either I'm dreaming, or something has really messed me up. I hope it's not a stroke or something. Can't be. Physically I feel fine. Let's see, I can roll my tongue. Good. I'm walking fine—no weakness. Damn, she is off to the races. Glancing ahead he saw that Courtney was already thirty feet up the walk and waving for him to hurry.

"Come on, Daddy. Get moving," she taunted. "You're a jogger—let's go."

⁂

Befuddled. That's what I am. Befuddled. What on Earth is going on? Tom Arnett contemplated. He had been sitting in front of the television for an hour—the Patriots game over, now the four o'clock game, and the Oakland Raiders and San Francisco Forty-Niners were doing battle. As had been their pattern this year, the Pats had pulled the game out in the waning minutes of the fourth quarter—once again Bill Belichick, coach of the Patriots, had stymied the ineffable Rex Ryan, the Jets' counterpart.

But Tom hadn't noticed, and he didn't remember. After going through the motions of putting the finishing touches on the wallpapering project and then cleaning up himself as well as the tools and trash, he had found the fifty-four-inch Sony HD television at just about the same location in the family room as it had been earlier in the day—before his world and his house had been turned upside down.

Where the hell did this stuff come from anyway? he wondered, surveying the room. There were pictures everywhere—his side of the family and a bunch of other people he mostly didn't recognize. The absolute strangest picture was Myra in a long, white wedding gown and him wearing a tux and a black yarmulke that was perched on the top of his long, blond hair. Next to Tom's feet was a cloth with shards of glass sticking out and glinting in the camera's flash. They both looked very young.

"Dinner is in fifteen minutes, Tommy." He looked over and saw Myra standing in the doorway. "Would you be a dear and set the table?" she asked. He was starving, now.

Set the table? On Sunday night when football is on? he thought.

"Myra, can I talk to you for a minute?" he asked.

"Oh, Tommy, honey. Can it wait? I'm getting everything ready right now."

"Are we having company?"

"I really do have to get back to the kitchen, darling…please…"

"Just a few—"

"Gotta go, Tommy…"

Myra whisked off toward the kitchen again. Tom looked at his watch. *Where the hell are Janice and the kids? This is our house, so where are they? Should I call? But who do I call? I've got to talk to someone.*

He jumped up and hurried after Myra. The blue upholstered rocker that he had been in bobbed violently back and forth. He could smell the aroma of what smelled like a fish dinner, which was totally foreign to him for a Sunday night.

We, or the former we that I knew just this morning, always have hot dogs and beans on Sunday night.

Just as he reached the door, he stopped and watched Myra. She was wearing an apron and flitting around the kitchen, busily at work. *Hmmm…she looks so good. Maybe this is some kind of a weird dream, and I've been given this unbelievable opportunity. So often I have wondered what it would have been like to have married Myra…*

Myra paused in the middle of the kitchen next to the island, part of the kitchen that wasn't there before in his memory, and gazed at him akimbo.

"Come on, come on. Set the table," she urged with that deep sensuality sprinkled with impatient urgency. He smiled and turned, unable to recall the last time he had set a table. *Maybe in Boy Scouts for a merit badge*, he guessed.

"Oh, and Tommy," she called after him. "Would you get my packages out of the car in the garage and bring them up to our bedroom?"

Our bedroom? He felt a tingle of nervousness followed by, or concurrent with, an involuntary physical manifestation of arousal. Then, just as quickly, he weakened from a shudder of guilt: a cartoon image flashed through his mind—the lily white ANGELIC Tom on his left shoulder and the fiery red DEVILISH Tom on his right, both whispering in his ears.

"Oh, and get the dessert from the freezer in the basement," she added.

Only about ten minutes until dinner, and she just gave me twenty minutes of chores. And a formal dinner on a Sunday during football season? This is really different.

Leaving the kitchen doorway after stealing one more glance at Myra's backside, he moved tentatively toward the mudroom that led to the garage. When he opened the door to the garage and switched on the light, he halted abruptly and gasped.

Oh my God. What the hell is this? Before him sat two new shiny, black CL class Mercedes Benz sedans. Even in the dull glow of a single seventy-five-watt bulb that illuminated the entire scene, the majestic vehicles reeked of luxury and affluence and seemed poised like two black panthers ready to pounce at a moment's notice. Tom stepped carefully down the two wooden stairs to the smooth cement floor and touched the first vehicle gently, then lightly dragged his fingertips of his left hand along the smooth, metallic surface. It was a sensuous feeling, much like that experienced when exploring the smooth, silky surface of a woman's delicately groomed leg. He tried the driver's door. It was unlocked. In the backseat he saw the handles of two shopping bags.

He closed the driver's door. The sound was solid and pure. He then reached over and opened the back door. Ducking in he took the handles of both bags—one clearly identified as coming from Nordstrom, the other from Talbots. As he pulled out and away from the car door with the bags, an unfamiliar youthful male voice addressed him. He grazed his head on the top of the doorframe.

"Did Mom get my new game?"

Tom stood looking up at a pimply faced what he guessed to be thirteen-year-old boy with blondish spiked hair and puffy reddish cheeks, wearing a black T-shirt emblazoned with some violent looking band reference, black jeans, and high-top black Keds sneakers. All of this was draped on a five-foot frame that still carried a fair amount of baby fat. The boy's slate-blue eyes darted from one bag to the other.

"I…I'm not sure," Tom answered uneasily.

"Did she forget again? What the hell is wrong with her? Did she have a stroke or something? MOM," the youth whined loudly as he turned and, backing off of the top step, disappeared into the house without waiting for Tom's response.

Who the heck is that charming little monster? Tom pondered as he closed the car door and struggled up the stairs with the two heavy bags. As he re-entered the house, two voices, one that he identified as belonging to the monster and the other Myra's, were engaged in a verbal skirmish. His head swirling, and not wanting to get involved in something he had no idea was about, he headed for the stairs leading to the second floor. At the top of the regally carpeted stairs—brass rods held what appeared to be an expensive Oriental stair runner—he walked slowly down the hallway in the direction of what was the master bedroom, at least what had been the master bedroom for him and Janice that morning. He passed by what was Carrie's, or rather now Courtney's bedroom. The door was wide open, and the comely teen sat at a computer rather studiously. She paused and looked over at Tom standing in the hallway.

"Hi, Daddy. Feeling better?" she asked carefully.

"Ah…yes, quite." His response belied his true state of mind.

"Will you be a peach then and read over this paper on Eastern European architecture for me? It's not due for another two weeks, but I want to get it done before next Friday. You didn't forget that I'm going away, did you?"

"Er…ah…no. I mean sure," Tom replied. The room was exceptionally clean, and pictures and sports paraphernalia covered the walls—nothing like the rat hole that Carrie occupied.

"Oh, and don't forget our shopping trip Wednesday night. Baby needs new shoes, ya know," she said, smirking. "College visits next month."

He nodded tentatively, thinking, *Based on the cars and everything else around here, I can only imagine what that means—big bucks. And college—he could hear ka-ching, ka-ching somewhere in his universe.*

As he continued on his way, he wondered how he would play poker and take her shopping on the same night. Wednesday had always been his night out for the last ten years—golf between April and September then poker all winter. He had lost last week and wanted to win back the fourteen dollars—and drink Lyle Warren's booze.

Opening the door to the master bedroom, he couldn't help but laugh. The room looked like a circus. Garish colors everywhere and a king-size bed that resembled an aircraft carrier. There was also a huge HD TV in the room—nothing that had ever been there before. A television in the bedroom was certainly not something Janice would allow, nor would he care about it. Just as he was about to drop the packages, he heard Myra shout from what he assumed was the bottom of the stairs.

"Tommy…I need the dessert from the basement and the table set. Please!"

"Yes, Myra. I'll be right there," he answered in a normal speaking voice, which he realized she could probably not hear.

"What?" Myra squawked.

"I'M COMING. I'M COMING," Tom barked.

He scuttled down the hallway. As he reached for the banister at the top of the stairs, he became aware that Myra was still at the bottom.

Jesus Christ. The commander is waiting, he thought.

"Tommy, you are going to have to have another talk with that son of yours. He's impossible. He is driving me crazy."

"Another talk?" Tom said as he started down the stairs.

"Well, before next weekend he is going to have to do a lot of growing up and studying. He has responsibilities. Rabbi Fischler has called twice today. My parents will be here Friday, and I don't want him like this. He needs a haircut, and that attitude—he is very disrespectful. I don't know where that comes from. And he'd better not act up for his Bar Mitzvah, or I'll embarrass him in Temple, in front of all of the guests, man or not. I'll spank him."

"What's wrong, Myra?"

Tom reached the last stair and was eye to eye with Myra. He could see more frustration than anger in her countenance.

"What's wrong? Tommy, this may not matter to you, but to my family this is a momentous occasion. If this kid doesn't come around, there will be hell to pay, that's what. He'll embarrass the whole family. Now get going—I asked you to help me with a few simple things, and you're still in a daze. Next time we hire out for wallpapering. I'm at my wits' end since that boy came home. He upsets the whole family. Please do something. Please."

Myra turned and hurried back to the kitchen. He glanced toward the living room and saw the monster with his dirty sneakers propped up on the coffee table—at least that was what its functionality appeared to be. It appeared to be an unrecognizable design of something that, to him, was very gauche, whatever it was. It sort of resembled a plastic driftwood that had been stuck in a toilet. Tom strolled into the room and confronted the teen. He didn't have a clue what to say or how to say it. He was totally lost—this kid was off the charts.

He fumbled looking for anything to say that sounded reasonable within the context of the situation.

"Um…you heard your mother, I suppose?"

The monster remained unresponsive as he continued playing with a handheld videogame, his thumbs dancing on a tiny keyboard while the gadget beeped, squeaked, and emitted various words that were indistinguishable to the average human being.

"Ahem…you…ah—"

"The name's Noah, in case you forgot, Tommy."

Whoa. This kid's a major wiseass. I'm supposed to be his father, and I get 'Tommy?'

"So, what's your problem, punk? And get your feet off of the fucking table."

The teen, apparently shocked and distracted by the sudden firmness, the f-bomb, and name, looked up at Tom curiously.

"Did you just call me a punk? And, did you say *fucking* table?"

"You heard me. You have a problem with that? Or should I shove that little gizmo where the sun don't shine to get your attention?" he growled, barely audible. Complying, the feet fell to the floor.

"Listen, that shit won't cut it with me, kid. Don't think for a minute I won't kick your little ass—"

"Tommy. Aren't you being too harsh with him?" Myra's voice, barely above a whisper, announced from behind him.

He turned and was looking at Myra.

"Huh? I thought you wanted me to administer some discipline and respect around here?" he implored gutturally through clenched teeth, his jaw set firmly.

"Yes, but there's no need to threaten violence and use obscenities—he's still a child, you know."

Out of the corner of his eye, Tom saw the feet go back up onto the coffee table.

"Myra, you're enabling him, don't you see? If you don't back me, he'll continue to treat you, or us, like dirt. I won't take it, though."

"Tommy, I've never heard you use that tone of voice with him."

"Dad's right, Mom. He's a little bastard," Courtney chimed in matter-of-factly, now having joined them in the living room.

"Courtney. That language. Please, you stay out of this. This doesn't involve you."

Tom backed away slightly as mother and daughter positioned themselves to parry. He knew female body language, and this looked menacing.

"Mom, he doesn't respect any of us or this house, and you know it. It's about time someone put their foot down without you coddling him."

"There's a right way and a wrong way to handle this, Courtney. Nobody knows more than I do that your brother can be unmanageable. And I am not coddling."

"He's a little creep...and his friends are losers."

"Shut up, Miss Goody Goody," the monster snapped from a still-seated position on the couch, royal-blue and lime-green fabric covered with plastic.

"Yeah, and I'll come over there and kick your wormy little butt," Courtney shouted, edging in his direction.

Myra jumped in front of her.

"Now, Courtney..."

"He's a little asshole."

"THAT LANGUAGE, YOUNG LADY."

"Yeah, and you're a slut," Noah grunted as he leaped from the couch. "Whore," he shouted as he ran out of the room through the far doorway.

Courtney grasped both of her mother's arms. "I'm gonna kill him."

"No, you're not. Tommy, do something. Don't just stand there. Do something."

"Take him to a reform school, Daddy. That's where he belongs." Courtney released her mother's arms and relaxed.

"Why does this have to happen every day? Now Tommy, go get Noah and get the table ready. Courtney, since your father obviously has his hands full, you get the dessert from down in the basement."

Good Lord. What a nightmare. I have to reign in that little degenerate—the daughter is the only one around here with any sense. Wow!

Tom followed the path of the little monster. He didn't have to go far. The bathroom door was shut and locked.

"Hey, Noah. Supper's almost ready. Wanna eat?"

"Go to hell."

"OK. Starve, you little snot. Maybe you can eat in a few days—maybe not. It looks like you can miss a few meals you lard ass."

Tom walked by his study and casually glanced in the door. The room, remarkably, looked as it should and pretty much always had. He wandered in and saw only a few things missing and some that had never been there before. One new item was particularly intriguing—a large old Zenith floor model radio probably from the '30s: just the kind of relic that Tom would love to spend hours exploring. The room itself was small, with dark-mahogany paneling. One window was at the far end; his mahogany desk was in front of bookcases filled with familiar books. There was also a bookcase across the room on the opposite wall. Beneath it was a black-and-red sofa. Standing behind the antique Windsor chair at the desk, which he had inherited from his grandparents, his eyes drifted down to the top of the desk.

Atypically, several credit-card bills were there staring up at him. Being a professional financial planner by trade, Tom was fastidious about credit cards and spending. But, looking at the balance of the statement on top from Capital One, he was paralyzed—$29,047.17. That was the statement on top. He reached down and picked up the Capital One statement and saw the balance on another, this one from RBS Bank—$35,458.91.

His stomach churned. There were more underneath, but he didn't dare look further in the pile. Suddenly he felt an urge low in his bowels, as if he were about to have an attack of diarrhea.

Holy Christ. And what about the cars in the garage? Tom's hands were trembling. *I don't make that much money. What is going on here? Did we hit the lottery? Does Myra work?* he wondered. *Are her parents subsidizing us?*

Tom grabbed the AT&T cordless phone from its cradle on the desk. He quickly punched his best friend Arnie Forslund's number. Arnie was a friend from high school. Although not day-to-day close, they had remained loyal to each other and still got together during the year with their wives and traditionally around the holidays, at least the Christian holidays. Someone picked up.

"Hello." It was Lois, Arnie's wife.

"Hi, Lois. It's Tom Arnett. How are you?"

"Oh, hi Tom. Great. How about you? We haven't heard from you in a while. What's up?"

Hmmm. Strange response. We just went to dinner with them in September, he pondered.

"Not a lot. Say, is Arnie around?"

"Sure…hold on. I'll get him."

Tom waited for what seemed an eternity. From the dining room, he heard Myra calling him again; this time he distinctly recognized impatience in her tone of voice. *My God, she's relentless. What has happened to that agreeable little waif?* He covered the receiver with his left hand: "I'm on the phone."

"Hi, Tom?"

"Arnie. Man, am I glad to hear your voice. This may sound kinda stupid, but can I ask you a few questions?"

"About what?"

"About me."

"About you? What the hell? Everything OK?"

"I'm not sure. Listen, is there some kind of a gag going on with me…as in a joke about who I am married to and my kids?"

"Gag? Not that I know of. Why?"

"You're not pulling my leg are you? Truthful?"

"Yes, Tom, yes. You know damn well that I'd be in on it if there was somethin' going on. Why? What's wrong?"

"Well, nothing, really." Tom held the phone away from his face and sneezed. Lacking any better remedy, he wiped his nose on his sleeve.

"God bless you," Arnie proclaimed.

"Thanks. Listen, I'm not sure about my anniversary and don't want to blow it. Can you tell me what the exact date is and how long I have been married to Myra?"

Arnie chuckled. "I don't even remember my own. Hold on while I ask Lois."

In the background Tom heard Arnie: "Lois, what is Tom and Myra's anniversary?" Lois's response was garbled. "How many years?" More garbled discussion this time, and it was obvious that Arnie had covered the receiver.

"Hey, Tom. Lois says it's June fifteenth. About twenty-one years ago, though. She'll have to look it up. I know we were there, though, because I was your best man. I thought you were going to cut your foot stepping on those glasses."

Suddenly Myra was at the door of the study. She looked less than amiable.

"Tommy. For once I cook a meal at home, and we don't go out. The least you can do is help me a little. Please…" Like fingernails on a chalkboard, her voice was excessively nasal and shrill. She turned away, but not before emoting her disgust and contempt. She had paid no attention to the fact that he was on the telephone.

"Hey, thanks, Arnie. I gotta go."

"OK, old buddy. Later."

"Bye." Tom clicked off the phone and put it back in its cradle. The red light came on, indicating that it had made a connection and was recharging. He pushed the papers on the desk into a pile and followed Myra to the dining room.

I got my answer—Arnie and Lois definitely said Myra and I are married, he concluded.

Now he was really in a quandary—and those bills, which he suspected were just the tip of the iceberg, were incomprehensible.

My God. Myra has really become her mother, he concluded.

In the dining room, he looked around for his liquor cabinet. *Boy, if I ever needed a stiff drink now is the time. No liquor cabinet. That figures, damn it.*

Myra and Courtney were at the table—it had been set, most likely by Courtney.

"Where's the booze?" Tom asked.

"Tommy, are you kidding me or what? You haven't had a drink in five years, and you want one now? I don't know what's gotten into you today. I'm beginning to be quite concerned."

"Five years?"

"At least. I just can't tolerate you having that problem again."

"Problem? Again?"

"Yes. I just don't like it."

"Well, I drink responsibly...er...at least I thought I did."

"We've had this discussion a thousand times. Please, not again. I don't want you ending up like my father—tipsy every night."

Her father? What is she talking about? He's a great guy. We used to throw them back when I was in college sometimes, but we weren't alcoholics. He and I always had a good time together—not even close to being drunks. What is she talking about?

"I have never known your dad to be tipsy every night. Maybe once in a while he and I would tie one on, but that was just...well, just guy stuff. Nothing that anyone should worry about."

"Call it what you will, Tommy, but I just didn't like you having a drink every day. That is bad stuff, especially around the kids."

"Aren't you being a tad like a zealot? A fanatic? Who are you, Carrie Nation?"

"Who?" Myra enquired.

"Carrie Nation. She was a prohibitionist. You know—temperance movement."

"Tommy, why must we go through this again? You know how I feel."

"But Myra, aren't you being a little radical? And hypocritical? Isn't that sort of extreme?"

"Well, no—but you promised, Tommy." Her voice was somber; her eyes were stone cold. It was a look that he had never seen in Myra's eyes.

"I did?"

"Why are you being so impossible? Let's just eat."

"Amen," said Courtney as Tom pulled out a plastic covered chair at the head of the table and sat; it was the same as all of the rest of the chairs around the table and the living room furniture. *This is certainly unique*, he thought as he tried to shift on the seat—he couldn't. He had to raise his bottom off the chair to change positions. *She REALLY has become her mother*, he decided.

Myra passed around what appeared to be pot roast. When Tom's plate was full, he poked his fork into a carrot: it was as hard as a rock. *So this is what smelled like fish when it was cooking? Uh-oh.* He paused and then stabbed a piece of roast and tasted it. *This is terrible. I want Janice back—she's no Julia Child, but she can follow a recipe and make a decent meal. What kind of hell have I fallen into? Myra is still as physically cute as ever, but the rest of this package is a bit rough*, he decided.

"By the way, what's the story with those bills on my desk? Is that some kind of a joke to go along with the rest of this charade?" he asked.

Myra hesitated before she spoke, as she looked up at Tom. She carefully laid her fork on her plate. "Charade? What charade?"

"This whole deal. What is happening around here?"

"Tommy, maybe you should call the doctor."

"Doctor? What, and ask him why we have credit-card bills that would choke a horse? Or why our son is a nutcase? Or why we have two of the most expensive cars known to man short of a Formula One racer in our garage? I need a doctor? Myra, darling, I need a winning lottery ticket, not a doctor."

"Tommy, now, you agreed that we wouldn't talk about finances in front of the children."

"What can we talk about in front of the children? Our sex life?"

"Tommy...please."

"That's OK, Mom. I would love to hear that one," Courtney said, sniggering.

"Courtney. Young lady—"

"Mom. I'm joking. Can't we have a nice, quiet dinner? We're never home together for dinner—you and dad are always eating out. And Noah isn't here. That's the best part."

"Talk to your father about that. I'm doing my best."

What in God's creation is going on here? I want my old family back—Carrie and all.

For the first time, as he looked at Myra's wrists and fingers, he realized she was loaded with bling—sparkling and shiny jewelry, and big. *She must have thirty grand on her hands alone*, he observed.

"Where's Noah?" Tom asked.

"Tommy, I asked you to take care of him and get him to the table."

"I suppose I could have shot him and brought him here."

"Why are you being so derisive? This is not funny already."

"That's not such a bad idea," Courtney interjected.

"COURTNEY!"

"Well, he probably already snuck back upstairs and is online with his degenerate friends, looking at porn," Courtney offered.

"I forbade him to do that again. No thirteen-year-old should be looking at that stuff. I don't care if he is considered a man, that isn't right. Tommy, I thought you had someone put a block on his computer."

"Mom, there's no way to stop it. Those rutting little slugs will find a way no matter what."

"Leave your brother alone. He's under a lot of pressure."

"Ha...pressure. It's just a Bar Mitzvah. He's a little pervert."

"Well, you shouldn't criticize your brother. At least he's not dating someone who is ten years older, like someone we all know, and already has had two pregnancy scares."

There was a loud clank as Tom's fork fell into his plate. He grabbed his glass of milk and took a swig—it was an audible gulp.

"MOM. Don't start on Jerry again."

"Who's Jerry?" Tom interjected, nearly choking.

"Dad? Wake up—Jerry. My soccer coach. What's the matter with you?" Then Courtney looked sharply back her at mother. "And I'm not dating him. Why do you keep saying that? We are serious—we're in love. He wants to marry me."

Tom tried to stop it, but his throat closed involuntarily, and milk came back up into his mouth. He grabbed his napkin and held it to his mouth. He felt some dribbling from his nose and quickly wiped it.

"Because it is no secret what has been going on with you two—the whole town probably knows. It's disgraceful. And I am against you going with him to New York City overnight to go to a soccer clinic next month. Your father agrees with me, don't you, Tommy?"

"He just admitted that he doesn't even know who Jerry is," Courtney railed.

"He knows who Jerry is. Tommy, go ahead, tell her what we discussed. We don't want to make this whole thing worse by our daughter running off with some *coach* in a scandalous affair. If this gets out, as I'm sure it will sooner or later, that is if it isn't already front-page news, it will be devastating to you and your family. No way."

"It's not an affair."

"Young lady, don't try to fool us…and yourself. This guy no more wants to marry you than jump in front of a train. He's using you for sex. Now, where is your brother, damn it? This nice dinner and he's off doing whatever…Tommy, please. Find him and get him here."

"Mom, how many times do I have to tell you? This is not what you think. Jerry is a perfect gentleman. Besides, what did you and dad do in college? Are you telling me that you were a perfect little angel? You could have gotten pregnant."

"That's enough, young lady." Myra's tone was firm.

"You're a hypocrite, then," Courtney declared, slamming her fork down on the table. "You and dad *lived together* in college." Tears were beginning to well in her eyes.

"I was in college. You are an eighteen-year-old senior in high school. Your father and I were a year apart in age—and he wasn't a teacher or a coach with a moral responsibility to his students, their parents, and his employer. You are talking about oranges and apples—a potential for a terrible scandal. Can't you see that, Courtney Sarah?"

"You and dad weren't screwing?"

"COURTNEY"

"DAD!"

"TOMMY!"

Tom took a long drink from his glass of milk, actually finished it, and set it down carefully on the white-linen tablecloth. He glanced slowly at each of the two women now glaring at him, each wanting him to side with her, and then looked back down at his plate. As he stared at the leathery pot roast and petrified vegetables, he became lost in his reverie, remembering the mention of the shared bedroom upstairs. He smirked, but the hint of a smile quickly dissipated. He squirmed uneasily on the unforgiving plastic of the dining room chair which made noises that were indistinguishable from farts.

This is bullshit. Jesus Christ...This reminds me of dinners at Myra's house with her parents and her brother and sister. What a nightmare. Wow! Oh well, let's see—if I have sex with Myra will I be cheating on Janice? If I knew what the hell was going on here, I might think differently. And what if I did have sex with Myra, and she gets pregnant? Maybe she's too old now. Oh my God, she could be menopausal. This is crazy. What a mess. I haven't been with another woman in over twenty years, and I've never really had the desire to be, either, except for fantasizing about being with Myra again. Sure, Janice's libido isn't exactly going to set the world on fire, and Myra was a wildcat many years ago, and what a body. We were at it night and day in college—anywhere and anytime we could be alone, like monkeys. There was even that time in a park with people around as she sat on my lap—we tried to be discrete under a blanket, attempting to blend in with the scenery. I think we were high. But Myra let out a couple of very audible gasps and a few fairly loud flowery expletives at the height of passion. That turned several heads. We ended up laughing hysterically. She nearly severed off my manhood she was laughing so hard. We were kids, though.

"Huh," Tom muttered, unaware that his mouth was open and skewed obliquely.

For the most part, back then, Myra and I would just look at each other, and the next thing you know we would be naked. But was that what our relationship was all about all those years ago? Was the rest just a fill in until the next romp in the sack, which many times was only a moment away – and several times a day? We thought we were in love—or was it just infatuation or lust? Or maybe it was a convenient outlet for our hormonal rages that was monogamous and safe from STDs and fit the societal norms at the time? Maybe I was too easygoing and just put up with or ignored the rest? Was I seeing and hearing only what I wanted to?

Well, I guess not as far as Myra was concerned. For a while I couldn't get away from her—she was obsessive. And Janice and I are best friends. Sure, we have our differences, but she and I have a solid relationship. We have adjusted to our life circumstances, like most people with family responsibilities, I suppose. Maybe my instincts were right all along—Myra wasn't the girl for me. Breaking up when I did may have been exactly the right thing to do. That decision may have been one part wanderlust, one part common sense, one part intuition, and the rest dumb luck. Still, here I am, and here is Myra. I wonder if that certain spark is still there. And she still has a great body in her midforties and after two kids. My God. Would Janice ever find out? I would never forgive myself if I hurt her that way. How many times have I fantasized about making love to Myra again through the years, wondering what it would be like if we had stayed together? It appears that I have been given the chance to find out, but there are more questions than answers. I am so goddamn confused. Man, do I ever need a drink.

⊱⊰

"Aren't you going to fill the dishwasher, Tommy? You know I can't do it with these nails," Myra whimpered as he moved toward the family room and the big-screen TV—and Sunday night football. "I did make the dinner, and… well, sweetie, you always do the dishes."

We go from the ridiculous to the absurd around this place, Tom thought. *It doesn't sound like I have much of a choice.* He was still starving. What Myra had served was unidentifiable and inedible.

"Yeah, I guess so," he answered, his voice hard, truculent.

"Tommy, I'm going to go to the mall. I need to get a present for Gloria. You remember she's having a birthday party in two weeks, and we've been invited. I won't be long."

Tom stopped and squinted at Myra, who wasn't standing more than five feet from him.

"Isn't it a little late to be going shopping? And how are you going to pay?" he asked, remembering the pile of outrageous credit-card bills on his desk while also recalling something ghastly that had stuck in his mind since high school: required reading in senior English class, the lurid description of debtor's prison in Dickens's *Pickwick Papers*.

"Now, Tommy, please don't start that argument again. We simply have to get a present. You'll just have to work a little harder," she stated perfunctorily and then flashed him a capricious grin. "Oh, and don't forget poor Putz."

"Who's Putz?"

"Are you doing this on purpose, Thomas Arnett? Putz is our black lab who just so happened to have had the misfortune of being sprayed by a skunk last Friday night. The kennel called and said they have taken care of the smell, and he can come home. You need to pick him up tomorrow. They said it's five hundred dollars."

Tom gnashed his teeth. He could not believe the scenario he was living: suddenly, unexpectedly—and without a history or point of reference. He was speechless as Myra reached into her Coach pocketbook and withdrew a jangling mass. He noticed what looked like a silver Mercedes Benz medallion and oval keyless remote dangling with the shiny, plastic-tipped keys.

"Thank you, darling," she said, rising from the table. She hurried out of the dining area, headed for the garage door.

Noah was still nowhere to be found, and Courtney had made several calls on her cell and was about to be picked up by a friend whose name or gender were not revealed. Meanwhile the dinner table in front of him remained filled with dirty dishes, silverware, and uneaten food.

Tom heard the garage door open and one of the Mercedes roar to a start. Walking across the living room, he saw Myra's taillights as she sped down the street. Then he looked back at the table—the rooms were not separated—and glimpsed at the disaster still stacked on the table.

"Good grief," he moaned.

Slowly he shuffled back and started clearing, scraping leftover food onto a single plate. Realizing he was still very hungry, he put down the dish and fork that he was holding and went into the kitchen. He opened the refrigerator door and stared in, hoping to find something to at least fill the very large abyss in his stomach. Other than milk the contents were sparse. He was not surprised by the paucity and wondered if he had enough time to order, have delivered, eat, and sufficiently dispose of any evidence of a combination pizza.

After searching the cupboards, the pantry, and every nook and cranny, he found himself sitting at the tiny kitchen table, which was nothing like the large, family-style country kitchen table that he and Janice had in the same room sans the island in the middle, eating Ritz crackers, peanut butter, and orange sherbet ice cream. That was about all there was.

⚜

The soft amber glow of the single small lamp on the bedside table created a relaxed ambience in the bedroom. Tom had showered quickly in basically the same yet now aesthetically unfamiliar bathroom he had known since he and Janice had moved into the house when she was pregnant with Carrie. Eventually he found the toiletries that were presumably his. Not exactly what he had left behind but workable. That was except the Old Spice deodorant—that was where he drew the line.

He lay under the sheet and single thin, light-blue blanket, wearing only his boxer shorts, his usual bedtime attire. He waited nervously—much more anxious than he had anticipated he would be. In fact Tom Arnett was very restless, his mind jumping from pleasure to guilt like a silver ball hurtling around a pinball machine; swirling from the bizarre events of the day and wondering what had happened. Try as he may to assimilate into his current surroundings and circumstances, he was hesitant. After all this was an adulterous proposition as far as he was concerned—and he was no bigamist.

The bedroom door opened slowly. Myra glided in without a sound. No doubt barefoot—Myra had always preferred to go barefoot whenever she could. She did not look at Tom, but he could not avert his eyes from her. She strolled over to the vanity, a piece of furniture Janice didn't own—it was obviously Myra's. The furniture, as it was in every room, was almost completely unfamiliar. He recognized only a few pieces that were from his family.

Yes, that's her walk. That hasn't changed one iota. With her back to him but glancing at herself in the mirror on the back of the vanity, she began unbuttoning her blouse. Tom felt his pulse quicken as a wave of anticipation grasped at him and clutched his gut.

What the hell am I doing here—and how did I get here? If Janice finds out, I'm dead meat. For all the times I have fantasized about having sex with Myra again here I am actually going to bed with her and having no idea where Janice and the kids are and actually feeling out of place in my own home and as guilty as hell. Where are they, and what am I doing here? Bedtime in my own house, and I am here with strange kids who are allegedly mine, one a misfit and the other playing with fire. I am missing Janice and feel sad that something terrible has happened and she has disappeared from my life. Now I am seriously entertaining thoughts of having sex with an old lover of mine. Tom was terrified and abashed, yet his prurient interests were becoming harder and harder to resist. The temptation was insufferable.

Myra reached slowly, deliberately around her back and undid the hooks of her brassiere. She peeled off each cup slowly, first the right and then the left, and then dropped the garment onto the vanity chair. He watched her reflection in the mirror, her full breasts, round and larger than he remembered them to be, flow downward, almost touching the sensuous rounded bulge of her tummy. She turned slightly, and he saw each fleshy bosom sway easily with her movement. Tom swallowed hard. He felt his heart racing. His arousal was manifesting itself in the usual diversion of blood.

Next she reached across, released a single button on the side of her slacks, and then, grasping the zipper between the thumb and forefinger of her left hand, slowly moved her hand downward. The top of the slacks loosened, and she wriggled out of them. They fell to the floor. She stepped out one foot at a time, bent over, and picked them up, her breasts hanging and swinging pendulantly. Tom saw that her legs were still exquisitely shaped and the flesh smooth and silky. She laid the pants carefully over the back of the delicately flowered chair in front of the vanity. She stood before him wearing only her panties. He leered at her through tiny slits of his eyes, afraid to let her see that he was awake.

I have to wait—play possum a bit. I can't initiate anything, he reasoned. *And if Myra does give me a sign or an opening, so to speak, I have no idea what I will do. Should I say the Lord's Prayer or something? God, she is still very much a hottie.*

Myra's body was exquisite; although not as youthful as a skinny twenty-one-year-old college student, she was in outstanding shape in just the right places. Without moving, he watched intently as she slid both thumbs under the elastic waistband on either side of her curvy hips. Tom was paralyzed—his breath caught in his throat and momentarily stopped breathing. He stayed completely still as she bent over slightly with her back to him, and slowly slid the silky, pink-lace panties down—and then stood revealing her shapely buttocks. She turned, stepped forward, now totally naked, and picked up a sheer nightgown from the end of the bed. She lifted it and pulled it over her head—her nipples stuck straight out as if they were about to pierce the material. Tormented, his breathing shallow, Tom felt himself twitch involuntarily when her bottom jiggled ever so slightly under the sheer material when she turned back toward the vanity. Finally she pulled out the chair. Myra sat down and began brushing her hair.

Damn. This is the moment of truth.

He heard a door close downstairs and chose to ignore its implications. Myra heard it too, cocked her head slightly, and then resumed running the

blond-wood Caswell-Massey natural bristles through her predominantly ra-
ven hair. Then she slowly rested the brush on the vanity and stood, framed by
the silver wallpaper covered with etchings of birds and flowers—it was hor-
rible: busy and extremely feminine. She looked at the door and stood listening
like a cat contemplating a mouse's silent footsteps.

"Court?"

"Good night, Mom," Tom heard the now-familiar voice respond from
stairway or the hallway; he couldn't be sure.

"Doors locked and your brother in his room?"

"Yes, Mom."

"Good night, sweetie."

During this banter Tom had opened one eye and watched her intently—
the nightgown left nothing to the imagination. Myra, though thicker and
fuller with age, looked better than ever. Holding himself completely still, he
stayed silent; he felt his heart pounding and knew he couldn't hide his enthusiasm if he had to get up. He quickly closed his eye and remained motionless.
Myra walked over and sat on the edge of the bed.

*The curve of her hips and buttocks, the shape of her back, and her square
shoulders are tantalizing if not downright delicious*, he mused dreamily. *Her
backside looks like an inverted heart. Perfect.*

She turned out the light. He heard her fumbling with something on the
nightstand. Suddenly there was a flash, and the room exploded with bright,
unsteady, dancing light. She had turned on the television.

"Tommy. Tommy," she whispered. "Are you awake?"

Oh God, oh God, oh God, he screamed in his head. *She is wearing nada
under that flimsy negligee. We could both be naked in an instant. And that skin;
that hair; that body; that girl who once loved to have sex with me—I can't take
this much longer.* He held his breath.

Tom Arnett was a millisecond away from reaching up and stroking her
hips and derriere when the events of the day suddenly dashed through his
mind like a movie on superfast-forward. He thought of Janice. He stayed
perfectly still and controlled his breathing. He waited. Myra slid into bed and
propped up her horrid floral pillows. Through the slits of his eyelids, he saw

that the room was now bathed in the blue moving light of the TV. He peered at Myra as she rapidly sped through the channels, finally settling on one. He listened carefully. It was a talk show, but the volume was low. He couldn't make it out.

Suddenly Myra got out of bed and walked delicately across the room into the bathroom. She left the door open—he could hear her peeing.

Tom opened his eyes. *Whew*, he sighed and closed his eyes again.

When Myra returned to bed, she left the TV on.

"Tommy," she purred. "I saw you peeking when I was undressing."

He remained excruciatingly still, unable to move. The BAD Tom was screaming to make a move: "Go on, take the chance, now goddamn it. Make love to her." The GOOD Tom was whispering for him to stay still—do the right thing. *But what is the right thing? If Myra is my wife, and my mind has short-circuited, how could that be wrong?* Tom contemplated.

"I'm sorry," she bemoaned. "I know it's me. Damn menopause. It just sapped me of the urge. I can't explain it. I just have no libido anymore. Doctor Goodwin said there may be some things that can be done. Maybe it will come back like before. He says sometimes it comes back with a vengeance! Wouldn't that be nice? But you know how I feel about taking drugs. I'm sorry. Not tonight."

Myra put the remote on the bedside table then snuggled down under the covers.

The television was never turned off. Tom dozed only intermittently. Once he awoke with a start from a weird dream where he was onstage in an ornate auditorium—perhaps an old, grand opera house—in front of a large, raucous audience, with Myra's family, as he had known them years before, in the front row. Ruth Winkler sat with arms folded across her chest and wore her usual supercilious expression while husband Joel looked on empathetically yet powerless to act and risk the wrath of his wife for offending her; older brother Louis, eyes glazed over, typical of his detached law-student bearing; and younger sister Sarah, analytical but wide-eyed and mouth agape—a bemused professional speech therapist. Tom was holding a golden bassoon that was unplayable—there was no reed, and, fumbling around, he discovered there were none to be found anywhere.

—※—

"Tommy. Tommy. Hurry. Hurry. Come here. Quick."

The blood-curdling shrieks were from Myra somewhere upstairs. He had just sat down to breakfast having made himself toast slathered with peanut butter—that was all he could find. Thinking he was the only one in the house who was awake at six o'clock on this Monday morning, he had stolen away to the kitchen. Still groggy—he had only dozed all night, and finally, after extricating himself from a clutching Myra who wanted only to cuddle, he circled the bed to get the remote. He clicked off the TV. Now he was startled by the urgency in her voice.

He raced through the rooms then grabbed the newel of the banister and vaulted up the first few stairs. He slipped on the third step and quickly caught himself on the stair with the palms of his hands. He scrambled up the rest hurriedly on all fours.

When he arrived at the top of the stairs, Noah and Courtney stood in the doorways of their respective rooms, Noah in his briefs and black T-shirt with "AC/DC" across the front (a rock group familiar to Tom) and Courtney in a terrycloth bathrobe, both looking at their mother standing halfway in the guest room at the end of the hall. Myra was wearing an orchid velour bathrobe.

"Tommy, I can't believe this. This is terrible," Myra whimpered. "My parents are coming in four days. What are we going to do?"

"Calm down, calm down," Tom proffered in a soothing voice, as yet unaware of the cause of her consternation and distress. He looked closely at Myra's face. Even without makeup and with her hair uncombed, she was extremely attractive—and her expression of horror made her seem so appealing: helpless, vulnerable.

When he arrived at the door, Myra stepped back into the hallway. He peered into the room, not knowing what to expect.

"Oh my God," he said as he walked into the guest room.

All of the wallpaper that he had painstakingly put up lay curled on the floor—not a piece, not one small, single strip had stayed on the walls.

"Tommy," Myra moaned, threading her arm in his and pulling herself close to him. "What are we going to do? Do you think we can get someone on this short notice? I don't want my parents to have to stay at a hotel on their first grandson's Bar Mitzvah, especially since my father has been so generous to us. You *have* to do something."

Should I ask or just assume that Myra doesn't work? The random thought crossed his mind suddenly. He presumed not.

"I'll call around, but if worse comes to worst, I guess yours truly will have to redo the whole thing."

"Tommy. I don't want my parents to wake up under a pile of wallpaper or a husband who doesn't know where he is or how he got there. You had better get professionals."

"Can we afford that?

"I don't care—that's your department."

"Yours too if we go bankrupt."

She pulled away and glowered at him.

"Tommy, that is uncalled for. You find a way, just like you always do. I'm depending on you. This is very, very important to me. I don't ask you for much around here, so please…please take care of this. For me and your son."

Myra wandered off down the hallway and into their bedroom. Knowing he should have turned away because he must have had a bemused look on his face, he glanced at both Courtney and Noah. Simultaneously they shrugged their shoulders and disappeared into their rooms, both obviously uninterested in venturing close to what might end up being work for them under their mother's supervision.

"Well, I'll be sure to get prepasted this time," he called after her, which he assumed fell on deaf ears. She had pretty much dropped the problem in his lap and signed off. He didn't think she would have any idea what he was talking about anyway.

Tom shuffled down the hallway and stopped at the bedroom doorway into which Myra had entered moments ago. She stood in her bra and panties, with her hands on her hips, gazing into a substantial walk-in closet. Having not looked inside before, the door had been closed, he saw that it was jammed full entirely with women's clothing.

"You want to pick out the wallpaper again?" he asked.

Myra glanced over her shoulder coyly and shifted her weight so that her bottom wiggled seductively. "Of course I do, Tommy. You're not to be trusted." She winked and smiled.

So that's how she always gets her way. She sure uses a lot of honey, he considered and returned the smile. *It will be tough to get used to this…especially at night. She has her wiles…and man, are they good. But is that it? Tommy do this, Tommy do that…because I'm a girly girl, pretty, sensuous, and maybe great sex will be yours for the asking again—someday? Now I understand how it works around here. Now what will my fantasies be like?* Tom shook his head. *Definitely Janice. Desperately Janice.*

Tom turned and went back downstairs to finish his breakfast, such as it was.

⚬

By eight-thirty Tom knew he would have to wallpaper the room again. He had totally forgotten that it was Columbus Day weekend. Nobody was working. Besides, with such short notice it was next to impossible to expect to find someone who would be able to size and paper a complete room. Especially for a customer who wasn't a steady patron. He had been down this road before.

Alone in the kitchen, he became aware that the house was quiet again. *Of course Noah and Courtney are back in bed and asleep. They're teenagers*, he thought. Myra was still upstairs, presumably getting dressed.

He called his office and heard the recorded message. Joyce, the voice on the recording, was still the receptionist, and Bob Gilbert was still his partner in their financial-planning business. And, remarkably, the telephone number was the same, and the office was where it had been for the last seven years. Fortunately, being a long weekend, he could reasonably take the day off. He knew he wouldn't have set up any appointments for a holiday.

Why didn't I think of this before? I should call my sister, he reckoned. He knew her number—she had lived in the same house in Waterloo, Iowa, for nearly thirty years. She was his elder by five years, and they talked infrequently. His right hand pecked at the buttons like the head of a pileated woodpecker, his wrist thrusting a wildly frantic yet accurate index finger forward. He held the cordless receiver to his ear. The other end was ringing.

"Hello."

He recognized her voice. "Dar?" he asked.

"Why, it's Silent Tom. And to what do I owe this unexpected and rare call at this hour, on a holiday no less? Who died?"

"No, no. Just wanted to say hello. Everything OK with you?"

"Ahhh…yeah. You OK?"

"Sure. Er…actually there is something on my mind."

"Usually is when you call. Oh, and I did send back our regrets for this coming weekend to Myra. I hope you're not upset about that. Just can't make the trip east with Ralph still in rehab for his back."

Tom sighed loudly. Ralph was her husband, and yes he'd had back surgery about a month ago. He knew that. *She mentioned Myra. So now she has confirmed this thing too. It must be me*, he acquiesced.

Myra presented herself in the kitchen. "Who are you talking to? Wallpaperers?" She looked exactly like her mother twenty years before: a clone. Even the gold shoes—slipper looking things. A matching gold handbag hung on her forearm. Her hair was perfect, and she had on more jewelry than he had ever seen before on one person. She looked gaudy.

"Darlene," he said covering the receiver.

"Oh. I think I forgot to tell you about the card she sent. Well, we knew she wouldn't make it for this weekend anyway."

Tom turned away with the phone to his ear once again. "Dar, I was just checking on Ralph and wondering how the John Deere factory is surviving without him."

"He's fine. Want me to get him?"

"No, actually we were just headed out the door. I'll call him back later."

There was a pause—the silence was obvious and uncomfortable.

"Tom. That's all you called for?"

"Sure, sis. And to hear your voice. Gotta get going now."

"Whatever. You are a very peculiar man, Thomas Arnett. Thanks for call-ing—it was…underwhelming."

"See ya." He pushed the red "clear" button and disconnected the call. *At least she's still a pain in the* ass, Tom ruminated.

"Are we going?" Myra asked, standing in the middle of the kitchen, lean-ing on the island.

"The store opens at ten. Are you going like that—I mean, all dolled up just to go to Home Depot?"

"Oh, stop teasing me, Tommy. Can we make a few stops on the way, sugar? I have a few small things I need to pick up."

"Ahh…I guess so. You want to leave now?"

"Yup. Let's go."

Small things? What, another Mercedes? A room of furniture? A place on Nantucket? How about a time-share on Mars?

Tom had never driven a Mercedes and had no interest in starting today. "You wanna drive? I don't."

"I think you're going through a change of life, Tommy."

"Yeah—to poverty."

"That's not funny."

"No, it isn't."

She yanked the now-familiar set of keys and such from her pocketbook as they headed for the garage.

⊶⊷

On the way to and from the Home Depot, everything was where it should have been, at least as he remembered it to be. Myra's driving was horrendous, and he kept his eyes and mouth closed most of the way. A few abrupt gasps and at least one violent sucking of air through clenched teeth and nearly put-ting his foot through the floor of the car as he pounded on a nonexistent brake were met with flinty sideways glances.

What was intended as a quick run to get new wallpaper turned into a shopping extravaganza, the likes of which Tom hadn't experienced since last

Christmas season. Now he wondered what holidays they celebrated—probably all of them besides the usual religious and holy days. He cringed when they pulled into their street and he saw the house again. It was a gray day, more like November, and the colored leaves on the trees were more muted than they would have been on a bight autumnal afternoon. As they drove down the street, they exchanged polite waves with the neighbors—strangely, all the same neighbors as the day before. John Connor, not surprisingly, looked like his usual disheveled and hung-over self while raking leaves. His wife may have left him years before if she wasn't as big a lush as he was. Moira kept inside with the shades closed, mostly. "Buzzy" Connor was one of the best criminal attorneys in the city, and only his vast reputation as a drinker had kept him from being seriously considered for an appointment to a judgeship.

The garage door took its time pulling itself up before Myra maneuvered the Mercedes into its stall like a sweaty thoroughbred following a solid workout several times around the track. The door closed automatically behind the car.

There were two clicks—seatbelts were unfastened. Tom watched Myra climb out of the car. Once again he admired her shapely curves. *She sure is still a treat to look at, but I'm beginning to miss Janice. Janice has an appeal that Myra could never have.* He started around the back of the car.

"Tommy, can you please get the bundles? I don't want to take a chance with my nails before next weekend," Myra whimpered.

Whoa. This girl is really delicate—and high maintenance. Maybe I knew she would be. I am not used to that. Janice is wonderfully not. And I'm perpetually hungry, just like basic training, he thought.

It took three trips to get everything in the house. He knew that all items had been charged to credit cards. She had justified every purchase as necessary for the weekend. He had watched Myra the whole time, seeing her mother in every move of her body, her expressions, and words—even her bickering with sales clerks. About every two minutes, his mind had flashed back to the bedroom the night before. He saw her body, heard her sensuous voice, yet remained stymied with guilt and his inherent probity. He missed Janice.

Tom Arnett was bewildered. Drawn in one sense and repulsed in another. But not revulsion born of horror or fear; but tortured by the very salacious thoughts that he had overcome years before. Temptation and lust were beckoning him, yet he was fighting himself, adrift in a sea of contradictions. Unsure of his circumstances, the familiar blended paradoxically with the anomalous—he was holding on precariously to what appeared to be reality while going through the awkward motions of someone who was unfamiliar and uncomfortable with his circumstances. For years he had conjectured and fantasized about something that was purely sexual—but to actually live that experience had now become a terrible gamble with a price that he was unwilling to tender—a genuine fool's errand.

"Dad, can I have twenty bucks?"

Tom suddenly awakened from his stupor. Noah stood before him, his clothes characteristically disheveled, and his hair tousled and shabby. Tom did not know this child, yet the child knew him. He did recognize that the boy needed tidying up before Saturday—that much was a given. Myra espied around the corner. Tom felt compelled to act firmly, fatherly.

"Ahem…when do you plan to get your hair cut?"

"Now, Tommy. He has an appointment with my stylist on Wednesday," Myra piped in.

Tom swung around to confront her.

"Every time I talk to him you answer. I forgot what his voice sounds like. Can I please have a conversation with him? You cannot be him. And why does he have to go to a stylist? What is wrong with a good old barber shop?"

"Tommy, nothing is to be gained by badgering him. He has enough pressure on him this week."

"I haven't seen him do a goddamn thing besides get pissed off because I exist and then barricade himself in his room. Now, all I get is 'Dad the ATM' from him. Who pays the freakin' bills around here, anyway?"

"Noah, I have twenty dollars—"

"Jesus Christ Almighty. What am I around here? Invisible?"

"Tommy, why must you be so unreasonable? And must you use that language?"

"Unreasonable? I'll tell you what is unreasonable. I know what I make, and I see the bills. Two Mercedes. New clothes. Nails. Hair. How soon before we are out on the street? Homeless?"

"Thomas Arnett. Stop it. NOW. Not in front of the children. You know that would never happen. You should have taken that job my father offered you years ago in his company if you want to be that way about it."

I'm not going to win this battle. In fact it looks very much like I'm losing the war.

"Forget it. Where's the wallpaper stuff?" Tom yanked at the bags on the floor between the dining room and kitchen and pulled out the prepasted paper and can of sizing. Looking up he noticed that Myra was crying. Noah was gone with his aforementioned twenty dollars.

"What? I'm sorry. Listen, it's just that…I mean…ah…well, it's just that I feel like a schmuck around here." He was glad he had remembered the word—it fit perfectly.

"Tommy…" Myra sobbed. He stood in front of her and reached out. She embraced him and put her head on his chest. He could feel her warm, wet tears as he held her instinctively.

"No, wait, Myra. I am sorry, but we do need to talk. I am just so…well, confused."

"Tommy…you know that Courtney's pregnant, right?"

He froze. *Holy shit. That girl seems like such a winner, and now she's screwing up her life with some asshole who is ten years older than her. She's only a kid. Plus she's delusional—wants to look at colleges? Maybe she should be looking for daycare instead.*

"Oh my God, Myra. I know I should know this, but how old is Courtney? I lost track."

"Eighteen."

Then statutory rape is out, he resolved.

"Tommy, my parents cannot know about this."

"What are we, or rather what is she, since she's a consenting adult, going to do about it?" he asked, pulling away and brushing her hair from her face. She didn't smell like Janice—sweet but different. She was, after all, in his mind, a different woman from the one he had known supposedly for the last twenty-odd years. It was a very disconcerting sensation consoling Myra as if he were her husband—but he was.

"Oh, Tommy, I don't know. Abortion?"

"First of all we have to get that soccer coach son of a bitch in here and ask him what he's going to do."

Myra suddenly sobbed louder. "Tommy—she's not sure it's his baby."

"Oh…that's marvelous. So our daughter is promiscuous? That's fabulous. Boy, you sure can't tell a book by its cover. Good grief. Where is she, by the way?"

"I don't know. She wasn't home here when we got home."

"Splendid. I'd better get started on that room, or your parents will be sleeping on the floor in here," he said as he pointed to the living room. Myra retreated into the kitchen. He could hear her whimpering, and it occurred to him that for some unknown but understandable reason he wasn't overly anxious to comfort her. Then it hit him like a ton of bricks—he lusted for her, but his feelings were empty, devoid of compassion and real caring. And that he really would be capable of empathy like that only for the woman he loved dearly and had been married to, he thought, for the last two decades. For the woman he truly adored and was comfortable with. The emotional and the physical became a human puzzle whose solution was akin to that of a game of connecting the dots.

"I'm going to start the room," he said, louder than talking but quieter than shouting. There was no reply. He headed for the basement door to collect the tools for the job upstairs.

⌐⌐

The sizing had dried quicker than he had anticipated, and the prepasted paper went up in a fraction of the time compared to the paper that needed paste applied. By ten o'clock, having stopped only for a peanut butter on stale wheat bread, as there was no rye bread in the house, Tom Arnett was climbing the stepladder and hanging the last piece in the same corner as he had the day before with the faulty wallpaper. Also, as he had done before, he smoothed the surface with the wide brush and then ran the seam roller up and down the edges, wiping off any excess watery paste on a rag.

His two feet back on the floor, he moved the ladder to the middle of the room. He made his way slowly around the room, rolling edges and putting the finishing touches on what he thought was a job well done in a crunch—as good as any paid professional and at a fraction of the cost. Which led him to think about the credit-card bills as yet untouched, or at least unpaid, on the desk downstairs. His mind also drifted to the refrigerator—always sufficiently stocked by Janice, not so now. He realized that his hunger pangs were beginning to sing, and he contemplated a late night run to McDonald's.

The radio was tuned to a classic-rock FM station, the volume on low—Steely Dan was filling the room softly with "Dr. Wu," and the distinctive alto sax solo of Phil Woods floated effortlessly in the air. Monday-night football had started on television, a fact of which Tom Arnett was keenly aware. The darkness outside painted the windows ebony in sharp contrast to the colors in the wallpaper, and the room was suddenly cooler than he had noticed while he was working—the windows were open, less than earlier but enough to permit an October evening breeze to filter in. Tom took the spotlight, unclasped it from the back of a chair that had been brought into the room for that singular purpose, and aimed it at the border added to the top of half of the room. It looked good—well installed. He heard footsteps on the stairs.

He shut off the spotlight and laid it on the tarp on the floor, assuming it was not too hot. The footsteps were in the hallway now. He knew that any second Myra would be inspecting again. Earlier she had stuck her head into the room and had given him a thumbs-up.

This time he anticipated her entrance and turned toward the door. It opened slowly. A single bare light from a lamp without a shade cast shadows throughout the room. Tom gasped and dropped the seam roller. It fell with a loud thud on the tarp-covered floor. He smiled broadly.

"JANICE," he shouted. "JANICE, I LOVE YOU."

Janice stared at him blankly, her auburn hair a bit mussed and her fin-gernails and toenails plain, but neatly trimmed. She was wearing plain blue shorts, an old Chicago Cubs T-shirt, and topsiders—and no makeup.

"Janice, you are beautiful, and I love you, and I want to make love with you tonight."

He rushed toward the door with every intention of sweeping her up in his arms and feeling her, smelling her, and wanting to hear her voice.

Startled at first—caught off guard—she smiled weakly.

"How about supper first, sweetie?" she offered. "This is a great job, but what the heck happened? Did the store make a mistake? This wallpaper is hideous."

He hugged her and then, in the one singular motion, picked her up and swung her around. One of her feet hit the portable spotlight on the floor and sent it crashing against the wall. Janice was limp in his grasp and heavier than she probably should have been, and he adored her for it. She remained com-pletely passive, not having had time to interpret or react to this spontaneous outburst of adoration and affection.

"Where are the boys?"

"Downstaits."

"Where is Carrie?"

"In her room."

"That is wonderful," he gushed.

"Tom, I do like your unbridled enthusiam, but what is going on?" she asked.

"Oh, never mind." He held her face in the palms of his hands and stared into her eyes. "I love you," he repeated.

"I love you, too, Thomas Arnett, but this wallpaper. It must be a mis-take," she said averting her eyes and peering sideways.

"Absolutely not. This wallpaper is wonderful, and so are you," he avowed as he felt warm tears trickling down his face. "Listen, I'm starving, and an-other thing—the wallpaper stays."

Then he kissed her.

NOVELIST

*All the world's a stage, and all the men and women
merely players. They have their exits and their entrances;
and one man in his time plays many parts*

—William Shakespeare, *As You Like It*

"So the interview went just OK?"

"As well as can be expected, I suppose. Those rag writers are always trying to make something out of nothing. Whores—anything for an angle. They're a pain in my ass, if you want to know the truth."

Just as the sentence was uttered, a gusting sea breeze nearly pilfered Blake Sheppard's hat—a jaunty, well-blocked gray felt fedora that was normally tipped fashionably to one side. Around his neck a deep-blue and white patterned scarf rustled wildly, the ends flapping like the wings of a huge hummingbird. He reached up and grabbed and held the brim then readjusted the chapeau when the wind subsided.

"Yeah, but we still need them. I suppose they are still bemoaning the demise of Dick Dragger?" asked Max Kreiger, horn-rimmed senior editor at Provost Smith, one of the largest publishers of fiction drama in the world.

Max was tall and slender; his carefully combed salt-and-pepper hair was parted in the middle; his nose sniped downward from, it seemed, the middle of his forehead and then swelled noticeably outward above the nostrils. The cadence of his discernably erudite speech and urbane mannerisms set him apart from others: people listened to him if for no other reason than what he said sounded interesting and important.

"Dick Draggit…Daggett…there, goddamn it, you have me screwing up my own protagonist's name," Sheppard bristled. "And yes, it seems that killing him off has been more devastating for some people than I anticipated. They need to get a life."

"You've given them life through a world of fantasy with your books, Blake. Now they're dependent upon you to sustain that imaginary world. You either fill a need in otherwise torpid lives or provide enjoyable entertainment. In some cases both, no doubt. And need I remind you who buys your books and has enriched you so splendidly? You have a good thing going with the Daggett series—made your bones with it. I still don't understand why after such a successful run you would kill the golden goose. After only seven volumes. Do you have any idea how many Perry Masons Erle Stanley—"

"Oh, the hell with Gardner, Christie, Fleming, Doyle, or any of the rest of them," Sheppard snapped, sharply cutting off Kreiger's uncompleted rhetorical question. "And that's all they did—serial popcorn. As a writer I simply don't want to be remembered that way. I want to be taken seriously as an *author* in a classic sense. I merely got my start with Dick Daggett."

Then Sheppard carefully raised a crystal martini glass containing mostly Bombay gin, a hint of vermouth, and two green queen pimento-filled olives skewered on a blue and red plastic sword with the initials "*QM*" as the hilt. With his index finger, he held the olive kabob against the side of the glass while tipping it to his lips. After setting the glass back onto the heavy wooden table, he extricated a silver cigarette case from his suit coat pocket and removed a single Camel Light, which he lit with a wind-resistant butane lighter—its function resembled that of an acetylene torch. He sucked in the smoke and exhaled quickly; streaks of smoke whisked away on a horizontal plane in what was an ever-present yet virtually imperceptible sustained wind—an ocean summer zephyr. The deck was awash in brilliant sunlight intensified by reflections off of light-colored objects and the water. Both men wore expensive sunglasses: Sheppard's were the legendary and always fashionable Ray Ban Wayfarers.

"Dickens wrote *The Pickwick Papers* as a serial; others too that eventually became novels but only after serialization," Max decried. "Those characters carried over from story to story. And Clemens first published—"

"More like week to week, and they were all chapters of the same book—started out as books and always intended to be books after they were serialized. Those were first published in newspapers to make money—sell newspapers. Apples and oranges, my persistent friend. Apples and oranges. You know damn well what I mean," Blake countered.

Sheppard was balding but combed the remnants of his wavy blond hair straight back in a delusional follicle charade. Now, having removed his hat before the wind beat him to it, the remaining strands atop his head flitted in the wind like wispy corn silk. He waved his cigarette demonstratively as he spoke, the smoke following in miniature circuitous contrails that dissolved instantly. Handsome and rakish, he had a flair about him. His cheeks and nose were crimson, partly from the writer's life but mostly, today, as a result of the sun and wind on the open deck of the great ocean liner.

"Max, those guys did what they did. That was their shtick. Plus, that was standard practice back then. Maybe they didn't get bored or disallusioned because they saw dollar signs and made more money. Who knows? Times have changed. That was a million years ago. I just want to move on to bigger and better things. Dick is dead. Period."

"You made that perfectly clear to us—you have us by the short hairs with that being the last book you are contractually obligated to do for Mother Provost. That being said, I do have in my pocket a contract extension that, as you are aware, is most generous—"

"Listen, I asked Mel this before. Why you people can't give me a little creative freedom and trust my talent, I just don't know. If I have to keep grinding out the same cookie-cutter pablum using the same overused characters, forget it. I'll move on. That's it. Talk to Mel—he's my agent, after all."

Kreiger looked up and took in the enormity of the *Queen Mary II*. It was a magnificent vessel—elegant and posh. He marveled at the sight and was envious of Sheppard. Stylish crowds interspersed with stewards bustled about, preparing for the transatlantic crossing from New York Harbor to Southampton, England. Always in a rush to meet some deadline or make a deal somewhere in the world, time was always of the essence to Max Kreiger, and the airplane was considered the only viable mode of transportation. He rued the day the SSTs were taken out of service—over a year's time it quite literally added days to his travel time between New York and London.

"Listen, Blake. I'm going to have get out of here in a few minutes." Kreiger reached out his left arm and glanced at his shiny, jeweled Rolex. "You're scheduled to shove off in less than an hour. What do I have to do to convince you to do just two more Dick Daggetts?"

"Max, you are not hearing me. I'm finished with Dick."

"Not just yet, my friend. You and I both know that the release date for number seven is in twenty days. How's this? Two more "Dicks" and then you can write two of whatever you come up with after that, and we'll go with it. I don't care if you write about the mating habits of the common housefly—anything you want. We'll publish it and hump it. How about it?"

Blake buried the tip of his cigarette in the bottom of a heavy, black onyx ashtray that was somehow attached to the table.

"I write fiction, goddamn it. I've made scads of money for Mother Provost and you and Mel. Now you make it sound as though I don't deserve to be rewarded—like I haven't pulled my weight. Well that's bullshit. You guys are greedy bastards. Go shit in your hat, Max. And pass that on up to old Gresheiser as well. That fat ass owes me. I've lined his Savile Row-tailored pockets with gold."

"I'm not wearing a hat," Max deadpanned, looking away with his arms folded across his chest. "You are." Blake chortled—Max looked and sounded like Jack Benny.

"I'm done with Dick Daggett, and Provost if this is the way it has to be. Advance orders for *The Tattler Voyage* are through the roof. I agreed to this Atlantic-crossing gimmick, now let me enjoy it. I must say it was rather clever to have me ride in the venue of the book. But that's it. When volume-seven promotion ends, so does my relationship with Provost unless Daggett is done and you give me two books of my own choosing now. I'll say it once again… Dick is dead."

Max rose slowly from his chair. He tightened the belt around his ecru trench coat.

"Dick Daggett is better alive than dead. Resurrect him somehow."

"Don't you mean *worth more* alive than dead, as in makes more money? How very mercenary but not surprising. Dick has gone missing. Sorry."

"Listen, contact me when the ship reaches Southampton. Then we'll talk money."

"Mel will contact you. He's going to be pissed when I tell him you chased me onboard this ship."

"The hell with Mel. Come on, Blake. We've been friends for a long time. You know damn well I wouldn't cut Melvin Fisher out." The corner of his mouth twitched in tandem with an involuntary blink of one eye. "This is between you and me. I'm just trying to cut through the all the crap and end-less communication—you know, the e-mails, texts, phone calls…blah, blah, blah…and expedite this thing while the Dick series is still on top. You've been in this business long enough to know that you strike while the iron is hot. Five years from now, something or someone else will probably have moved in to fill the void and grabbed the fans, and an attempt to pick up where we left off will probably fail and lose money. Bottom line, buddy—the *big mo* will be gone. So let's close the deal now and save everyone a lot of headaches and cash. Hey, it's not like we aren't being fair with you—we're lining *your* pockets with gold, too, for God's sake."

"It's not about the money, Max. I want to leave Dick while he's on top and move on before I'm thought of as just the author of the Dick Daggett series. You know, stereotyped. Then anything I do after that in an attempt at serious literature will be ignored."

"I understand that—"

"No, you don't. After all I have said today, you still don't. You're a fucking salesman and don't get it. I'll call you when I—"

Just then the ship let off two successive thunderous, concussive blasts, and the words were lost. Blake was momentarily distracted in his response as he watched a very shapely female derrière, clothed in tight, lime-green slacks and attached to what appeared to be a mid to late twentish brunette, undulate past him. Watching Blake, Max rolled his eyes.

"Same old Blake we know and love—incorrigible. That's heartwarming. I do have to admit I was somewhat surprised when you agreed to this publicity stunt—sailing to England like this. Our London office is extremely pleased that you're doing this," Max acknowledged.

The brunette paused, turned, and briefly made eye contact with Blake. She offered a wispy smile.

"What was that, Max?"

"The London office is pleased you agreed to sail on the *QM* for this promotion." Max repeated.

"I thought it was a really cool idea. I wouldn't say sailing—I hate sailing. I haven't the patience and it has absolutely no allure for me. Never has. No sails on this monster. Anyway, I agreed it should generate some UK sales, me showing up in Southampton on the very ship that is the scene of Dick Daggett's last hurrah. I have to hand it to Provost. I've always sold better in the UK anyway. Better marketing on their home turf, I guess. Definitely know how to sell these popcorn books," Sheppard responded, his expression sardonic, snide, as his eyes finally returned from their lascivious flirt.

"Hey, no question we can sell pulp, my friend," Kreiger answered bluntly.

"Some are better than others in certain areas, aren't we, Max? Oops, looks like last call before we shove off."

"All right…be well," Kreiger said, a tinge of frustration evident in his tone as he extended his right hand.

Without standing Sheppard gave a less than convincing handshake, although his deep-blue eyes—intense, resolute—were sincere when they made contact with Kreiger's.

"You too, Max. Oh yeah, and what I just said about shitting in your hat— you know I'm only half serious," Blake said with a smirk.

"Right—only because I'm not wearing a hat."

Both men guffawed as their hands fell away from each other's grasp.

"TEPs are tops," Max said as he turned and gave a thumbs up, referring to the fact that both men were fraternity brothers of Tau Epsilon Phi—but different colleges, different years.

Visitors were streaming past, moving quickly down the deck and off the ship. Kreiger gracefully entered the flow of humanity and, glancing back at Sheppard, nodded before stepping up onto the gangway leading to the pier. Blake returned the gesture while adding a casual two-fingered salute then looked back to his right. Amid the chaos swarming on the deck, he spotted the girl in the lime-green pants and noticed she had stopped and was looking at him again.

⁂

As he drew the maroon-velvet drapes open slowly to his left, they revealed, through the glass slider, precisely nothing—Blake could see no farther than the small balcony of his luxury cabin several decks above the waterline of the great ship. The ship had been under way for an hour; it wasn't long out of port when it had encountered the unusually thick fog bank. After unlocking the glass door, he discovered that it was stuck. When he nudged it with his shoulder, it slid, and he was met with a cool, moist wisp of air. Stepping outside Blake Sheppard was encircled by a dancing, whirling mist. He had always enjoyed fog—it was the sensation of floating inside of a cloud that captured his imagination. Suddenly he hesitated. Something was odd—quaint. He felt a strange sensation and, as more of a reflex than intention, reached for his cigarette case in the pocket of his cashmere sport coat.

The coincidence was unnerving as he brought the hissing sterling-silver butane lighter to the end of another Camel Light. He recalled a line from his latest, the seventh and last in the series of books featuring the infamous detective of his creation, Dick Daggett:

"A murky mist enveloped the *Queen Mary II* as soon as the ship was beyond Montauk—a dense, sinister fog that breathed mystery and intrigue: danger."

"My, my…that is very strange now, isn't it? What are the chances?" he muttered to himself while exhaling a billow of smoke. Seeing no further reason for being on the balcony, he jettisoned the half-smoked butt—it disappeared immediately into the haze. He spun around and reentered his cabin, slid the door closed and locked it, and then glanced over at his suitcases on the bed. Lying next to his two-suiter and a nearly empty vial of antibiotics that had been prescribed two weeks before—he'd had bronchitis. The doctor had told him to stop smoking; Blake had ignored him. A pesky cough lingered, though much abated.

The indirect lighting in the cabin seemed eerily harsh as he walked over and reached for the phone. Although equipped for international use, that feature was unnecessary now for the call he was about to make. Following a sequence of purposefully synchronized punching motions on the keypad, he raised the phone to his left ear. At first there was a hesitant silence, and then it engaged and began ringing. There was a click.

"Ahh…here he is. What took you so long, lover?" purred a sensuous female voice dripping with promise of carnal pleasures.

"Well, I did at least wait until we disembarked, but that took an enormous amount of willpower after drooling over those green slacks," he stated boldly.

"Oh, honey, I knew they would get you—plus a little extra wiggle thrown in for good measure!"

"I think you tried to kill me right there."

"That will be later."

"Kill me, kill me, baby…please," he begged naughtily.

"So, did Max talk you into it?" she said, less kittenish and a bit more inquisitive.

"Why are we wasting time like this? I'll tell you over champagne at the Veuve Clicquot."

"Mmmm…I'll bet you will, sweetie. See you in a few."

"You bet, baby." Looking up into the mirror ahead, he chuckled at his salacious grin. If only she could see it. Then again, she probably knew what kind of a look he would have on his face.

Marge Olsen, never married, was a buyer for a New York women's store and was heading to London for business. At twenty-seven she was half Blake's age and only three years older than his only offspring, a daughter—the product of his first marriage. His first two marriages had failed, and number three was essentially DOA due in large part to of the trappings that accompany success as an author at a relatively young age: notoriety, fortune, extensive travel, and a seemingly fatal flaw—an insatiable quest for prurient satisfaction. Marge was young, exciting, and the possessor of a near-perfect female body. She was the latest in a long succession of lovers who stirred a voracious libido that had always bubbled near the surface, but in recent years, could only be aroused, it seemed, with random illicit relationships with younger and younger women. Still handsome and appealing, this modern-day Don Juan was resurrected—creative-writing juices that had languished for the last couple of years were suddenly flowing again as a result of his dalliances. He had recently begun working on a novel again that he had started years before—even before Dick Daggett.

As with most of his mistresses, Blake Sheppard imagined that he was in love with Marge Olsen. All his life he had had difficulty separating lust from love, hence the impulsive marriages and ultimate connubial failures. It seemed to be a quest, and perfection in a woman to his liking was an improbable and impossible enterprise. Marge was the latest and by far the youngest to have willingly succumbed to his romantic overtures. Sheppard had convinced Marge to accompany him on this transatlantic publicity cruise; she had quickly consented despite having met him only a month before. For the sake of appearances as well as plausible deniability in his latest nasty divorce proceedings, Marge had booked her own stateroom on a lower deck.

Excited, mostly in anticipation of finally consummating their relationship and indulging himself in that which was contained within the lime-green slacks, he quickly ripped open his baggage and changed his clothes.

Forget a shower…later we can take care of that, and I will get more than just my back washed! he contemplated licentiously. He felt a broad, conniving smile pull his facial muscles.

A loud double knock on his cabin door startled Sheppard. Glancing at the bottom of the door, he noticed a Cunard letterhead envelope on the floor sticking halfway under.

"Who is it?" he barked. There was no answer. "Who is it?" he repeated. Again there was only the familiar background sounds that he had already assimilated from his new environment. No answer.

It hit him. This was suddenly getting a bit weird. Another line from his latest book echoed in his head:

"Just as Daggett buckled his belt, the silence was shattered by a knock at the cabin door accompanied by the appearance of the corner of an envelope that had been furtively slipped under the door."

"What the hell is going on here?" Blake mumbled, reaching for the door. He eased it open and saw that there was no one there. He stepped carefully forward and, bracing himself on the jamb, peeked out in both directions. There was no one in the corridor. This time his own words from the book leaped off of a virtual page in his head:

"Daggett looked both ways, but whoever had deposited the envelope under the door had vanished into thin air."

"Wait a minute. I'm getting way ahead of myself…letting my mind play games on me. Horny old bastard," he said aloud. "Let's see what that little envelope contains—probably just a menu or program from the ship. That's all. Isn't that what they do on these cruises? Calm it down, pal." When alone, he was inclined to carry on conversations, verbally, with himself.

Blake Sheppard closed the door and bent over to pick up the envelope off of the brown carpet adorned with wavy white and blue lines. After standing, he strolled into the adjoining room of his Princess Grill Suite and carefully tore the end of the envelope, reached in with his thumb and forefinger, and pulled out the single sheet of folded Cunard stationary. He opened the note slowly, deliberately. It was not what he had thought it would be—instead it was a handwritten note that read: "Darling, I followed you onto the ship and know the mission, as usual. Provencher is aboard as well and not alone. I am also aware that you are not alone. You little devil—thought you were so clever.

But do please meet me in the Commodore Club at eleven—alone. And be very careful. You and your little chippy could be in grave danger."

"OK. Who's the comedian?" he pondered aloud. The note read exactly, word for word, as the note in the book. *It must be Max's people at Provost Smith*, he concluded. *Good grief—I totally forgot about Marge.*

With that he brushed his hair and grabbed the navy checkered linen sport coat that was on the bed, dashed into the hallway, and, after making certain that the door was securely locked, wrestled an arm into a sleeve of the coat as he sprinted down the corridor.

⚓

As soon as Blake Sheppard entered the lounge, the first thing he noticed were Marge's shiny, slender, crossed legs as she was already seated. He could see that she wasn't wearing stockings or panty hose. Their eyes met; hers flared coquettishly and then blinked alluringly. He felt his entire body tingle. Her soft brown hair had a slight wave, glimmering in the ambient light of the room, and flowed gently onto her light-blue Halston off-the-shoulder cashmere sweater dress. She wore light rouge on her high cheekbones, and her glossy lips puckered naturally. Erotic imagines of her flashed through his mind.

"I was beginning to wonder if you were going to stand me up," she said softly as he sat down across from her in a lightly upholstered, leather-accent chair identical to the one she was seated in. A small table separated them.

He leaned forward just as the waiter approached.

"Sir..." the waiter asked.

Blake looked at Marge. "Have you ordered?"

She nodded. He then addressed the waiter. "Mimosa, please."

"Thank you, sir." The waiter bowed deferentially, then turned on his heels and headed for the bar.

"It's the weirdest thing," Blake began. "First it was the fog then the knock at the door—"

"Sweetie, what on Earth are you talking about? You seem agitated."

"OK. Let me backtrack. Since you haven't read the manuscript for my latest Dick Daggett mystery, I'll have to explain. You do remember me saying that the venue of the book is the *Queen Mary II*, this ship, on a transatlantic voyage, don't you? And you also know that the publisher, as a publicity stunt, booked me on the ship to arrive in Southampton to a lot of hoopla."

"Yeah, I know all that," Marge acknowledged with a slight nod.

"Well, things have been happening just like in the book. I think Max Kreiger is behind it—some sort of charade, like a live version of the book. Oh, I don't know. They've been pressuring me big time to do two more Daggetts. I wouldn't put it past them to have something up their collective sleeve on the cruise to create more buzz—more publicity, you know. To be perfectly honest, I'm starting to get a bit weirded out."

The mimosa arrived, and the waiter placed it on a Cunard Line cocktail napkin. Then he vanished as quickly as he had appeared. Blake reached forward and picked up the glass. He smiled at Marge as she raised hers, and they clinked their glasses together.

God, she looks incredible, he thought.

"To five simply superb hideaway days," Marge whispered excitedly.

"Let's hope. Here, here," Blake avowed. "Say, little girl," he added with a sneer, "maybe you'd better go get your toothbrush and nighty and move in. Daggett's girlfriend gets kidnapped in the story and held for ransom. I think you need the protection of me in my suite. Don't you?"

"Hmmm. How could I refuse?" she whined, feigning fright. "Especially if the big bad wolf is at my door. But one thing…"

"What's that?" Blake asked.

"I didn't bring any nightgowns!"

Sheppard stopped—their eyes were locked. He guzzled down his drink.

"Uh-oh," Marge moaned softly. "Was it something I said? Now look at our glasses—they're so dangerously low."

Blake's mimosa and Marge's champagne seemed to come in champagne glasses that had holes in the bottom, and hunger pangs soon became more than just a vague notion. He motioned toward the waiter, who was across the room waiting on another table. Nodding discretely at Blake, the waiter returned his attention to his current customers.

"Love, I thought for tonight, our first night, we might start with the Princess Grill Restaurant. I trust you will want to go and freshen up and get dressed. I have my tux to wrap around me. Then we must get your luggage upstairs."

"Darling, any freshening up and dressing or otherwise will be done in your cabin. I have already arranged to have my things delivered while we're here," Marge declared.

"So much for prudence," he stated, disingenuous.

"You are so silly. First of all, who will see us or know us now that we're out of port?" she offered as they stood. He helped her by lightly grasping her forearm.

"Well, the staff does now, you can bet on that. And apparently someone else does too, from the looks of it."

"Who else?" she posed quickly, her eyebrows kneaded quizzically.

"Ah…whoever sees us together," he quipped. He thought of the author of the note under the door and Provencher.

"They don't know us."

"Don't forget that this is a publicity trip, sweetheart."

Marge clutched his arm as they walked out. They paused as they met the waiter. "Number 5322," Blake said as he smiled.

"Thank you, sir," ackowledged the waiter accompanied with a sincere nod.

The gratuity was included in the bill.

As they continued out of the lounge, something caught his eye. Something red—a voluptuous platinum blonde in a brilliant red dress, sashaying around a corner. She glanced back at them, and was gone. Blake's pulse quickened. Another passage from the book jumped at him:

"As Dick and Marge exited the lounge arm in arm, he caught a glimpse of her shoulder-length platinum-blond hair. It was, of course, Marcia Hackett-Brown in her signature scarlet hourglass

dress. Marcia glanced over her shoulder and for a split second made eye contact with Blake just before she disappeared around a corner."

⊶⊷

"Listen, baby, I need to make a couple of quick calls. I think someone is playing tricks on me. They've gone to great lengths, obviously, to stage this charade." He spoke rapidly and fumbled with his smartphone. "Goddamn these things—they can be a real pain in the butt."

They stood on the plush, multicolored carpet in a common area of the deck as a cacophony of voices enveloped them. Just a single decibel above the din the muffled first movement of Beethoven's ninth symphony was audible.

"Oh God, that's mine," Marge announced, and, resting her bulky silver pocketbook on her knee, she bent over slightly and rummaged inside. Blake turned his back to her and, with his phone pressed to his ear, covered the other ear with his right hand. He paced nervously within only a couple of feet of her in the majestically appointed lobby that gleamed with polished brass surrounding sculpted wood and alabaster. The ship was magnificent: a throwback to the golden age of ocean travel—just as only the privileged classes had experienced many decades before.

They glanced at each other intermittently holding their phones to their ears as their eyes darted around the lobby, taking in the exquisite surroundings and the sea of bodies in their midst. They were no more than ten feet apart. At one point he saw that she seemed exasperated with whomever she was speaking. He, on the other hand, was able to experience only frustration as the only connections he was able to establish were with text messages.

Blake saw that Marge had terminated her call, yet her smartphone remained in her hand. He moved closer to her again.

"That was the concierge. They said I couldn't move my bags into your cabin."

"I'll handle it, then. I spoke to the bell captain or whatever the head guy's title is as soon as I got onboard and gave them specific authorization to let you do that," Blake answered sharply. He turned quickly and looked the other way and then back at Marge.

"I know you did, but they just told me there is no Blake Sheppard on the ship's manifest—you're not registered, and that is not your room," she said, dropping both of her hands to her sides in exasperation. Her pocketbook slid from her shoulder, and she awkwardly juggled it and brought the strap back into place.

"That's ludicrous. Give me your phone. I'll call them back since you have the number right there. Plus how can they argue if I call them on your phone?" Before she handed him the phone, she pressed a key that recalled the last number engaged.

"Hello? Yes, my name is Blake Sheppard, and I was there before we left port—" He quickly placed the phone against his chest and snapped at Marge, "What do you call it when a ship leaves the pier? Boat off?"

She chuckled. "I don't know…it doesn't matter—just talk," she urged.

"Hello, hello. Yes, I'm sorry. I was there at the steward's desk or whatever you call it and talked to a Steve Prescott. Is he still there?"

"Yes, sir. One moment, please, sir." It was a youthful voice—he sounded no older than fifteen. There were muffled voices, and then someone cleared his throat, presumably preparing to speak.

"Ah, yes, sir. This is Steven Prescott. May I be of assistance, sir?" Steve had a thick British accent.

"Hi, Steve. This is Blake Sheppard. I met with you earlier—I was the one who authorized the luggage move for Miss Olsen to room fifty-three twenty-two."

"Sir, I do recognize your voice, and thank you. Thank you for calling. However, I must ask if you are mistaken and have registered under another name?"

Blake pressed the phone against his chest again to prevent the listener on the other end from hearing.

"I gave the son of a bitch a hundred-dollar bill to do this. He just asked me the same thing you said about some name confusion. This is getting crazier by the minute." He looked up at the ornate ceiling in frustration and put the phone to his mouth again. "I don't understand. What are you talking about?" he pressed on.

"Well, sir, I am not at liberty to do this when there is this sort of conflict, however, in this case I will make an exception, having met you—I do recall your voice."

"Goddamn better or I'll come and take my Ben Franklin back," Sheppard growled under his breath, inaudible to the concierge on the phone. Marge frowned.

"Blake Sheppard is definitely not the name registered to this room," Prescott stated with reserved British aplomb.

"What name *is* it then?" Sheppard implored.

"Ahem…that would be a Mr. R. M. Daggett, sir."

⛨

"I am at a loss to explain this one," Blake Sheppard sighed as he stared at the rippling sea, the tops of the waves blazing orange in the evening sun that was dropping from the sky somewhere behind the massive vessel. Surrounded by uncompromising luxury in the Princess Grill dining room, the two not-so-clandestine lovers were seated across from one another, waiting for their initial drink order. The polished silverware glistened; the Cunard Line fine bone china gleamed.

"Can't you forget about it, sugar? Maybe it's just a weird coincidence," asked the nubile beauty with dangling diamond earrings that glittered with even the slightest movement.

He looked at her arms, shoulders and neck—he knew her skin to be incredibly silky soft and smooth. For a moment his mind drifted into the not-too-distant future—later that evening, alone in his cabin after several wines. Suddenly something caught his eye just over her left shoulder. It was the face of a man standing several tables away. Then the owner of the face turned and was silhouetted against background light. Blake knew that face and that profile; it belonged to no one else. He knew it so well, in fact, that among the surroundings and the circumstances, another line of the seventh and final Dick Daggett novel leaped into his head:

"He was enthralled as he stared at her delicious loveliness and considered his lustful intentions for a later hour, when suddenly his quarry and nemesis, the international jewel thief Nigel Provencher, appeared like a ghost in the distance, and then like an apparition was gone in an instant."

"Excuse me for a minute, sweetheart. I'll be right back," he snarled as he jumped up and moved quickly in the direction where he had spotted Provencher. He turned a corner and saw the profusion of humanity in the crowded room—voices, people seated and those moving about—and near the kitchen door the frenetic waitstaff pulled him in and consumed him like an eddy. Provencher was nowhere to be seen. Blake realized that the elusive character he had created was just that—a master of disguises and as slippery as an eel. Yet he was sure that the man he had seen was the personification of Dick Daggett's antagonist, especially in volume seven. This was all becoming more and more bizarre by the minute. Believing that this was all a hoax, trick, or mere haphazard string of coincidences was beginning to be abundantly more difficult to abide.

"Oh my God," he muttered, loud enough for several people within earshot to hear and turn their heads. He scurried back around the corner and felt his stomach twist as he looked at the table where he and Marge were seated. She was gone.

Goddamn it. I wrote the book. I knew this would happen just like I know what is going to happen tonight and tomorrow. Damn it all. Can I change destiny now, or is it too late—and do I want to at least change some of it? he pondered as he looked around, nervously rubbing his chin with his right hand. This was a conundrum.

His head spinning, Blake raced forward, nearly knocking over a wine steward and a waiter carrying a silver platter heaped with escargot. As he arrived at his table, he looked down and saw the note. The one he had expected to see. The note Dick Daggett had found the same way in volume seven—under the exact same circumstances. He read it quickly: "Mate, your lovely friend is safe with me...for now. Please reconsider my entreaty regarding the materials in question. I shall be most pleased if you do, and not so pleased if not.—N. P."

Blake Sheppard fell heavily into the cushioned chair as his waiter approached.

"Sir, would you and the lady wish to order?"

Blake looked up. He knew exactly what he was going say, and he knew how the waiter was going to respond. He knew every line. He also knew he would be meeting the shapely Marcia Hackett-Brown in less than two hours at the Commodore Club.

Marcia. Marcia…under these circumstances. And now I can't avoid her because I need her. Damn, he reasoned as another paragraph from volume seven paraded through his memory:

"Daggett gazed blankly at the dusky sea and contemplated his situation. Marge had now fallen within Provencher's grasp, and he desperately needed and would soon, once again, seek the aid and comfort of the inimitable Marcia Hackett-Brown."

Blake knew that the ficticious Marcia Hacket-Brown was not only a talented sleuth, but also a dangerous woman whom Dick Daggett could never seem to avoid. Dangerous not because she presented a physical threat or breach of security, but rather she symbolized personal commitment and a self-indulgence that Daggett, for one reason or another, was unable to accept after so many years of freedom and independence as a bachelor. It was a complicated relationship that had developed over the first six Daggett books in the series.

"No, I'm sorry my good man. I…rather, we…have changed our plans. Not feeling well, you see. A touch of seasickness," Blake explained credibly in clipped phrases. He knew the waiter's name was Gerald and that he would be complicit later on in an attempt to flush out Provencher and rescue Marge.

Damn. Tonight of all nights, Blake mused. Then he contemplated Marge's predicament and the fact that Provencher, although a very successful and notorious jewel thief, was not prone to violence. In fact that feature was an anomaly in Provencher's line of work. His was a business that depended more upon cunning, deception, and virtual transparency to succeed. Master jewel thieves like Provencher rarely got their hands dirty and tended to ply upon the rich and famous with impunity—most losses were immaterial to the owners and went unreported to shun publicity and embarrassment. Besides, other than Lloyd's of London, very few insurance companies would touch them, and if they did the deductibles were so high that anything other than extraordinary losses, generally in the millions, went unclaimed.

Still, it was entirely possible that Provencher had one of his accomplices with him, perhaps one or two of the goons he had used in the past who were quite ruthless. There was a pair of particularly unpleasant Samoan brothers who traveled with him occasionally, usually for jobs involving heavy lifting or the like. They would be hard to miss—they were massive and covered with tattoos.

Still, on a ship like this, in the middle of the Atlantic at night, no one would be the wiser if a gagged and weighted body plunged into the sea. Chances are it would go undetected.

Provencher was also keenly aware that Marge wouldn't be reported missing for days or maybe even until they reached port. And that eventually she would be connected to Daggett and their surreptitious liaison. Meanwhile Daggett would keep quiet so as not to expose his mission or the unsavory escapades onboard. The cruise line would also remain mum if they were to find out—notoriety of such goings-on could frighten future passengers away. As usual Nigel Provencher was clever and smart.

Lastly Provencher was an incorrigible womanizer incapable of letting a female dripping with such sexuality as Marge to sit or idly lie about while in his possession.

Blast the day I made Provencher an immutable ladies' man capable of seducing just about anyone. I have really created a monster—and this was supposed to be Daggett's and now my week of romping about my cabin. Son of a bitch, Sheppard groused. He knew his Provencher character could charm a dead woman out of a cemetery or would use any method at his disposal to get what he needed to satisfy his uncontrollable libido, including drugs.

"Shall I keep the tab open then, sir?"

"No…No, thank you. I'll sign. It's cabin fifty-three twenty-two." Blake sighed, now aware that he may have become trapped in his own creation—that somehow he had been inserted in the middle of the seventh and last volume in the Dick Daggett mystery series and was living vicariously as Dick Daggett.

Gerald stood off to one side. "Are you all right, sir?"

"Yes, Gerald…just need a stiff drink."

"Have we had the pleasure of meeting before, sir?"

"No, why do you ask?"

"Well, sir, you know my name, and we're just out of port. I'm not wearing my name tag yet."

"We must have crossed paths at one time."

"Have you ever taken this cruise before, sir?"

"Only in my mind, but don't try to figure that one out. I guess you looked like a Gerald." Sheppard smiled weakly and casually brushed a speck of lint from the satin lapel of his tuxedo with the back of his right hand. He knew because he had invented him and gave him that name—and Scotland Yard credentials.

Blake glanced around the restaurant—it was the scene he had painted for the readers and that in which he was now embedded. The fact that he had killed off Dick Daggett in this book began to weigh heavily and more seriously on his mind.

⊶⊷

Back in his cabin, Blake ruminated about the circumstances of his story. He knew it all because he had written it a year before. Trancelike, his eyes were fixated on Marge's suitcases stacked on his bed. He mulled over the events of the last four hours. Sheppard had all but abandoned the notion that this was some elaborate hoax perpetrated by persistent editor Max Kreiger or longtime agent Mel Fisher. Or even the publisher despite the fact that they had the means with which to pull it off. Blake had tried to roust Kreiger and Fisher on his phone several times but to no avail. In his many years of association with them, they had nearly always returned his calls within a couple of hours. At that, and the fiction publishing business, they were exceptionally proficient.

Blake Sheppard found it amusing that as precocious and supercilious as he could sometimes be, he could now be living within the pages of his own novel—and the story was playing out in real time with himself as his own protagonist, just as he'd written it. Sheppard now knew that it could be perpetrated only by the select few who had actually read the book—it was still a manuscript being finalized for printing. But to remember minute details and as precisely as described in the story and interpreted exactly as he, the author, had envisioned them in his mind's eye was not only improbable—it was impossible.

Blake Sheppard had never been more confused in his life and momentarily entertained the thought that he was possibly going mad.

The ship's phone rang abruptly, spiking the relative silence like a mace meeting a solid, metallic object. He jumped, startled out of his reverie, and lunged for the receiver on the bedside table.

As a matter of habit, he paused for a split second before speaking. He had known who it was before he answered.

"Hello?"

"Dick, darling. Why must you keep avoiding the girl who is willing to give you anything and do anything that your little heart desires? And you know what *anything* means."

Blake's entire body tensed. The voice was unmistakable—words spoken in a deep, throaty murmur, seductive and alluring, much like the smoky saxophone played by Paul Desmond on Dave Brubeck's classic jazz standard "Take Five." There was no question who was on the other end of the line. He had imagined the sound in his head a million times, through seven volumes of Dick Daggett mysteries. The woman who had pursued Daggett in an eternal cat-and-mouse game and had then somehow always played a major role in solving his cases—the woman who had not only pledged her unflagging loyalty to him professionally as another private eye but also had promised herself to him emotionally and physically, a bargain that had manifested itself in more than one fling over six previous volumes. Yet Marcia Hackett-Brown, transplanted to New Jersey as a child from her native Essex, England, had always defiantly defended her independence and fought dependence. This made for an odd and contradictory situation between them. Their relationship was complex, with a nebulous vacillation between the professional and the personal. It had been that way since chapter one, volume one. Still, her inescapable allure, the vixen bait of the flesh and total surrender, was her hook, and Dick Daggett knew there were barbs on that hook.

Then, before Blake could respond, more lines from volume seven dashed through his consciousness like a streaker, naked and moving with deft quickness:

"Her voice seethed and oozed like dripping, thick, sweet cream— a whispering mezzo-soprano. It was as voluptuous as her figure. Those dulcet tones could belong to only one female human being: Marcia Hackett-Brown"

"Marcia?" Sheppard asked, groping for what words to say next, unable to connect any with his thoughts at this moment in spite of knowing what would be said and how—even envisioning the punctuation and inflection.

"Dick, my sweet lover, you *must* meet me at eleven at the Commodore. You will be there, won't you? Now, don't be a naughty boy. You know I will never apologize for following you, but this time we'll both be glad I did. You can't let me down, can you, darling? There was never a more serious or better time for us."

"No, I'll be there," he spluttered, feeling embarrassed at having been so taken in by what, to now, had been a fictional character that he had been enamored with since he had first visualized her.

"Do you have the briefcase with you?" she asked, abruptly: More business-like. Her engaging remark trumped his notion of her as a fictional character. He thought for a moment. The briefcase. The one that currier Dick Daggett was bringing to Scotland Yard—the locked leather briefcase with the alarm that contained indisputable and irrefutable evidence of Nigel Provencher's complicity as the premier international jewelry thief and the top of the most wanted list in Great Britain. The decoded information would splash his face and name throughout the world and could, if apprehended, send him to prison for a long, long time—possibly life. That was if they could hold him; he had already escaped rather easily from a Moroccan jail ten years prior. He changed disguises so often and well that the Moroccan authorities were totally befuddled and unsure who or what they were after. It seems he had left the country without question as an Australian diplomat—female, no less.

"Oh, yeah…Maybe I do," he responded carefully.

"And you know our man is on this very ship?"

"I do. I read your note."

"Hmmm. You said 'I do.' If only I could get you to say those two words in the proper setting," she said, her voice like liquid love and divulging the remnants of an English brogue learned in childhood and never expunged completely from her American diction. "And you are with your latest precious concubine?"

"We'll talk more in the lounge," he countered defensively, "but about Provencher and his antics. You should also be very wary—he knows you're aboard if I am. And he could try to get to me through you. Remember he is a chameleon and can look like anyone, male or female."

"Oh, how sweet. I can take care of myself, however. darling…eleven then? Alone?"

"Eleven. Alone."

⌗

Blake arrived twenty minutes early. She was already there. He had hoped to give the place a thorough going over, to case the joint, as it were, before she appeared. But that was her—ever the cat, ever vigilant; a super sleuth. As he approached the booth, a mahogany-looking table with plain tan leather-upholstered seats, he was shocked that up close she looked exactly as he had written.

Why wouldn't she? After all, I did create her, he reasoned.

Marcia Hackett-Brown was intensely alluring, yet, as Blake—or Dick Daggett—knew she was also exceptionally cunning and sharp. She was gifted. Still, for all of her skill and wiles deployed trying to snag Dick Daggett through six prior novels, he remained elusive—the fox always crafty, forever wary and sly. But now, nearly face to face with the irresistible, perfect female he had seen in his mind and created...and secretly desired, Blake Sheppard was rubber legged. Her shoulder-length, bleach-blond hair, though knowingly from a bottle, was refulgent, her white skin shimmery smooth and like that of a porcelain China doll; her eyes were hypnotically pale blue, and although she was seated, a full, voluptuous figure that was a composite of the best parts of Marilyn Monroe and Jennifer Lopez aroused him to distraction, just as he had imagined when he'd written about her. And all authentic parts.

Marcia had changed from her trademark scarlet to a more appropriate ebony evening dress—the neckline plunging just so and highlighting her ample bosom such that it was virtually impossible for a member of the opposite sex to look at her, much less carry on a conversation, without his eyes involuntarily dipping downward for a breathtaking quaff, to imbibe of nature's natural beauty.

"Ah...my lover arrives," she purred, offering up her puckered, full, pastel-red lips for his gentle buss.

Obliging her, their lips met—hers were soft, warm, wet, and delectable, just as he had dreamed they would be when he'd imagined her in his mind.

"I have a big problem...and need your help," he began.

"Where have I heard that before, lover?" she answered softly.

My God, she is everything I wanted her to be—alluring and irresistible, he bemoaned. *Working with her is going to be impossible.*

"Darling, I have already ordered your cocktail," she offered competently.

"Thanks," he answered. He folded his hands together and rested them on the table. "You look fabulous." He knew what was coming next.

"Before we go an inch further, you know I love you and always will," she professed.

"I suppose. You have mentioned that before." It was more of an impulsive retort caused by nerves than a seriously snarky response. He knew it because he had created those feelings intentionally.

"Gee, thanks for the enthusiasm. And you do know that I WILL get you someday, my little pretty?"

"I'm quick…and you are the furthest thing from being a witch."

"I'm quicker! That was just an affectionate phrase, although I may have supernatural powers," she added with a wink.

He knew she was always a step ahead of everyone, even Blake Sheppard.

"And…I already know about your problem—and I have some ideas," she offered.

"How could you—"

"I know all about your little cumquat gone missing, darling. And, yes our man Provencher also knows that I am onboard this ship as well. This was shoved under my cabin door about an hour ago," she said with a more serious countenance.

Another passage from the seventh and final Dick Daggett novel scudded into Blake's head:

"Delicately plunging two slender fingers into her gaping cleavage, one finger adorned with a small but flashy diamond and ruby ring that Dick Daggett had given to her years before, she carefully withdrew what was obviously a piece of the ship's writing paper folded enough times to permit storage in her cleavage. It was the same ship's stationery that had been slipped under his door by Marcia or whomever Marcia had put up to it."

Having removed the note just as Blake had written, and holding the paper between her index and forefinger, she handed it to him. He opened it quickly, the crispness of the fine linen stationery crepitating softly, and read:

Dearest Scarlet,

Though a bit naughty, and not without a salacious thought or two, I have taken into my possession the latest object of your partner's oft-time desires. She is a dear, sweet thing, and it would be most unfortunate and, to my way of thinking, a bloody shame if something harmful should befall her.

In that regard I ask only that you assist in convincing your "dear friend" to relinquish to me that for which your lad is acting as courier. Only original documents, mind you, as encryption can be tricky. Please be a good girl, now, and don't the two of you try to fool this old forger with anything but the genuine articles. To do so would prevent all of this from coming to a happy ending.

All my love,
N. P.

"Scarlet?" Blake posed, looking up from the letter and peering over the top of his reading glasses perched on the bridge of his nose. "He still refers to you as Scarlet?" There was a tinge of annoyance in his tone, and he knew it. But now she was with him in the flesh and a nerve was struck—a jealous streak.

Marcia smiled coyly but didn't respond. She was not about to give him the satisfaction of knowing about her past, though he knew it all. He understood her as a woman—he had to.

"So what's next? We're on our own here, you know," he said. "I'm still not one-hundred percent certain that this isn't an elaborate hoax designed to blow my mind and promote the book."

Marcia had a startled, flummoxed look on her face. "What are you talking about? Are you OK, Dick darling?" she asked.

"Dick?"

"No. Dick, darling," she added with a coquettish smirk. She knew how to get to him—just the way the character was designed. If Dick Daggett or Blake Sheppard had an Achilles heel, it was her come-hither smile—and her dreamy bedroom eyes. Blake had pictured her face in his mind thousands of times—he could even smell the fragrance of her skin. That smile and her brilliance as a private investigator were dauntless. Rarely had she ever been fooled, and even more infrequently had she not been able to ferret through clues and evidence to get to the substance of any case—or him.

"OK, OK. How can we get to this guy? I suppose you should know about the briefcase. Oh, and that the girl moved into my cabin. If we don't resolve this thing quickly and safely, there will be hell to pay," Blake warned, knowing that the plot was of his own design.

A very British waiter arrived with their drinks—she a vodka Collins; he a Gin Rickey. They remained silent as he carefully placed cocktail napkins emblazoned with the letter *C* in old-English calligraphy. Lowering the tray in his left hand, he set down first the lady's drink and then Blake's.

"Will that be all, sir?" the waiter asked deftly as he straightened again, his accent pure—indulging the ears of listeners with an imagined ancestry of having also served others similarly. His sharp features and aquiline nose more or less confirmed his heritage—concocted from a Blake Sheppard perception of British waiters and domestics experienced in real life and old movies, most notably of an Arthur Treacher ilk.

"We're fine. Thank you," Blake replied.

The waiter nodded, a stifled bow actually, turned, and was off, immediately blending into the scene that was the glitter and glimmer of opulence adorning the gilded dining room.

"You *do* realize we need to be suspicious of everyone," the platinum blonde whispered. "He's the cleverest of the clever or something like that. I think this waiter is a spy for him. In fact, it could be him!"

"Hmmm…" Blake groaned contemplatively.

"We don't know who's with him at this point, and he will absolutely try to divide and conquer," she added with a subtle smirk that was impertinently playful—the flare in her eyes and delicately pursed lips obvious clues to her innermost and most intimate intentions.

"Meaning what?" he followed after taking a hearty swig from his condensation-covered glass.

She smiled, an adorable dimple on her right cheek belying a calculating countenance that was utilitarian as well as captivating.

"Meaning that one, he may have others with him, and we don't know what means he will use to accomplish his end. That information in the briefcase will incriminate him and make him notorious throughout the world. Second, he has the girl somewhere on this ship, and we don't know what he'll do. Third, he, or they, may make a move to get me out of the picture, leaving you isolated and alone—and incredibly vulnerable. Now, you might not be terribly affected by losing me, but you know I can help you and I have…" Her voice lowered as she winked salaciously. "Certain, shall we say, benefits that I can impart should we bunk in together."

"Shack up?" he offered carelessly.

"Let's just say it is a working relationship for now. It's no secret, is it now, darling? You have varied and important needs that are begging for fulfillment right now, and you just know I've always been the gal who comes through for you. Maybe, pinch hit, shall we say?"

"You are very talented and are blessed with incomparable resources and assets," Blake responded with candid capriciousness. "I'm not that easy, you know." That was a joke. His heart was racing, and he had broken out in a cold sweat at the thought of spending the night with her, something he had only fantasized and written about as a writer. She was a character in a book and now sitting before him in the flesh. His intense arousal was quite noticeable but fortunately only to him.

"Dick Daggett, you are an impossible fish—is there not any bait or net that can catch you?"

"Can you cook?"

"You know I can—I'm a gourmet chef."

"Oh yeah…I forgot. It's been a while. But what of the girl? It seems rather cruel and opportunistic to use this situation to abandon her."

"As I see it, you're doing nothing of the sort. You are trying, within the constraints of the situation, to do what you can. You're not committed to her—at least I don't think—so all's fair in love and war, eh? So trust me. You won't break her heart. She isn't madly in love with you. You're old enough to be her father, for goodness' sake. In fact I checked—you are actually older than both of her parents. And don't kid yourself. You are in that relationship strictly for the exercise—sex and an ego boost. Besides, right now as always, Mr. Daggett, we need each other. You know in your heart that you love only me, anyway. Consider this, lover: If Provencher thinks she is insignificant to you, or rather that he misjudged the relationship, she becomes less important, and her value as a pawn diminishes considerably. She becomes more of a burden to him, and to do anything to harm her is irrelevant and an unnecessary risk. Besides, knowing him, he will try to bed her, and he can be very persuasive if not downright criminal with an arsenal of drugs. Don't you recall how he uses that drug that is administered for colonoscopies, where the patient becomes totally compliant and participative but doesn't remember a thing afterward? Do I make my point?"

Damn it. Why did I make her so irresistible and so smart? Blake considered. She shifted in her seat, and another line from volume seven eclipsed his brain:

"He watched intently as she wriggled carefully in her seat—her movement exuded steamy femininity—and Dick suspected he could no longer deny or resist her wiles or her genius. He sighed. It was a relief to finally free himself from that tension."

⚏⚏

Blake had come to the stark realization that somehow, in ways he didn't and probably could never comprehend, he had been trapped by his own words—his own imagination. But a more ominous concern was looming ahead. Just as he had written, he awoke the next morning with Marcia Hackett-Brown lying naked next to him. Gazing at her incredible beauty, or Blake Sheppard's very own personal interpretation thereof just as he had chiseled with his words—his Galatea with her milky, ivory skin; her pouting full lips, hypnotic eyes, and sculpted face; her legs, arms, breasts, exquisitely rounded hips, and plump derriere: some would say chunky, with lovely dimples and soft, nearly imperceptible ridges that could be a precursor to cellulite. It mattered not to him—he found her physical features to be incredibly erotic. Marcia was simply exquisite to Blake Sheppard. He knew without a doubt that he had made her to exactly fit his own very personal fantasy—full of personality and vitality, a shining intellect, warm and centered emotionally, and physically a full figured woman—very curvy; *embonpoint.* Blake Sheppard had built a fictional female who was irresistible to him.

From the first volume in the Daggett series, *Trinkets, Tangents and Trouble,* she had been the perfect woman for him, and therefore his alter ego—Dick

Daggett. He'd lusted for her as he wrote. Marcia was the love he desired intensely both figuratively and literally. He built her to have a burning, unquenchable passion for Dick Daggett. She was always positive, adoring, and astonishingly brilliant, inordinately sagacious and incredibly intuitive. The kind of woman, a star if you will, to whom a million men would want to hitch their wagons. Bryn Mawr—Phi Beta Kappa, Georgetown Law, the FBI…Her father, with his brother, a successful grocer; her mother a stay-at-home mom until Marcia and her Down syndrome brother, Alex, were older, then a champion for the rights of the mentally challenged. But as portrayed by Blake, Dick would embrace her only when he needed or wanted her. Daggett had avoided commitment at every turn because he knew subconsciously that if he let himself fall, there would be no return from love's abyss. In Dick Daggett's mind, by proxy, she was the woman to whom all others were compared—the gold standard who, despite being a fictional character, was the *one and only*. Marcia Hackett-Brown was impossible as well as improbable perfection for one man. Still, as parsimonious as the covetous author could be with her affections, he had tolerated the occasional tryst with his protagonist.

Now, in the morning after an evening that was short on slumber and long on lovemaking, Blake Sheppard was awakened by this revelation of his unbelievable good fortune, but also his impending fatalistic future. He was trapped in his own novel and knew what was coming next. Yet somehow he needed to give Marcia what she wanted because he now understood it was what he also wanted. Yet she was make believe, imbued with his own very particular set of specifications—an invention of his mind. And he was in love with her. He always had been, from the time she first came to life on his computer. But, none of this was real, at least he thought so, but he still had to try to slog through it all and figure it out. And the other girl—she was possibly in great danger, and here he was finally where he had always wanted to be. It was a dream, and he was aware of that, yet in the last sixteen hours not a word, not a sentence, and not a paragraph had been out of place. He stopped and looked at Marcia's cell phone on her side of the bed and thought about what would happen in a few seconds and the question he would be asked. The next line came to him:

"As Daggett sat on his side of the bed, contemplating his next move, Marcia's cell phone buzzed alive and began hopping across the bedside table next to her flowing, flaxen hair."

He glanced at the iPhone in its pink case. Suddenly it jumped, and the vibration made it dance across the bedside table. The sound startled Marcia from her silent repose. She reached over without looking, instinctively, and grabbed it. Blake knew who was on the line and what the call was about. Marcia rolled from her back to her side, facing away from him. Blake stared at her and watched: Her ample, supple breasts shifted and rippled as she moved with erotic gracefulness.

The call was quick, and she looked over her shoulder at Blake. Then she twisted onto her back, clutching the phone to her chest, the call had obviously ended.

"He gave us a deadline. Surprise, surprise! He wants a swap…said he will call back in an hour with the instructions."

Blake cleared his throat and looked into her eyes. He knew what was coming next and why.

"Ahem…I guess there's nothing else for us to do until then. We can ping his call and maybe get a location," he said perfunctorily—an investigator's first instinct.

"That won't work—he's too smart for that. Dick. Did you mean it? Last night, I mean?" she said, unexpectedly changing the subject.

What the hell am I going to say now? She's a master at catching people off guard, especially me. I have to say what I feel. I really do. But this is not real—it can't be. Still, I know what I want. Whether she is real or make believe. Have I trapped myself in my own words—my own novel? With my own mind, have I have crafted an unresolvable scenario that, one way or another, cannot end the way I now want it to? he ruminated.

"What do you mean?" he croaked.

"Did you mean it when you said you love me?"

"*Bien sûr, je voulais dire…Vous avez la seule femme que j'aime et que vous souhaitez faire l'amour avec pour le reste de ma vie.*" There was no other answer left for Blake Sheppard or Dick Daggett.

"Et je vais aimer aucun homme ni aucun autre homme ont mon amour in-conditionnel et la loyauté, ou avoir moi comme vous le faites, Dick Daggett. *Je prêter serment pour vous..."*

"I love only you, I desire only you," he whispered softly, holding her cheeks gently and gazing into her eyes.

"I'm sure you have said that to many women in your life in the heat of passion."

"Listen, Marcie, this is different. This is not the heat of passion. You're different, and you know it. I've been running from you for years. It's not a question of giving in to your persistence for the sake of getting you to stop—you are the woman I've wanted all of my adult life, but I was afraid of a final commitment. Something that men call fear of the 'last vagina.' It isn't that. It's that I love you and want to be with you. Simple as that. Surrender, yes—but happy and willingly, something very unique for me."

"I'll say, Dick Daggett," she squealed as she threw herself onto him. "Darling, my darling," she cried quietly, "I'm yours, all yours. It has been so long. And you haven't called me Marcie in years, sweetie."

Wait...I really do love this woman and have ever since I made her come to life with my words. What happens when this fantasy ends—or am I now the doomed Dick Daggett?

"I want to make love to you again—" Marcia moaned.

"There isn't time..."

⚜

When they finally pulled apart from their embrace, Blake felt the tears of joy that had cascaded from Marcia's eyes.

"OK. Now we have a problem to solve, sweetheart," Blake stated. "We've lost another half hour."

"Was that half hour not pleasurable?" she responded.

"Beyond description, Marcie. But now have to get going."

"Yes, sir. Aha, suddenly the tables have turned, my love. Now who's the task master? As soon as we wriggle out of this one, I want to go somewhere with you and lock ourselves away from the world for as long as possible. But listen to me. I think I have a reasonable plan."

"I'm all ears, kid," Blake said, knowing full well what it was.

Her eyes glazed over, as they usually did when she was deep in thought. She brought her left hand to her chin carefully. "I know how this guy thinks. Provencher will call back in an hour. Now, let me finish—" she started, her eyes flared as she raised her index finger.

"Go ahead," Blake encouraged, just as Daggett did in volume seven.

"You answer the phone. You ask where her luggage is to be sent. Maybe not like that, but make the point to make it sound as though you aren't particularly invested in her. We'll think of some clever wording in the meantime."

She sat up, crawled across the bed, and sat next to him on the edge. He felt the warmth of their bodies touching.

"You'll have to get dressed—I can't concentrate," he admitted.

She stood and walked around the bed. He couldn't take his eyes off of her.

"Isn't that rather cruel? I mean, what will she think?"

"Dick, darling, if it saves her life, is it worth it? We need to make her insignificant to Provencher."

"—Or if he decides to dispose of her, as she is someone in his way who may know too much? he declared, cutting her off.

"Not his style, lover. He is a very pragmatic man. Nothing unnecessary, pointless, or useless. He doesn't want blood on his hands—and not on an ocean liner, where he has few escape options while at sea. He's a captive. Even with all of his disguises and tricks, it would be tough to avoid detection. No. He wants things nice and quiet and does not want to draw any attention to himself."

Blake frowned and remembered what was next in volume seven:

"Daggett watched her pull a navy-blue turtleneck over her head. When she had straightened her hair, she looked over at him tenderly. 'Oh, lover,' she sighed, smiling broadly. Marcia Hackett-Brown knew she had finally captured her prey."

"Dick, darling. One thing before we go on with this. Let's start making plans for *our* future as soon as we can?"

"Marcia, I promise. But first things first," he avowed.

"OK. I'll save my exuberance, but I don't know how," she conceded.

"You do know that the empty briefcase is in your cabin?"

"WHAT?"

"And the goods are hidden in Marge's room. There's a false bottom on her armoire."

"But...how did you...Dick Daggett, you are a crafty one," she said, followed by a peck of a kiss on his cheek. "I should have surmised something like that. Oops," she offered apologetically as she recoiled. He chuckled and stood to get dressed.

"And you have the passkey card to Marge's room in your pocketbook. It's behind the mirror of your compact."

⊰⊱

The thickening mist enveloped them, swirling in concentric circles around Blake and Marcia as they hustled along the third deck, the agreed-upon rendezvous location. Barren except for the infrequent hooded passerby, cooler than expected temperatures and clinging dampness at sea served to keep all but the heartiest of ocean travelers belowdecks in the controlled environment and luxury of the ostentatious surroundings of the *Queen Mary II.*

Neither was certain that Provencher had taken the bait on the last call. Blake, or Dick Daggett as he was now known to all, had answered the ringing ship's phone as planned, played his part, and delivered his lines just as he and Marcia had written and rehearsed them:

Daggett, *confident*: Who is this?

Provencher, *confident*: Ah...a familiar voice from my checkered past. The venerable Mr. Richard Daggett.

Daggett, *forthright*: So what do you have up your sleeve this time, Provencher?

Provencher, *mocking*: Oh, I just love a sense of drama, old boy. There's no need to be so bloody cheeky. You know it adds some spice to this otherwise mundane lifestyle that we lead. Downright boring at times, mate. Oh, and the girl…don't worry about her things. Until we have a happy ending, they might as well stay with you, you know—depends upon whether she needs them after today. Not to worry, I'm always quite equipped to accommodate female guests, as you are undoubtedly aware. Just ask your faux blond friend…"

Surpised at his angry reaction to his own words from Provencher, another passage from volume seven slid inauspiciously into his consciousness:

"Daggett suddenly realized that Provencher hadn't taken the bait—the bluff didn't work. There seemed to be something more ominous in his ordinarily languid British tone. Both Daggett and Marcia were listening in on the call. She glanced up and frowned, knowing they had been outsmarted, and plan A was obsolete."

Daggett, *more intense*: So what is it, Provencher? What's the deal?

Provencher, *with élan*: Good heavens, Daggett. Must you continue to be so priggish among friends? Really, now. Scarlet, love, can't you tame the feral beast in your man?

Daggett, *steely*: Cut the sweet talk, Provencher. What do you want?

Provencher: The goods, Daggett. I might have them in possession by now if they were jewels, you know. You have one hour—we'll make an exchange on the third deck. Sorry that it's nearly steerage, but that shouldn't matter now, should it? Follow the blue ribbons. Be prompt and have the briefcase—we will check the contents before we release your lady friend, which will be somewhere on the ship. You have my word.

Daggett, *serious*: Release the girl first or no deal.

Provencher, *resolute*: Hardly, Daggett.

Daggett: What assurances do we have that she's OK?
Provencher: Here. I'll put her on.

There were muffled voices and the sound of the phone exchanging hands.

Marge, *tentative*: Dick?

My God…it's her voice. But I was never Dick to her—only Blake, he thought.

Daggett: Marge, are you all right?
Marge, *diminutive*: Dick? This is Mindy. Who's Marge?

Sheppard, panicked, looked over at Marcia standing across from him. She shrugged her shoulders then took a step forward. Cupping her hand over his ear, she whispered: "Just go with it. I know you don't understand, but it's not important."

Daggett, *shifting uncomfortably but voice firm:* OK, Mindy. Has he got someone—

There was a sound as if the phone was snatched from the woman's grip.

Provencher, *assertive*: That's enough, my friend. Third deck. One hour.

And so it was that Blake and Marcia now found themselves at the final blue ribbon, knowing it to be such because of a tag hanging from it that said: "Daggett, party of three, meets here." It was a narrow alleyway with only a railing on one side and a long white wall on the other—more of a passageway than anything: isolated, noiseless from anywhere else on the ship. Marcia stood several feet away from Blake, both arms to her side and wearing a fashionable scarlet raincoat, Blake with the narrow brim of a brown fedora pulled down over his eyes, sporting a matching trench coat. They waited, not knowing from which direction Provencher would approach. The fog thickened. The only sound was the barely discernable steady flow and swoosh of the great hull cutting through the hills of the Atlantic Ocean.

"Ah, right on time, I see."

It was Provencher's voice, but he was as yet unseen. In an instant he sauntered ahead from the fog, wearing odd-looking black goggles and wearing a crisp, white steward's uniform.

"Oh, don't be alarmed. These are fog glasses—latest thing. Work like a bloody charm. In my business one must be prepared for anything, anytime, yes?

"Dick," Marcia gasped.

Turning quickly he saw a large figure in a black jacket looming just behind her.

"Oh, yes. How rude of me. That is my 'assistant,' Moogalatant. He and his brother are Samoan friends of mine who came along with me on this trip. As you can see, they are providing me with invaluable services." Provencher sneered as the giant stopped just short of them.

"Where's the girl?" Blake growled.

"Before we get into any more details, you will be ever so kind as to surrender the briefcase to me."

Blake hesitated then pitched it in the direction of the jewel thief. As he did he moved forward quickly to grab Provencher but suddenly felt a searing pain in his right calf and felt his leg go numb. Unable to support himself, he fell to his knees. The briefcase smashed onto the deck but remained unopened. There was a gash on one of the leather corners.

Lying on his side, Blake felt his calf and pulled out a small dart. Marcia was kneeling next to him while the larger, hulking Samoan had moved closer. He stopped and came no closer than ten feet.

"Go to hell, Provencher. Keep your dog at bay, or Marcia will put a hole in him," he hissed through gnashed teeth.

All glanced quickly at Marcia, who was now holding a small, twenty-five-caliber automatic in her right hand, which had been hastily retrieved from her small, crimson designer clutch when she turned away for an instant moments before. She was quite practiced at such maneuvers in sticky situations—Blake had seen to that.

"Now, Richard. That's not like you to make a foolish move. And there's certainly no need for profanity with a lady present, and such a fine one at that I might add." He leered at Marcia. She was unimpressed by his arrogance. "Let's see what we have in here," Provencher announced playfully as he tried to unsnap the latches of the case. They were locked. "OK…We can play this any way you want, Richard. The key, please, or Mooga—that's my boy's nick name—will have to work his magic with your lady love… in private. Might I add a little history lesson while I am at it? Back in the late nineteenth century, I think it was, the United States Army commissioned the Colt Firearms Company in Hartford, Connecticut, to come up with a handgun that had more stopping power that the thirty-eight-caliber revolver. The reason was that in some skirmish or another, attacking giant Samoan warriors could not be stopped with one or two shots from a thirty-eight before they let their deadly spears fly. So Colt came up with the forty-five-caliber automatic, which offered a higher caliber bullet, faster muzzle velocity, and therefore better stopping power. They fired more rapidly as well. Marcia, your tiny pop gun is no match for Mooga and his darts or my own forty-five that I have under my belt."

"Where's the girl?" Blake barked, attempting to stand. A quick ruffling noise from behind Marcia and then another shooting pain, this time higher in the same leg—in his thigh—dropped him again as he struggled to stand. It was another dart, both having originated from the direction of Mooga.

"Unfortunately, Dick, old boy—and Scarlet, my dear; oh, what fondness I have for you, Scarlet—I have some rather bad news for you. Oh, Scarlet, I will always cherish my fond memories of our time together, when you were such a sweet, young kitten. Anyway, as I was saying, I am sorry, but that poor girl was a ruse. Stephanie, love, come hither."

Moving along the railing as the fog tightened around them came the girl. She walked up next to Provencher, and he draped his arm over her diminutive shoulders. It was Marge, or Mindy. She wearing a tight skirt and open blouse—not a lot was left to the imagination.

"Sorry, my good man and fair lady. You've been snookered. Tight lime green trousers and all. Happens to the best of us," Provencher gloated. "Now, Dick, my boy, Mooga, wants to have a word with you."

"You bastard, Provencher," Marcia snarled. "Not so fast. Where Dick goes, I go."

"Now, isn't that sweet." Provencher chuckled, revealing a sinister dimple on his right cheek.

"Listen, Provencher. I want ten minutes with Marcia—alone. Keep your goon at bay. Oh, and by the way, how you and these clowns expect to get off of this ship is anybody's guess," Blake admonished.

"Elementary, Daggett. No one knows we're here in the first place. Just give me the key, man. I am growing impatient."

"Except that I contacted Scotland Yard," Dick gloated.

"I rather doubt that since your phone was disabled in New York. And to contact the captain and crew would be ludicrous as well."

"Ah, but you forget that this is a big publicity stunt, and there are a lot of people who know about this," Blake said, grimacing from the floor, where he had inched his way and was leaning against a wall. He knew he couldn't stand on his totally numb right leg. He remembered that he couldn't reach anyone on his phone since they had left port.

"I have no idea what you mean about publicity, but did I mention that Scarlet's phone is also unserviceable? We waited for her to come aboard, your lovely shadow. You know, Daggett, I have to tell you something. Years ago I knew what I was up against when I made love to her, and she would call out your name in her sleep—that she loved you, Dick." He emitted a menacing chuckle at the crass double entendre.

"Shut up, Provencher—"Dick growled.

"Yeah, don't give yourself so much credit, lover boy," Marcia added sharply.

"Oh, now, children," Provencher rebuked. "On second thought, no ten minutes—Mooga, dispose of him, and take her away, please. I've lost my patience. Maybe she alone…" He glanced salaciously at Marcia. "Will be more cooperative given the right circumstances—and persuasion."

Mooga hulked over Dick and grabbed him by the back of his jacket while sending Marcia stumbling back with a swat of his other massive arm.

The gun flew across the deck. The balding giant was unshaven and had dark, rough features. Dark tattoos covered all that was not covered except his face. He reeked of body odor; his black clothing was rumpled was soiled.

The goon dragged Blake about twenty feet away. Marcia chased after and tripped—she fell on top of Blake and furtively pressed her cell phone into his hand. It had been a pratfall with a purpose. She straightened up while purposely hitching up her skirt.

"Dick, I love you," she whispered as she squirmed to her feet making sure that she purposely exposed enough of herself to create a distraction that would carry eyes away from Blake.

He rolled onto his side against the wall. With the thickening fog as his cover, away from Provencher, he began pressing the cell-phone keys as rapidly as possible. Marcia moved back over and slumped down next to him and pretended to be providing discreet convalescence to him and his paralyzed leg. She glanced up and saw Provencher hand the briefcase to Stephanie. He punched out his left arm, shooting his cuff to look at his Rolex, and then started walking in their direction.

"We must get lovely Scarlet to Mooga's room," Provencher ordered. Miss Scarlet, you will thoroughly enjoy your stay with us—Mooga is quite a tatoo artist, as you will see. It is a custom that Samoan men, and women as well, cover their bodies with tatoos, even their faces. There is symbolism behind it all, of course. Should you continue to be uncooperative, surely Mooga will demonstrate some of his indelible artistry on your face, and other places on your anatomy so that you, and anyone else who sees you clothed, or otherwise, can forever be reminded of this day, Mooga, and me, Nigel Provencher, particularly. Now, I ask you—isn't that thoughtful and considerate, my love? That smooth, exquisite white surface will provide an exceptional canvas for our very large Samoan friend, eh? I do hope he doesn't get too carried away, or excited, touching all of that warm, silky skin, if you know what I mean. He hasn't been alone with a woman in months." Provencher laughed out loud—sinister, lascivious.

"Not on your life," she snapped back instantly and, falling forward slightly, pushed closer to Dick, concealing him.

"She felt Dick slide the small cell phone quickly up her skirt and along her inner thigh—she moved slightly to enable him. Then, squatting while concealing her right hand, she surreptitiously twisted and turned in such a way that that device had become completely undetectable."

Mooga grabbed the back of Dick's collar and dragged him toward the railing on the side of the boat. Marcia clutched Blake's leg desperately and slid along the deck with him. Out of nowhere she was throttled by tremendous pain and force as the giant Mooga delivered a thunderous, crashing blow to her head. Suddenly she felt the cold steel of a gun barrel pressed against her left temple.

"Sorry about that, sweetheart. I so hate to force myself upon you, but I'm certain we will have some jolly fun until you tell us where the key is. Plus you're my collateral. There's no doubt you know where the key is, and even if this briefcase is a decoy, you will lead us to the goods. I know you will, love."

Marcia glimpsed over and, through streaks of blood running into her eyes, saw the dastardly double dealing Mindy pick up her gun. Marcia's nose throbbed with pain, and she rubbed it with the back of her hand and saw that it was also bleeding.

"Just a moment, Provencher," the to-this-moment silent Stephanie said, barely above a whisper. She was holding two guns—one a Glock nine millimeter, the other Marcia's twenty-five caliber. She smiled with twinkling irony.

"Nigel, dear," she said with a heavy British brogue, "perhaps *you* should throw your weapon over here. And Mooga, free Mr. Daggett, if you will, please." From a distance, several footsteps, hastening, became audible—they were drawing closer.

"You see, Nigel, Dick, and Marcia, my real name is Sally Southwood. I am a special operations officer for Scotland Yard. Nigel, you see, you are the one who got sloppy...and then snookered. Sorry, Richard, I was a plant. Yes, I wasn't supposed to get so far so fast with you, but you were such a perfect gentleman, and fun. Sorry, Nigel." She looked askance at Provencher, "He's the real deal. I just might have gone through with it—he's very persuasive. Occupational hazard, you might say. She winked in Dick's direction.

Nevertheless, I had a suspicions about how he felt about his sidekick. I saw it in his face when he spotted her. It was just a matter of time before he surrendered. Marcia, you're a lucky bird, though I do know it hasn't been a picnic."

The hastening footfalls grew closer.

"Why, you little strumpet," Provencher sneered. "How totally egregious and unfair of Scotland Yard to compromise their morals so."

"Ha! That's a laugh. Look who's accusing someone of being less than respectable!" she spouted. The footfalls were closing in.

"You may all like to know that the documents have been in Mr. Provencher's room since I came onboard and discovered them in my cabin. Of course they are now in the hands of Scotland Yard. Richard, I'm sorry, the skin-tight lime-green slacks were meant to be a diversion—to purposely draw attention to my adorable little bottom. You know, inconspicuous by being conspicuous. I changed after coming onboard and pulling the document switch, and then I left and reboarded. I knew the last place you would have looked is in your own room, Nigel, dear—you slept on them last night!"

Sheppard, in pain, recalled the next passage of volume seven vividly a split second before it happened:

> **"Suddenly Provencher grabbed Marcia and spun behind her, using her as a shield, the gun now at the back of her neck. Her dress had ripped and fell off of one shoulder, exposing her Victoria's Secret bra and practically an entire breast. In the commotion, the giant Samoan, in one fluid motion, hurtled Blake over the railing. It seemed like slow motion as he fell toward the water. He heard a gunshot from above as he spun and then hit the surface of the water."**

⊰⊱

Fortunately for Blake Sheppard, years of competitive diving in high school were put to good use. Even with a partially paralyzed leg he was able to quickly grab his thighs in midair and get himself into a pike position to negotiate the forty-foot drop. He straightened his body, arched his back, and entered the water head first, with arms outstretched. As he plunged deep into the rolling, frigid ocean, he rather generously awarded himself 9.5 points on the execution, considering the circumstances and the fact that he was very rusty. Just as he realized he needed to move away from the great ocean liner or the drafting action of the current would draw him under the hull and into the giant screws that powered the ship, he felt something pulling him toward the surface and away from the *Queen Mary II*.

Blake bobbed to the surface and saw the fishing boat, one of hundreds that made their way daily to George's Bank and the Grand Bank, some of the most fertile fishing regions on the planet. The thudding of the boat's powerful engine was a shocking yet welcome noise. He climbed the net as it was hoisted and then closed. The boom swung it over to the deck of the boat—the pungent odor, a blend of diesel exhaust and fishing boat, filled his olfactory facilities—he smiled with delight. He heard the voices as he was lowered and the net opened.

"Blake Sheppard, I presume?" a baritone voice bellowed. Blake looked over, searching for its owner. A tall, husky man with a pitch-black beard, wearing yellow-slicker overalls and rubber boots stained with fish gore, was smiling. His arms were crossed on his chest. Blake presumed he was the captain—he looked like the kind of a man who would be the possessor of a voice like that. Blake's feet reached the deck as he tumbled from the net, the numbness in his leg suddenly gone. The wide, ebony bearded man stepped forward and reached out his hand. Blake shook it.

"Glad you could make it," Blake said, reassured that the events of the last ten minutes were in part due to his hurried and cryptic rewrite of the ending of *The Tattler Voyage* and that he had somehow altered his destiny—rather, Dick Daggett's rendezvous with the grim reaper. The rest he wasn't certain of but wished for the best.

"No problem, my friend. I'm Captain Frank Diaz out of New Bedford, Massachusetts. Welcome aboard *The Minnow*."

"*The Minnow?* Blake laughed. "Someone has a sense of humor, As in *Gilligan's Island*, I assume. I don't know how to thank you, Frank."

Blake glanced around at the crew gathered on deck. Judging them to be mostly Portuguese-Americans, he accepted a blanket that had been thrown over his shoulders. He looked up and watched the stern of the *Queen Mary II* disappear into a thick, rolling fogbank.

"We received an SOS from an international source that there was a man overboard from the *QM*, but we didn't expect it to happen right in front of us. That's very odd," proclaimed the burly seaman. Sheppard knew different.

"Cap'n," called a crewman leaning outside of the cabin. "There's a call spliced in from London for Mr. Sheppard."

"Wow. News travels fast," the captain stated, surprised. "We just wired the New York Coast Guard that we had you." He stopped and looked at his nautical watch. "Not ten minutes ago."

Blake walked over to the cabin and ducked inside. He took hold of a receiver held out to him by a slim, young, unshaven fisherman wearing a dull-green knit cap, with a half-smoked cigarette hanging from his lower lip.

"Hello?" Sheppard asked as he nodded in appreciation to the seaman.

"Blake. Yes, Blake. It's Gresheiser. I just want to personally thank you for agreeing to another five Dick Daggetts. That was unexpected, to say the least. I got the message not fifteen minutes ago from Max. And bravo for your performance falling overboard. But then Max did mention something about you being a championship diver in high school or university or something. Came in handy, yes? Quite the touch to the publicity end—I'm sure Fleet Street will be buzzing by the time you arrive, and Dick Daggett volume seven will be all the rage. We offered that fisherman a tidy sum to get you back to port in one piece. It was eerie and incredibly fortunate that they were so close. Lucky, what? There will be a plane ticket for you to London when you get onto port"

"Mr. Gresheiser, how did Max get my e-mail and so fast?"

"Damned if I know—just know it was great news. One thing Kreiger mentioned, in fact he was quite amused about it. He told me that the name that appeared on his caller ID was Marcia Hackett-Brown. How the hell did you arrange that gag?" he said, chuckling.

"The devil is in the details—or the writing, if you will, Mr. Gresheiser. Dick Daggett lives," Sheppard declared, thankful that Marcia always carried several clandestine, untraceable phones with her when traveling.

Blake handed the phone back to the radioman. Looking straight out over the rolling waves, he became absorbed in the moment—fascinated by the metaphor of the restless, unpredictable, and mysterious sea. The pit of his stomach was knotted, not because of seasickness but because he'd been with her in the flesh: loved her and made love to her. And now she was gone. He had to write about her again, and now she would be alive as his wife and forever lover. He just knew it. Marcia had been everything he'd ever wanted her to be. He shuddered and then felt an uneasy quaintness. He had written to Max on Marcia's cell phone that Dick would not be lost at sea, but would be rescued by a nearby fishing boat. He would live to exist in many more volumes of the Dick Daggett series, with Marcia—books as yet unwritten.

Blake Sheppard, the stoic with a notorious reputation for intemperate panache and overconfidence, stepped humbly back out onto the slippery and unsteady deck, the salt water being sprayed in a heavy mist with every wave that pounded at the starboard side of the boat. Walking alone, he wiped the tears from his eyes with his right hand. What had seemed important forty-eight hours ago was now irrelevant—now only improbable fantasy seemed to have any significance, but that was his new reality.

In those critical moments aboard the *Queen Mary II*, Blake had sketched a rough outline for the ending of volume seven, revising the story, and sent it hastily to Max Kreiger. Provencher's goon died. Provencher released Marcia as he faced an inescapable situation and was captured by Scotland Yard, and the hard evidence against him that courier Dick Daggett brought onboard had been in the possession of the cunning Sally Southwood since just after the start of the voyage. After leaving port, when they were together, Sally had seen Provencher in the restaurant at the same time Dick had and saw her chance to steal away and snare her real prey when Dick impulsively pursued the cagiest international jewel thief and Scotland Yard's most wanted.

Faking her abduction, Sally drew Marcia Hackett-Brown into the plot, knowing the history with Daggett and a woman's intuition of the combustible romance that was about to be ignited. Southwood then took advantage of Marcia's absence from her cabin to find the briefcase and replace the contents with forgeries. Later the plan she presented to Provencher provided the cover she needed to entrap him as well and pull off the perfect double deal.

⚌

Marcia would reunite with Dick in London, and the romance would carry on fabulously, with Blake's alter ego living the life that his imagination, through his fingertips, provided. The new ending of volume seven now promised much for the future both in adventure as well as companionship and romance.

But before surreptitiously sliding the cell phone high up the soft, fleshy inside of Marcia Hackett-Brown's thigh to be safely ensconced in the delicate silk of her undergarments, Blake had left two other messages on the phone.

Although grasping the futility of his delusion, he'd left a telephone number in London where he could be reached when he eventually made it to the United Kingdom. The other, which he hoped that Marcia, real or imagined—the true love of his life—would see was his last message on her phone: "Marcia, I will love U forever. Until we meet again…Blake."